The Good Shepherd

*Fourth in the Angel of Death
series.*

Now Available:

Angel of Death Novels:

IN THE BEGINNING
FALSE IDOLS
VEILED COMMANDMENTS

Angel of Death:

The Good Shepherd

Stevie Jo

CHAPTER 1

CASHING IN

Bane was in quite the pleasant mood by the Time he was ready for dinner. He had been searching for the mystery Mortal for the last few hours to no avail. There was no rush; the Guardian did not appear to possess the strength or concentration needed to bond with her completely, so Bane had Time. He would find the Mortal soon enough, then he would put Hope's Guardian skills to the real test.

As he walked into his kitchen for a well-deserved meal, he was startled to see Samuel waiting for him. Instinctively, Bane's black wings spread behind him, curving around his shoulders as a shell of protection. This new habit the Pied Piper had of dropping in on him this way was quickly turning laborious.

"I guess Evey finally got tired of you."

"Actually, I had enough of her." Samuel raised his eyebrows and folded his arms over his chest. "I didn't hate ending her fun. And, in case you were wondering, yes, her punishment has already caught up with her."

"What the Hell did you do to her?" Bane demanded, angrily.

"Relax, big guy," Samuel smiled. "Evey will be released shortly, I have no doubt. It's nothing deadly. Just a little task to help some of my Defenders at the Pearl Gates. A little humility will be good for her."

Bane gaped in utter disbelief. "How can you do this? You don't have the authority."

Samuel just shrugged and maintained his smile because he wasn't done yet. "Yet, you think you have the authority to sneak around in Heaven?"

"I don't have the slightest idea what you're referencing," Bane lied, attempting to cover up his crime.

"Come on, Bane. You've been around a long Time. You should know, by now, that Fate shows me everything. Even when I'm not there to see it."

"I have been around a long Time, Pied Piper. Longer than you. And I don't think you know shit about my whereabouts."

Samuel inhaled, sharply, narrowing his face. "Well, it sounds like Eveylynne isn't the only one who could use a crash course in humility…"

"Are you kidding?" Bane laughed, turning his back on the Piper to pour himself a glass of white wine. "Evey is one of the least humble Angels in the Three Realms. Nothing you do will phase her. As for me—I think you're forgetting who my master is."

"Lucien doesn't scare me, Bane," Samuel insisted, though his voice cracked on a tremble. He was walking a fine line between protecting the best was out of his scope of authority. Only the Higher Powers could manage Divine Rule, but Samuel liked to think he could ask for forgiveness later.

"Well, he should. You know how he gets when his authority is undermined." Taking a sip of wine, Bane shrugged. "Maybe you should spend more Time with Evey. She'll tell you all about it."

Samuel paused for a beat to contemplate his predicament. Bane was not normally so arrogant. His former Life as a Guardian kept him humble and considerate. Most of the Time. Samuel supposed it was likely the loosely-ruled environment of Hell could alter Bane's attitude toward Fate and Divine Rule.

Regardless of Bane's attitude, the Dark Angel was right. Samuel could not punish Bane just for going to Heaven—if that was what he actually did. Lucien had a real penchant for doing it, and there were no consequences for him. In fact, Samuel knew Divine Rule permitted such visitation as long as Fate was not compromised.

Presuming Bane had gone to Heaven was an educated guess, but not a fact that Samuel could prove. Not while Fate was un-wielded. Yet, he figured it was a safe assumption, given Bane's close relationship with Lucien. After all, wouldn't the Dark Lord himself use this opportunity to spy, if he could? Samuel could not fault Bane for aligning his thinking with his master. It was, actually, quite clever. And precisely what Lucien would want his Dark Angels to do.

Even so, the Pied Piper could not be undermined in such a way by a Dark Angel. It was bad enough Fate seemed to be undermining all of them; Samuel had to regain control somewhere. If nothing else, Bane should have stopped Eveylynne from chaining Samuel up and plucking a pile of feathers out of his wings. Whatever Bane may have done on his own, allowing Eveylynne to perform such a heinous act on the Pied Piper was out of line.

"Bane, the fact that you didn't step in and defend me from Eveylynne is punishable by Fate," Samuel said, confidently. He even went so far as to snag a glass from Bane's cupboard and pour himself some wine. He had to show these Dark Angels that he was a force to be reckoned with and not some grey-winged punching bag. "So it's Time for you to pay up, my friend."

"When Master Lucien sends for me, you'll get your payment." Bane retorted without missing a beat. He knew the game the Piper was trying to play and it would not work. So Bane swallowed the rest of his wine and scoured his pantry for something tasty, although he would go with something other than cheese tonight.

"That's where you're mistaken," Samuel corrected. "I'm a neutral force here, Bane. I have to do whatever it takes to secure the peace and Balance of Power."

Bane raised his eyebrows and turned back to the Pied Piper empty-handed. "Sure, that's your Purpose. But we both know I didn't violate the Treaty or Divine Rule. Not my fault I have more power than your precious Guardians."

Samuel smirked. This Dark Angel was smart. A lot smarter than the others. The sly little devil of an Angel shoved the loophole in Samuel's face with confidence. If Lucien were there, he would laugh with pride.

"Well played, Bane," Samuel commended. "I'll go easy on you this once, if you pay up now."

Bane narrowed his brows. Somehow he thought this was no longer as much about his illicit trip to Heaven as it was about an old debt acquired from The Fall. One that haunted Bane's subconscious thought for thousands of years.

"Do you recall how Eveylynne came to Hell?" Samuel grinned as he polished off his wine and dared to pour another.

Bane laughed heartily now and handed the bottle to Samuel; it was precisely as he thought. "That's an awfully old debt to cash in. Truthfully, I hoped you forgot."

Samuel moved around the kitchen to a tall-backed chair at the dining room table. "Fate never forgets, so neither do I. And it just so happens I do need a way to keep the Balance from tipping too far."

"What if I don't want to restore the Balance?" Bane asked as he joined Samuel at the table, sitting across from him. "I rather like having this kind of control."

"I know you do, but we all have to live within our restrictions. You know it's what's best for the Treaty. For Fate."

Bane laughed again. The Pied Piper was so predictable. Always in it for Fate, if nothing else. Ever the neutral force, nothing ever could sway Samuel to one side. Not that Bane could think of, anyway. Of course, he was always willing to test that theory.

"Is there nothing that won't cause you to tip the scales a little?" Bane asked, sitting back in his chair, comfortably.

Samuel smiled, proud that he was an immovable neutral force. The Pied Piper was, in fact, one of the rare Angels whose only dog in the fight was the only one that mattered. Fate was all that mattered in the end. So Samuel stayed neutral to keep an open mind for all Three Realms.

Narrowing his eyes, Bane leaned forward to really try to get inside the Pied Piper's head. "Surely, there's something that can move you. Something you care about more than the Balance of Power or Fate."

"You've known me from the moment I took on this role, Bane. There is nothing that matters more than the perfect Balance of Fate."

"I've known you long enough to know everyone has a weakness," Bane snickered, folding his arms. "You just haven't encountered yours yet. But you will. You will."

"Be that as it may," Samuel attempted to return to his mission, "we don't have a lot of Time and I do need your help."

"I'm flattered." Bane batted his eyelashes at the Pied Piper, teasing his desperation.

"Bane, make no mistake, if I could handle this myself, I would. As it stands, I cannot and you're the only one I trust."

"And this is what you're positive you want to use your one free pass on?" Bane asked, skeptically. "You know I'll refuse any future requests from you."

"I'm in dire straights here," Samuel confessed as his face fell minutely.

"Well, then, I'll accept. What do you need?"

"I need you to be a Guardian to a Mortal. A Heavenly favor." Samuel paused, awaiting the confusion that he was sure would plague Bane.

"You can't be serious," Bane gaped in amusement. "You do remember I'm a Dark Angel, now, right?"

"I'm perfectly aware." Nor did Samuel find it an amusing situation. But Bane would learn just how dire the situation was before too long. "I need help from someone strong and skilled in breaking bonds."

So that was the key, Bane thought. He knew how to make and break bonds well. A small gift given to him for his loyalty to Lucien.

Angel-Mortal bonds were relatively simple to form in mind. Body and soul were a bit more challenging, but could be achieved with hard work and no interference. Major Mortal Life events certainly helped. Heavy emotions were key to making the connection despite the narrow window of opportunity. Mortals were the most vulnerable to Angelic persuasion when they were at the height of their emotions. Positive or negative. Most of the Time, at least.

The trick was breaking the bond once it was formed. Even if it was only in the mind. A strong force was required to sever any sturdy Angelic bond. If all three requirements were not met, a Dark Angel or Guardian could do it with a bit of elbow grease. But, if the Mortal Trinity was achieved, it required the interference of a Higher Power like Lucien.

"Bane, you're the only one I trust who is strong enough to break this bond without forming one of your own."

"I appreciate that, Samuel," Bane nodded sincerely. "However, you're asking me to play the role of a Guardian. That's not my skill anymore."

"But it was," the Pied Piper reminded. "Once you see the Mortal and feel Fate's influence on her, I'm sure it'll all come back to you. Just remember to leave her soul intact."

Bane stared at him silently for a beat, wondering what was so special about this Mortal. It was starting

to sound like the same one Hope was after. But that couldn't be right. Surely, Samuel would not discourage the future Wielder of Fate from forming a bond with a Mortal? It could be her Divine Purpose or her Leap of Faith. Rightfully, no one was to interfere with either of those.

Perhaps Samuel was more easily swayed than he believed, Bane thought with a smirk.

"You have to understand, Bane," Samuel continued. "This is no ordinary Mortal. Fate is intricately tied to her, and I need her to be free of influence when Fate claims her."

"Who is this Mortal, Piper?" Bane asked, more intrigued now than when he went to Heaven. "It's unlike you to want no influence. Not even from a well-aged Guardian."

"You only need to know she is tied to Fate. Dangerously so. It's my job to ensure Fate does not suffer losing her. To any Angel."

"Does this have anything to do with your troublesome Wielder?"

Samuel sighed. Bane really was smarter than he got credit for. "Heaven is at risk. *The Hand* won't reveal much lately, but this is something I've seen coming for quite some Time. I've finally received the signal to act and make the necessary correction."

"Okay, so I break the bond," Bane nodded and shrugged. It should be relatively simple, anyway, for someone as experienced as him. "What if I form my own? Maybe she's worth something to me."

"I'd advise against it," Samuel warned. "As I said, she should be relieved of all ties to any of the Realms. But I know I cannot stop you if it does happen. I'm not naïve. You very well could want her for yourself. Most of you would, if you knew her worth."

Bane contemplated deeply for a moment, lacing his fingers together and gazing into the next room at nothing in particular. "Why me? Why not Evey? She spent all that Time with Lucien, so her dark power is probably stronger."

Samuel shook his head adamantly. "It has to be you. Eveylynne is not skilled enough to know when to let go. You will know what to do when faced with the crossroads of Fate."

Bane made fun of Samuel for only thinking of Fate, all the while knowing he had his own vices. His loyalty always got the better of him. If nothing else, Bane had to keep his word and repay his debt. It was what Lucien would ask of him, and Bane never cared to disappoint his master.

Sticking out his hand, Bane knew he had no choice but to agree to the mission. It was his solemn duty for the Balance of Power, even though he wished to hold on to this tip in Hell's favor just a little longer.

"Just remember, Bane," Samuel stated, holding onto Bane's hand to seal the deal, "You must complete the task. If you back out, I'll have to take your debt another, more painful way."

"It won't come to that, Piper," Bane warned firmly. "I'll complete the task."

"I hope that you do. I'd hate to have to send Eveylynne to *The Hollow* where she belonged in the first place."

Bane gave one hard shake to Samuel's hand before releasing it. A soft ribbon of blue encircled their grip, tying a knot with a strand of grey, solidifying their deal. Marking the consequences, should either side falter.

But Bane would not falter. He could not do that to Eveylynne. Hell, he couldn't do that to himself. Regardless of his loyalties, Bane had fallen in love with Eveylynne, and Samuel was willing to exploit it. That sly Pied Piper knew Bane hated to lose. Look who was choosing a side after all.

CHAPTER 2

THE DEATH LAB

Two weeks was far too long to sit in a hospital bed. Getting shot in his left bicep was no laughing matter, but James knew it was not serious. The bullet lodged itself in his humerus, cracking it like a windshield after a pebble struck it on the freeway. It hurt like Hell, and he was left in a cast and sling for four more weeks, but James wasn't concerned.

What he was concerned about was the last four days in bed at home. He had been trapped there, a prisoner at the mercy of not one, but two wardens. Sylvia and Harper tended to him well; he could not have asked for better home care. But four days bedridden?

No. It was Time to get out of that bed and push things along with the Conquisitors. Time was running out, after all. There was only a week and a half until the July Fourth picnic. They had to have something concrete. And they had to have it now.

James tried not to wince when he climbed out of the front of Sebastian's shiny new government paid white Mustang. Repositioning the sling around his cast, James' freshly pressed blue dress shirt was wrinkled all over again. He inhaled deeply and slowly released it, hoping the pain and frustration would go with it. He didn't care what the doctors said about strenuous activity. He had an election to win and a species to save.

While Sebastian agreed that this was a must-win situation, he still wished James would take it easy. The day after James was shot by Sonny McCoy, Sebastian presented his formal proposal to start a new law enforcement group in Murlance. It was supposed to be Sebastian's gentle way of forcing the injured mayor to relinquish a little control.

Whether it was the post-surgical morphine or his own fear of being hurt again, James did not hesitate to sign the order. Sebastian thought that meant James would slow down. Sebastian thought wrong.

As it turned out, Sebastian actually needed James' help. Because the Human Protection Agency was no ordinary law enforcement group, they were struggling to recruit new agents. They needed men willing to be specially trained in Creature combat. It was a dangerous Life to lead and Sebastian knew not every man was willing to sacrifice both his family and his Life just to protect a Conquisitor or a Jericho—beloved as they were.

So Sebastian used James' resources to reach out to the military. Young, unattached veterans who were willing to be a twenty-four hour security guard volunteered to help the cause. Thank goodness, too. The HPA—as it was coined around town—needed soldiers, men who knew what it was like to kill, and they would not hesitate if they had to do it again.

Assisting his father-in-law into the secret elevator leading directly to the depths of VerHum Labs was somehow more difficult than recruiting for the HPA. Sebastian was used to seeing James stand tall and commanding, but the injury to his arm still made him slouch his shoulders ever so slightly in an effort to keep it steady. James was older than Sebastian realized, and he wondered how much longer the aging mayor could put up the good fight.

"Mayor, we can get a wheelchair from the hospital upstairs, if you need," Sebastian suggested.

"Don't be ridiculous!" James spat. "I got shot in the arm, not the leg. And we can't afford to show those Melatrommi lunatics any weaknesses."

Sebastian nodded and pressed the only button that took them down. The hidden tree elevator was not known to the public, so they were safe from prying eyes this way. He stood up straight and smoothed out his black uniform.

Unlike his Murlance Police uniform, the HPA did not wear badges or name tags. It was not critical everyone knew who they were. The name of the Agency was embroidered over their heart, but that was all. Discretion was key. The men even wore military grade combat boots since they were expected to be ready to fight at any Time in any condition.

The only decoration they had on their uniforms was a utility belt, which carried their cell phones, three different calibers of guns, and silver bullets in matching calibers. Handcuffs were not necessary since no one planned to arrest a Creature. Creatures who got out of line were dead on arrival. Simple as that.

Since the shooting two weeks ago, security at the Lab had to be increased both inside and out. In fact, that was the first place Sebastian sent his new Agents. It was worth every expense, too.

When the Melatrommi picked up on Sonny's unaffectionate term of "Death Lab," they flooded the media with it. And the public flooded the main lobby of Healing Hands Hospital, unable to get directly to VerHum Labs in the basement. Thank goodness for that pre-existing protection. The massive protesting to release Subject Alpha and shut down the Conquisitors was frightening.

Although Julia was still alive, the "Death Lab" name stuck and the once scientifically proud lab was reduced to nothing short of a haunted house at a theme park in October. That was ongoing public perception. No one had gotten hurt during the protests and the public still crowded the main lobby, but it was better now than it was two weeks ago.

"Was" being the operative word. James' release from the hospital prompted more protestors to swarm the lobby, waiting for the opportunity to tell him how they felt. To spit in his face and wish ill upon his Conquisitor family. The Subject Alpha situation was getting personal.

For that reason, alone, Sebastian wished James would have pressed charges against Sonny. It would have shown these obnoxious protestors the mayor was not someone to be messed with.

Not only did the old farmer bastard try to kill the mayor of Murlance and Falshooke Mountain, but he defamed the government entity entrusted with his wife's Life. Evidently, none of that mattered. James refused to listen to Sebastian's legal recommendation. Not when Harper had an opinion on it.

Harper's recommendation not to press charges came from a politically sound place, but Sebastian wanted justice not politics. Who cared what the public thought about Sonny? They all knew Julia would be cured and then Sonny would be the liar, the joke. The attempted murderer.

Who cared about the public? Mayor James and Dr. Kordelia Danes, that was who. Although those people in the main lobby would gladly hurl stones at the mayor, he needed them. James and Kordelia both needed the public to trust the Conquisitors in spite of the vile "Death Lab" nickname. At least Sebastian had convinced James to obtain an Order of Protection for himself and the Lab. It wasn't much, but it was something to prevent Sonny from coming around again.

Harper waited for them at the base of the secret elevator with a smile. She refused to ride in the back of the HPA squad car like an imprisoned Creature, so she drove herself. Her short hair was flat-ironed down today, but her face was made up pretty as a picture. The denim skirt and sleeveless flowered blouse were just as cheerful as her demeanor.

It annoyed Sebastian on a daily basis.

Harper smiled at both men and reached out for James' hand. She kissed his lips, softly, careful not to hug him too tightly as she touched him for fear of hurting him.

"You look pale," she said, caressing his face, tenderly. "Why don't we go sit in the conference room? I'll get Kordelia."

James shook his head, adamantly, again. "I'm just fine, darling. Been sitting too long lately."

Harper smiled and linked her left arm through his right, leading him into the loud, busy hall of pods with Sebastian trailing behind them. She knew it was important to James to see the progress of Subject Alpha, but she wished he would take just a few more days to recover at home. They could do a video update. But he was stubborn and determined. The weeks were winding down and Harper knew James feared losing to Elias. All the Conquisitors did.

Walking down the long white hallway with pods and Creatures around every turn, James winced at the roars and calls of the various beasts who wished to be Human. He could only hope for either a speedy recovery or a merciful Death. It was the only ounce of pity he had for the disgusting Creatures who were destroying his county.

Armed members of the HPA stood at the entrance of each pod, unwavering in their protection of the assets behind them. Conquisitors were pushing carts and discussing charts. It was a completely different world from the quiet examination area that James knew was on the other side of wall straight ahead. Part of him longed to go there and take some of his pain killers, but that would be a weakness. These vile Creatures could smell weakness a mile away and he would not allow them the satisfaction.

Amid the loud voices and cries, Kordelia's familiar stomp of high heels could still be heard, silencing the Creature noises as she approached. Some Conquisitors believed the director wore high heels every day to intimidate her subordinates. While that might have been subconsciously true, Kordelia simply liked the way her legs looked in the shoes.

She rounded the corner from the last set of pods on the right and smiled when she saw the visitors standing in front of her.

"Mayor James," she cooed, taking his un-casted hand in hers. "It's so good to see you up and about again."

"How are things going, Dr. Danes?" James asked, squeezing her hand in a loving gesture.

"Let me show you."

Kordelia led the way down the last hall to the pod on the left where Subject Alpha was kept. Quiet and asleep in bed was Julia. She was radically different from the last Time James and Harper saw her. Instead of wild eyes and deformed limbs with claws, she was Human.

Her long, dark hair flowed softly down the side of the bed as she lay prostrate. Her legs were smooth and separated from each other. The shape of each and every joint appeared normal. If James hadn't known better, he would have thought this was a regular Human being kept prisoner. The only reality check rested in the dialysis machine and numerous other intravenous medicines hooked up to her.

"Delia, you've done it!" James grinned, uncontrollably. "You've cured her."

Kordelia pushed her glasses up her nose slightly and shook her head. "Not quite, Mayor. Granted, she isn't feral anymore, but she also isn't Human."

"So the dialysis isn't working?" Harper dared to ask, amazed that she was looking at the same Julia McCoy from just two weeks prior.

"That's a complicated question." Kordelia lifted the chart from the bin to review their notes over the last two weeks. "We've taken her off it four Times. Each and every Time, her body reverts right back to its natural state. Quickly, too. Much quicker than before."

"So she turns back into a Creature," James concluded, disappointed.

"Unfortunately, yes." Kordelia put the chart back in the bin and turned to James with worry written all over her face. "And it's not feasible to send every Creature in Murr County home with a dialysis machine."

James frowned deeply, creating thick lines in his already wrinkled forehead and around his aging mouth. "What do you need, then? There has to be something we can do. We've got a week and a half left."

"A cure, Mayor," Kordelia said, emotionless. "We need a cure or she will have to remain on dialysis forever just to maintain a Human physique."

"You have a cure! You wrote an entire report on it." James waved, emphatically, with his good arm in the direction of the examination labs. "Just take some of Skyelar's blood and mix it in there and see what happens."

"And risk killing Subject Alpha?" Kordelia shook her head. "Believe me, Mayor, I wish it was that easy. But if you'll recall from our report, we can't use Skyelar's blood as it is. It's toxic to everyone. We have to modify it to find a cure. And that takes Time."

"Time we don't have," James huffed. He turned away to stare at the pod across the hall where a large wolf sat and stared right back at him, hunger in its eyes.

Disgusting.

Kordelia remained unmoved at James' emotional display. Sure, he was frustrated. They were all frustrated. If everyone would have just listened to Kordelia from the start, they wouldn't be in this mess right now. Of course, she would never say that to the mayor. She was doing her job, and that was all they could do.

"We will find the cure," Kordelia said with forced confidence. "Everyone all but lives here, anyway, so a few extra hours in each shift shouldn't hurt."

"Put Chloey Jo on it," James said.

Harper's eyes widened in confusion. "James, this is Kordelia's lab, and she assigned Peyton to that task. That is her sister, after all."

"Peyton is weak, and we can't trust her. For all we know, she's been holding out on a cure just to protect that vile Mythic. Isn't that correct, Dr. Danes?"

Kordelia's lips parted for a moment in hesitation. Her daughter—the one she would dare say she loved —meant everything to her. Peyton was all Kordelia had left. That little wolf-girl was part of the reason the Conquisitors were able to even look for a cure.

"If that's what you want, Mayor," Kordelia agreed, sadly. "I'll transfer everything to CJ this afternoon."

James took a step toward Kordelia and took her hand, gingerly. He could see it plastered all over her perfect demeanor. The sadness and fear that wrinkled her flawless face. She was worried about her little family, but James knew that what they were doing in that Lab was for the best. Surely, she understood that.

In a rare show of affection between the two authority figures, James pulled Kordelia into his good arm for a soft hug. "You'll make it through this, Delia."

Kordelia pulled away and stared into James' light brown eyes with glossy ones of her own. "As I keep saying, we don't have a lot of Time—"

"Delia," James frowned. "You know what I mean. I heard you've moved out of the house."

Inhaling as deeply as she could to press the tears back into her eyes, Kordelia straightened her back and kept her head held high.

"It doesn't mean anything." Although she was matter-of-fact when she said it, her voice betrayed her with a thick crack. "Nole's just upset. We will get through this as we always do."

"Do you plan to sign the paperwork?" James wondered, worried for his daughter-in-law.

"Absolutely not," Kordelia insisted, proudly. "In spite of his drastic tantrum, we are not getting divorced. I'll move back in when this is all over, and we will be just fine."

CHAPTER 3

ON THE PROWL

In the early morning hours, while James and Kordelia were conspiring, a wolf set out for breakfast. Her fur was a light shade of brown that almost blended in with the trunks on the trees in Liberty Forest. Had it not been for a soft shimmer of yellow when the light hit her, most prey might not even know she was there.

Loud chuckles sounded from five hundred feet away. She had smelled them three miles back, but chose not to pursue them. Campers, probably. A lot of people in neighboring counties came to Liberty Forest this Time of year. Murlance had the best beach in eastern Kentucky. Not to mention their consistently outstanding fireworks display on July Fourth. Summer tourism was a great thing; it helped fund that spectacular show.

The fresh scent of kerosene and burning flame filtered into the wolf's nose. It was pleasant and meant that food was being prepared, but the wolf remained uninterested. She would not dare attack Humans in broad daylight. No breakfast was worth that risk.

Besides, she wasn't even craving Human flesh right now. Not after her little binge last night. By the light of the full moon, all Lycans craved Human flesh like their lives depended on it. Much to her surprise, last night's full moon was particularly scrumptious. Since last month's full moon, the wolf was more docile and easier for the Human within to tolerate. It made hunting the night before that much more enjoyable. This morning, however, she craved something softer. Something with a little less work involved.

Hunting Humans was tiring and she needed a snack that wouldn't fight back so hard.

So the wolf shook some of the leaves off her smooth, soft coat and started on her leisurely stroll through the depths of Liberty Forest. The Human campers would be free to carry on as they pleased without the slightest suspicion of what was lurking just beyond the thick trees of the forest.

The wolf sniffed at the bushes and the dirt path in front of her. Something smelled odd here. Some kind of scent that seemed both familiar and strange. Alarmingly comfortable. Wet beast and Death rolled into one stench that wafted around her. If she had to guess, the source of the stench was about one hundred yards away.

Odd, she contemplated. She recognized the scents of all those who ran these parts of the dense forest on the full moon. Both alluring and abhorrent. This scent was neither those Creatures she knew nor was it Human.

Her large paws left prints in the dirt larger than a Human's foot, and crushed small flowers as she padded lightly, trying to locate the owner of the strange scent. She was still hungry, but she could not eat if she was being stalked like prey herself.

A rustling in the bushes behind her startled her and her tail went down as she turned and snarled at it. Poised for attack, the wolf was taken aback again when a rabbit hopped out of the thorny bushes and into her path.

Temporarily forgetting the pungent odor, the wolf did not hesitate to give chase. Because she was so much larger, she caught up to the rabbit in a matter of seconds. Swiping at its fuzzy backside, the rabbit was flown off course and sent hurdling into the nearest tree with a loud crack. Its spine would be severed, which was good for a wolf who did not want to put forth a lot of effort this morning.

As she tore into the thin flesh of the rabbit to devour what little meat was on its tiny bones, the wolf's ears perked up. She jerked her massive head around at the sound of a vicious roar echoing in the distance. She had not gone that far from the campers, and, when she heard them scream, she ran back to their location, blood still dripping from her jowls.

The wild roar of a cat sounded again. By the Time the wolf got to the campers, a jet black panther had them cornered against a large tree trunk. The fire was still burning, but the food had been overturned into the dirt and the tents were ripped to shreds.

The wolf growled loudly, gritting her teeth to get the panther's attention. There was no distracting it. That panther's entire concentration was bent on the Humans it was about to kill. Although the moon set two hours ago, this beast behaved as if it was still under the moon's spell.

One of the campers screamed at the top of her lungs when she saw both massive Lycans in front of her. Humans knew Lycans existed, but they never really understood how much of a threat they were until face-to-face with them. Frantically dialing for emergency services, these Humans knew they never wanted to see a Lycan in the flesh again.

The panther took the scream as a sign of forfeiture of Life and boldly leapt forward. Without hesitation, the wolf followed suit and barreled its thick, sturdy body into that of the panther. The two Lycans clawed and bit at each other's hide, only causing minimal damage. The panther was strong, but not strong enough for this fight. As the wolf pinned the panther beneath her, the foul odor returned. Closer now than it was before.

Looking up and behind her, the wolf was distracted enough that the panther swiped a giant cat paw at her face. Claws breaking the surface just behind the wolf's ear. With a whimper, the wolf stumbled off the panther in Time to see the beast emerge from the Forest. It was a deformed beast with muscular limbs and a broad chest. This thing was unlike any Creature the wolf or panther had ever seen, and, for a moment, they both remained in their positions, fearful of what was entering the fight.

The face of the beast was distorted with a long snout like a wolf, but sharp, pointy ears and oval eyes like a cat. When it opened its mouth to growl and roar, a frightening sound escaped like nails on a chalkboard amid the roar of a truck engine heard through the amplifier of a bullhorn. It pierced their sensitive ears, causing them both to cower.

Swiftly, before either the panther or wolf could react, the strange new beast took one long leap forward and pinned itself on top of the panther. The panther cried out in pain as the beast swiped with its massive front paw.

Unwilling to let something so wild and strange attack one of its kind that way, the wolf growled and started to charge forward. The beast saw her coming and kicked out one of its unnaturally long back legs, digging its claws into her chest as she was sent flying backward.

Turning its attention back to the panther, the beast lifted its drool-covered lips and dug its sharp, pointed teeth into the shoulder of the panther.

The sound of sirens approaching nearly mimicked the sound of the campers' screams. Unwilling to get caught by the MPD or the HPA, the wolf rolled over and ran back into the woods, trying her best not to limp. When she looked back, she saw the other two Creatures doing to same, but a thick trail of blood followed the panther's path.

CHAPTER 4

THE MAGIC OF THE FALLS

Ava's panther ran as fast as she could through the sprawling woods of Murlance. It was the long way to her house in Falshooke Mountain, but it was the best way right now. The section of her neck right above her left shoulder was bleeding profusely. Burning like a hot iron brand that was stuck to her skin.

This was abnormal; she should be healing by now. No blood should drip to leave a convenient trail for her assailant. That was one of the perks of being a healthy Lycanthrope, wasn't it? Ava was aware enough in her Human brain, however, to know nothing about that morning was remotely normal.

The hunger she felt for those Humans well after sunrise was no surprise. Ava had a number of new and surprising cravings over the last month. While her father had taught her not to hunt Humans outside the light of the full moon, Ava was starting to enjoy their taste. Not to mention the reward she received for exterminating yet another enemy to the Melatrommi cause.

As a result, she took more risks, allowing the craving to capture her taste buds long after the moon set for the day. Her body count was up to six now—with no plans of slowing down.

In truth, it was invigorating. Ava had never felt so alive!

Being with Lilith had shown her a whole new way of Life. Ava's beast would be forever grateful to the freedom in Lilith's control. Never, in her wildest fantasies, did Ava believe the Lycan-Alpha bond could be this way. So liberating. So exciting. So complete. Now, she understood why so many Lycans risked their lives for it.

Unfortunately, right now, Ava was relinquishing some of her liberation and completeness to whatever bit her. All at once, the high that kept her going, that made her heart light, faded away. It sunk to the bottom of an endless pit and she was helpless to stop it.

All she could do now was run. Fast. She was almost home, but the closer she got to Falshooke Mountain, the slower her pace. Her gusto ran out three miles ago, yet she trudged forward. No, she thought, with a snarl. She had to keep pushing. Had to keep fighting.

Why did she ever think it was a good idea to move so far away from her hunting grounds?

Well, after today, Ava had to be willing to try new hunting grounds. Most Lycans kept to the forest of the Mountain, anyway. Surely, that boded better than

Liberty Forest. It meant fewer Humans to attack, sure, but it also meant fewer Humans to try to kill her in that vulnerable Time right at sunrise, when her beast was full and resting.

It might also mean she would never encounter that Creature—whatever the Hell it was—again. Good. She never wanted to live through an attack like that again.

Trotting through the thick trees behind The Devil's Fountain, Ava could hear the roaring waters of Alchemic Falls. Her limbs were on fire, burning so hot she might melt from the inside. That left shoulder was certainly swollen and it made her limp, shortening her gait. Her throat was starting to swell as well, tightening and drying up.

Slowing down to a steady, thudding limp, the panther approached the bright blue waters of the Falls. The smell of the fresh mountain water filled her nose and her tongue dangled out of her mouth, salivating as she approached.

The panther laid on her stomach, placing most of the weight on her right side, and stretched her neck out to lap up the water. It was difficult to swallow, but she forced her esophagus to cooperate and push the liquid into her dehydrating body. The utter crispness of the chilled water burned her throat as it forced itself into her system. But she welcomed it as it cooled the flames singeing from within.

After five large laps of the magical water, Ava rested her chin on the rocks to bask in their coolness.

Her body temperature was rising; she could feel it in her ears as they reddened and heated her face. Of course, the late June heat was no help at all. What she really needed was an hour in a cool bath, but Ava didn't have the energy to run the rest of the way home. Not yet.

The magic of Alchemic Falls flowed through her and lessened some of the pain, but it wasn't quite enough to provide running energy. She had to get out of this fur. The panther was strong and could protect her from whatever infection she had, but it was hot. The fur attracted the rays of the sun even through the shadows of the large trees that canopied over the pool. She had to be Human and bare for just a minute. Just a minute before she ran the rest of the way home.

The wolf skin peeling away was more painful than it should have been. Like being slapped on top of a third-degree burn. Everything about this was more painful than it should have been. As her muscles shortened and her bones snapped and broke back into place for a Human skeleton, Ava shivered in the warm sun.

Bites from one Lycan to another were not supposed to feel like this. They would hurt for a while, but Lycans were immune to the venom in the fangs of their own kind. Then again, Ava did not altogether remember what species of Lycan that was.

It should not have mattered what the disgusting beast was. Even the bite from another kind of

Lycanthrope was not known to cause this kind of fever and infection. An aching with the potential for vomiting, certainly. But not whatever this was.

Now that she was Human again, Ava could better examine her wound. Groaning on a whimpered cry, Ava stared at the gaping bite on her clavicle, oozing yellow puss and thick, red blood down her naked chest. Oh, God. Oh, God! It was more horrible on her Human flesh.

Touching her right hand to the area around it, Ava could not withhold her cry of pain. Yes, that was, indeed, some of her bone boldly exposed as the muscle connecting her neck to her shoulder was ripped in two places. This was a pain unlike anything she had ever felt before. It burned all the more as her teardrops splashed into the open wound uncontrollably.

Biting her lower lip, she caught a glimmer of sunlight on the gentle wave of the pool next to her. It was so tempting to dive in and let the magical water do its work. Ava debated. Typically, it was discouraged to swim, fully submersed, in the pool of Alchemic Falls. The threat of the Mer-folk was too great. Their magic was believed to be as ancient as the Falls themselves.

Mer-folk were fun to talk to on the surface or at Creature Comforts, but they were dangerous. The siren call of the Mermaid was said to be a most deadly weapon.

So many Humans and Creatures alike had gone missing in the woods around Alchemic Falls, their bodies never found. Ava knew just as well as any other Creature that they were taken by the Mer-folk. Humans were just in denial over something they did not understand. What else was new?

Even knowing the great danger to her, Ava decided she was in too much pain not to go for a swim. She wanted a cool bath, didn't she? It didn't get much cooler than Alchemic Falls.

Using her legs and right arm as if she were still the wolf, Ava crawled her way into the pool of magical water. It was impossible to reach the bottom; no one knew how deep the pool went, so Ava was forced to hold onto the rock ledge with her good arm. In minuscule movements to avoid aggravating the injury, she used her left hand to cup some of the water and drip it directly onto the wound.

It stung at first, then the cooling sensation filtered through her lacerated skin like Novocaine, numbing her from the inside out. In only a matter of seconds, Ava's shoulder was smoothly mobile again. No strain; no pain. The wound was still gaping, but the bleeding stopped for the Time being. Finally, she was comfortable enough to hold her own body weight in the deep waters of Alchemic Falls.

Kicking her legs forward in slow, gentle movements, Ava leaned back and allowed herself to float on her back. She dared to close her eyes and enjoy the calm of the small waves made by the loud waterfall just thirty feet to her left.

The heavy crashing of water onto water should have rocked the little pool more than it did. Ava did not question it. Alchemic Falls was one of those magical parts of Life that she did not have the capacity to comprehend. Like the innate magic of the Mythic or the hypnotic spell of a Mermaid call.

Or the frightening deformity of an unknown Creature in Liberty Forest.

Whatever that beast was, it had to be found and stopped. Creatures did not attack other Creatures without just provocation. It was one of the many ways Humans were wrong about them. She made a mental note to call her mother about it when she got home. Lola would put a group of Melatrommi together to make sure the beast was found, but not murdered.

Never mind the lingering fear tickling the frontal cortex of her brain. She would not think the "f" word. There was no way. It was just an estranged beast. Maybe it came from a neighboring county where the Creature population was too dense. Sure, that was it. Territorial Creature attacks happened, didn't they?

Besides, Ava was just tired. A little magic from the Falls was a good remedy. She couldn't stay long, though, since Lilith was coming to get her soon. Ah, Lilith. If anyone could heal her, it was that beautiful Creature.

Not so long ago, Ava relied on her cousin, Skyelar, for healing. Since meeting Lilith, however, Ava learned there were more powerful sources of magic in Murr County. Lilith was one of the strongest Mythics Ava had ever met. Granted, she only knew three Mythics, but she had a hunch Lilith was a little stronger than her cousin. Surely, Lilith could heal her without plants and potions.

Opening her eyes to gauge the sun, Ava sighed. She floated too long. If she stayed much longer, she risked tempting the Mer-folk to investigate her presence. Ava did not want to take that chance after the morning she had.

Swimming to the rock ledge, she pulled herself out of the water with ease. For now, she felt strong enough to finish the trek to her house. Changing back into the panther, Ava was thankful Lilith would be over soon; then, she would really feel better. Lilith always knew just what to do to make Ava feel better.

CHAPTER 5

HUMAN PROTECTION

Peyton stepped out of the shower, dripping onto the plush mat beneath her feet as she towel dried her hair. Lifting her left arm was a bit of a struggle, but at least her face healed without a scar. For once. The cool water of the shower was refreshing after going out that morning. Her muscles were much more sore than usual.

She dragged her feet across the carpet in her bedroom and went to the closet where clothes were piled everywhere. She should put them away, but exhaustion overwhelmed her. Reaching into the pile on the floor, Peyton sniffed out a pair of yoga pants that did not smell like she ran a marathon in them. Hanging in front of her were the clothes that were actually clean. After tugging the yoga pants over her hips, she yanked an over-sized pink shirt off the hanger and threw it on over her bare chest.

Wesley sat on the couch in their living room watching the morning news before he went to work at VerHum Labs. He still maintained his role as junior pastor at the Church of Life, but the Lab was quickly taking over. If anyone asked Peyton, she liked Wesley a lot more when he was just a junior pastor.

Feet propped up in one of the recliners that extended from their grey fabric couch, Wesley watched the news intently. He was dressed in his black slacks and a navy blue polo tucked into the pants. His dress shoes were on, even as he reclined. Clearly, he was ready for work, but got distracted by the news.

He was hopeful to hear any kind of breakthrough from the Lab. Just because he worked there part-Time now, didn't mean he was in on the genetic happenings. In fact, Wesley's role was rather limited to working with Kaylee on their little engineering side projects for the mayor.

"There you are," Wesley said. He patted the couch next to him as Peyton entered the living room. "They just announced a bunch more military guys joining the HPA. Has your mom mentioned anything about it?"

"Briefly," Peyton nodded. She leaned against him on the couch, curling her knees under herself. "She said I'm supposed to get mine today. We'll see."

Wesley grumbled at the thought of another man coming in to protect his girlfriend. That was his job. No one knew her better than he did. No one had more reason to protect her than he did. If everyone was worried that Wesley couldn't handle it, they could guess again. He was determined not to fail this Time. Determined not to lose another woman he loved to a bunch of damn Creatures.

Admittedly, though, Wesley knew he was spreading himself thin. Between working for the Conquisitors during the day and Nole in the afternoon, he was booked solid!

Then, there was the little issue of his deal with Elias. Wesley felt strongly that Skyelar—of all Creatures—didn't need protection. More importantly, she didn't deserve protection. Not from any sane member of society. Mayor Jericho should just get some of the new HPA to bring her in. Flex his authority. Show the rest of these vile Creatures that the Jerichos meant business.

Yet, Elias was on his back about protecting Skyelar, and this was serious. Wesley could not just ignore Elias as if he were a patron of the Church complaining about their neighbor's trash bins. No, this was about Wesley's Life. This was about everything Wesley worked so hard to correct four years ago. If he didn't find a way to keep Skyelar safe from the Conquisitors and everything they stood for, Elias would reveal Wesley's secret to the world.

It was counter-intuitive, but he couldn't take any chances. Not with Peyton on the line.

Too many times, Wesley had almost slipped up on his own and revealed everything to Peyton. The burden of his secret Life was getting more difficult to keep. Still, Wesley's gut instinct told him if Peyton found out about his lies, she would leave him. Even if he explained that he only did it to protect her, she would never understand.

Peyton had the tendency to be hot-headed. It was that wretched beast inside her that got the better of her sometimes. Most of the Time, actually.

Wesley stood by what he did years ago. It had been a grave mistake that Peyton would never have forgiven him for if she knew the truth. The way she treated Skyelar was a clear indication of that. Just because Peyton seemed to have a change of heart, lately, toward her sister, did not mean she would go so easy on Wesley.

As far as Peyton was concerned, Wesley was disposable; Skyelar was not. If he was going to keep the love of his Life around, Wesley had to be willing to make sacrifices that withheld the truth. Even now, he prayed for help so he did not have to be the one watching over Skyelar.

"Wes," Peyton laughed. She'd been whispering his name for the last three minutes, but he was in such a trance. "Wes, can I have a drink?"

"Oh, sorry," Wesley smiled.

Without thinking, he reached for his glass of sweet tea and handed it to her. Peyton gladly took it. She didn't even bother sipping; she simply gulped it down. What she really needed was water. The sweetness of the tea would only make her more thirsty, but she opted for laziness.

As far as anyone in her family knew, Peyton was caged at Skyelar's last night during the full moon. Then, she took her routine morning jog all around Falshooke Mountain and Murlance to burn off the excess energy.

It was the second Time she told that lie to the ones who wanted her caged, and she had no regrets. What were they going to do? Come into the woods and check on her? Yeah, right. Some days, she wished they would.

Wesley took back the empty glass and shook his head with a smirk. He started to say something about it, but she nestled closer into him and he did not want to ruin the moment. Putting his arm around her shoulders, they just sat for a few minutes in pure peace. If he didn't know any better, Wesley would dare to say they were having one of those moments like a real, happy couple.

It was so rare that they were close like this anymore. One of them was always working or living a Life independently of their Life together. When Peyton wasn't working, she was out. Sometimes with Skyelar; sometimes in places Wesley did not want to know about.

That was the base issue between them. There were too many things neither of them knew about each other. Secret lives that grew more secretive with each passing day. If Wesley could just get this one project finished with Kaylee, he could make more of an effort with Peyton. Maybe he could start revealing little pieces of his past to her to feel her out.

Until then, he supposed he would have to trust whomever her Human Protection Agent was.

"I just thought of something," Wesley said at last. "Maybe I should join the HPA."

Peyton chuckled softly. "No, I don't think that would be good."

Removing his arm from around her, Wesley pushed the recliner into the couch and rotated in his seat to face his girlfriend. "Why not? It makes perfect sense. I work with the Conquisitors, so I'm already trusted. Plus, we're dating. Why shouldn't it be me that protects you? Sebastian's doing that for Kaylee."

"Well, that's his wife, so that's not a good comparison. And, Wes, you work so much as it is." Peyton sat up a little straighter, trying not to grimace at the low throbbing on her rib cage. "I don't think you'd have Time to do this and everything else."

"I'd quit everything else," Wesley insisted. "Or I'd scale back, at least. You're more important than all that."

Peyton forced a smile. She tried to be gentle in her hints to him, but he wasn't taking the bait. The truth was there was no world in which Peyton wanted Wesley around that much. He hovered and he was over-protective. Hell, the only reason she was able to tolerate him this morning was because she hadn't seen him in almost three full days thanks to her own work schedule. The convenience of the full moon was a huge help, too.

If he became her HPA...Peyton feared she would be trapped in a prison worse than the cage at her sister's house.

"I appreciate that," Peyton said, trying to tread lightly. "But Sebastian is assigning me an HPA, remember? Let's just let them do their jobs and we'll do ours."

Wesley opened his mouth to speak, but was distracted by the news report of campers attacked at Freedom Park. Returning his attention to the television, he listened to the theories that there was a feral Creature on the loose. Although it should have frightened and angered him, it did not. In fact, the report gave him a mild sense of peace.

"I wish they would quit making Creatures look like monsters," Peyton mumbled softly, interrupting Wesley's thoughts. She rose from the couch and grabbed the empty glass on her way to the kitchen. It didn't matter how lazy she wanted to be. A morning "jog" like that required copious amounts of water afterward.

"Why would you say that?" Wesley wondered, narrowing his eyes at her. "I thought you felt the same way. That's why you're a Conquisitor."

Peyton closed her eyes and sighed as she leaned against the counter, clutching the full glass in one hand. How could she make him understand that things could change? There was something in her heart that did not want to see Skyelar hurt. Moreover, this new calming feeling with her beast made her actually want to stay this way. It gave Peyton hope that she could live as a Lycan and still have a full Life.

Well, almost full. The only disruption to her peace seemed to be her boyfriend, and she resented him for it. This was precisely the reason why she did not want him around her more than he already was. He pretended to understand her plight, but Peyton knew better. For crying out loud, they could barely enjoy some quality Time on the couch before arguing over something stupid! That was their Life, lately, and Peyton was growing weary of it.

Wondering what Life could be like without Wesley in it occupied her mind more and more. Was she finally ready to move on? Had Wesley finally served his purpose? He helped her through the hardest part of losing her ex-fiancé. When was Peyton going to let go of everything else and be the Creature she was born to be?

Thankfully, her contemplations were interrupted by the doorbell before she could go too deep and say things she might regret. With a huff, Peyton stomped her way to the front door, taking another swig of the water as she threw the door open.

As the doorknob thudded hard against the living room wall, Peyton looked at the person on her front stoop. When her mind finally registered who was standing in front of her, a shriek and gasp escaped her lips. She released the glass so both hands could cover her mouth. As the water glass fell from her hand and crashed to the floor, Peyton choked on the last gulp she took, shocked at the man who had the nerve to ring her doorbell.

Rushing into her house to help her, without waiting for an invitation, was the one person Peyton never thought she would see again: her ex-fiancé, Derek Noble.

CHAPTER 6

EX MARKS THE SPOT

In what felt like another Life, Peyton was in love. Really in love. When asked, she did not hesitate to tell everyone that she found the one who tamed her beast. She found the one who understood her like no one else. She was going to marry him and they would live, happily, as the Creatures they were because he did not shame her for it. She was free to be who she was born to be.

Then, just a month before her wedding, Peyton found herself more alone than she had ever been. The only man she ever loved—the man who claimed to love her more than Life itself—vanished. He dropped off the face of the Earth without a trace. The story was he enlisted in the military as a way out of the relationship.

Peyton didn't believe that for one second and it plagued her heart every single day since. When her uncle volunteered to look for him with a few of his officers, Peyton secretly wished they would find Derek's body, lifeless and cold, rotting from being abandoned in the woods or the Mountain. Death would have been easier for Peyton to grasp than pure abandonment without a trace. Without a reason.

Miraculously, that was when Wesley returned to pick up the pieces. What he could, anyway. For the first two years, she kept him at arm's length, unwilling to let anyone in to hurt her again. Most of the pieces of Peyton's heart were so shattered that he couldn't put them back together again no matter how he tried.

Much like the glass she dropped on their living room floor. And Peyton had no intentions in letting Wesley back in her Life after their break-up so many years before. Yet, there he was: a scrapper seeking the remnants of what Derek left behind. Did he ever receive the value he hoped she would bring him? Peyton could not say.

It was no secret that Wesley Todd had been the last person Peyton wanted to share a bed with again after their destructive relationship years before. He made her beast feel inferior back then, and he guilted her for loving who she was. Letting him back in after Derek disappeared was a calculated choice. Wesley was to be nothing more than a rebound. She needed someone to fill the void in her heart left by Derek Noble. Wesley was a willing and able specimen. What could it hurt?

A lot, was apparently the correct answer, because Peyton was stuck in the same vicious cycle from over a decade ago. Though, this Time, they could not use college as an excuse to break-up. Wesley swore he would be different, but, if Peyton really sat down and thought about it, she would realize the only thing that was different, now, was her willingness to give up so easily.

That was why she refused to think about it all.

For four years, Peyton just lived the motions of her Life, determined to kill what no one except Derek would love. Almost a month ago, Peyton's eyes opened a little wider when she realized she was worth more than she imagined. Skyelar had been right. It took four damn years, but Peyton was finally trying to figure out how to be comfortable in her own skin.

Just when she was learning to be on her own, today, of all days, the one man Peyton ever loved was in the house she shared with Wesley. Derek patiently held her arms above her head so she stopped choking. The strength of his hands warmed the flesh of her wrists, unnervingly. Whether this would help or hurt her inner progress, Peyton had not even considered. The involuntary reaction of her body gave her a hunch, though.

The only thing Peyton knew with certainty was she never thought she would see Derek again. The angry part of her hoped he died in war, if he really did join the military. Yet, the beast within never wanted harm to come to him. The beast within always held out hope that he would return to her one day.

Who knew that day would be today?

Here Derek was in the flesh, smelling as delicious as ever. Like fresh mowed grass uplifted by a breeze on a warm summer night. The strong pheromones of his beast danced through her nose, and old memories that she tried so hard to bury came flooding back in a rush of emotion. All the hunting; all the hope and promises; all the incredible sex. It made her giddy.

She hated herself for it.

Derek led Peyton to the kitchen where he sat her at the dining room table. Her coughing finally ceased and he made himself at home to find her another glass for water. Peyton ogled him as he moved. Every tiny muscle fiber flexing and stretching, rippling through his skin. He was more muscular than he had been when he left. Peyton would never complain; it suited him perfectly. She recalled with ease what it was like to have those muscles wrap around her, and a chill shot down her spine, fluttering between her legs.

What was wrong with her? She was supposed to be angry at him. This man hurt her deeper than anyone should ever hurt someone they claimed to love. He abandoned her before they could even start a family. Yet, when he turned to bring the water to her at the table, Peyton had to wipe at her face to ensure she wasn't drooling.

His eyes were light brown like caramel and his skin was tanned to almost a perfect match. His once long, dark hair was cut short like most men did in the service. Somehow, Peyton didn't mind. The shorter hair let his sharp facial features with that strong jaw stand out on their own. Stop, she scolded inwardly.

With great effort, Peyton ordered herself not to lick her lips when he sat across from her.

"Are you okay?" Derek asked, still concerned for her.

Peyton took another gulp of water and nodded her head. His deep voice was like music to her ears. A song almost forgotten. Was it hot in here? She felt like it was getting hot in here. Glancing over her shoulder, she caught the rumble of the air conditioning. Perhaps the thermostat was broken because she was starting to sweat.

Returning her gaze to Derek without a word, Peyton supposed her recently found inner peace was preventing an angry tirade of questions and accusations being thrown at him. For now.

Cleaning up the shattered glass in front of their front door, Wesley looked up when he heard Derek speak. Peyton's heart was thumping so loudly and quickly that he practically heard it on the other side of the room. That irked him. Her arousal draped itself around the room like a thick, warm winter blanket. That irked him more. If Wesley could smell her desire with his weakened senses, he knew Derek would barely have to try.

Wesley grumbled as he stood, sweeping the last of the glass into the dust pan. Derek Noble was never supposed to come back. Peyton belonged to Wesley and he was sure as Hell going to see that it stayed that way.

"It's good to see you again," Peyton said, finally feeling her throat whetted enough to speak.

"No!" Wesley shouted. "Absolutely not."

He dumped the shattered glass in the trash, violently, and tossed the broom and dustpan aside so they clattered onto the floor near the back of the couch. Stomping over to the dining room table, Wesley grabbed Peyton by the arm and lifted her away from Derek. Possessively, protectively, he stood between them, ensuring Derek knew Peyton was his.

"Get the Hell out of my house," Wesley demanded.

Derek rose from the table and held his hands up. "Wesley, I'm not here to start trouble."

"Too fucking late," Wesley almost snarled.

"Wesley!" Peyton scolded from behind him. She used her wolf's strength to push him out of her way so she could get pulled back into Derek's orbit. It was more comfortable there. "Why are you being so rude? And don't you have to go to work, anyway?"

Wesley let out a twisted laugh that was almost a howl. "If you think I'm leaving you alone with him, you're insane."

Peyton waved her hand in an attempt to ignore him. Standing in front of Derek, she had to restrain herself hard not to rub her hands along his twitching arm muscles. His beast longed to break free as she saw the smallest flakes of amber whimsically floating in his eyes. Derek always had been a pro at keeping the beast active, yet docile. Just beneath his Human skin.

It was a trick he had taught her once, but she lost control when he left and struggled to regain it again.

Of course, standing so close to him made her beast stir. Whether Wesley went to work or not, Peyton was tempted to give in to the desires of the wolf. They were on such good terms, recently; it deserved a reward.

Her heart thudded hard against her chest, and her palms began to sweat. Peyton used to roam Liberty Forest with this man. There were so many nights when they woke up naked and covered in leaves and other forest brush. Derek was her lover once; her body had not forgotten him. Clearly.

Although she tried to remind herself she was supposed to be mad at him for abandoning her, for never getting to see—No. None of that was needed right now. Peyton's heart insisted she let it go. Save it for another Time.

"Sorry about him," Peyton laughed, nodding toward Wesley as if he were a child meant to be seen and not heard. "So, what brought you back?"

Derek smiled softly as she touched his arm. The warmth of her hand woke the beast. For the last four years, all he thought about was her and the moment when he saw her again. It was the only thing that kept him going when he was numb to all else.

It didn't matter if he came back and she hated him. He just wanted to see her. To know that she was still thriving. He, actually, thought Wesley would have convinced her to marry him by now. Noting the absence of a ring on her finger, Derek wondered what Wesley was waiting for. Four years was a long Time to be in a go-nowhere relationship when they had already been down that road once before.

If Derek were in Wesley's shoes, he would not hesitate to commit himself to Peyton. Then, he would take her away from here. The toxicity of Murr County ran deeper than she knew. He longed to take her somewhere else. Anywhere else. As long as they could be together.

Alas, Derek was not in Wesley's shoes. He was, in fact, an outsider. Remembering what it was like to hold her and kiss her. Unsurprisingly, a little jealous that someone else got to do those things instead. Someone more worthy of being tossed six feet under for what he did.

Patience, Derek reminded himself on an inhale. He had to bide his Time and tread carefully.

"Peyton," he began, resisting the urge to hold her hand. "I'm so sorry—"

"I said get the Hell out of my house." Wesley did growl it this Time and it startled both Peyton and Derek. Neither of them had ever heard him growl like that before. It was less man, less Human, and more Lycanthrope.

Wesley pushed Peyton aside once again. He had to prove he was the Alpha in this relationship. He stood toe-to-toe with Derek, but Derek was bigger than

Wesley. Taller and more muscular. It was intimidating, for sure, but that wouldn't stop Wesley from putting up one Hell of a fight, if he had to.

"Wesley, I get it," Derek said, hands up again. "But I'm just here to do my job. I'm Peyton's Human Protection Agent."

"Over my dead body," Wesley laughed in disbelief.

He saw the light sparkle in Peyton's eyes. He had to put a stop to this now. His relationship with Peyton was strained enough. Wesley was not willing to let Derek sneak back into her Life and ruin what was left.

The last thing they needed was for Derek to live under the same roof, tempting her into an affair. Peyton was weak, which was why Wesley had to be strong. She would be angry. She would pitch a fit. But she would see that it was all for her own good. For the betterment of their relationship. Wesley let her go once; he was not inclined to do so again.

"Oh, for fuck's sake, Wesley," Peyton sighed, slapping her hands to her thighs. "You can't stop him from doing his job."

"Watch me," Wesley dared, going to the living room to retrieve his cell phone.

Anger bubbled deep within him and he had to work hard to keep it suppressed. Making the phone call was the right thing. Ripping Derek's throat out was the wrong thing. Wesley could do it if it came down to it. He could do it quicker than Derek could change; before anyone in the room could blink. But it was the wrong thing to do.

If Wesley kept telling himself that, no one would get hurt. Derek Noble was not worth it. If that was true, then why couldn't Wesley ease the sickness filling his mind with dark, dangerous thoughts of the future. A future without Peyton. While the guttural rage that might kill Derek could be controlled, the fear and jealousy stabbing at his heart were a little tougher.

"Wesley, I promise you I'm here because Sebastian assigned me here," Derek insisted. "I have no intentions of ruining what you and Peyton have. Her happiness and safety is all I want."

Wesley scoffed as he pressed Sebastian's name on his phone to call him. "Your wants don't mean shit, Derek. I'm going to be Peyton's HPA."

"Wesley, you're being childish," Peyton insisted, panicking that she might lose Derek yet again. And so soon. A quick flash of alarm, Peyton seriously considered taking Wesley up on his offer to kill him. Anything to keep her heart from splitting in two again.

While Wesley made his phone call, Derek took Peyton's hand and held her back. He suspected if she fought this, Wesley would make her pay later when no one else was around. Although Derek found Wesley to be the most unsavory man to walk the Earth, he could not share that with Peyton.

Still, Peyton's cavalier attitude toward the situation was a dead giveaway that she had no idea what secrets her boyfriend harbored. Derek knew. It was tempting to tell her, but he could not do that. Not within minutes of returning to her Life. It would hurt his chances of redemption more than anything.

If Peyton was able to read Derek's mind the way Mythics could, Wesley's days would be numbered. But she wasn't thinking of that right now. With Derek's hand holding hers, Peyton's entire body tingled with long-lost desire. When he glanced down at her and winked, her knees buckled.

Hanging up the phone from his absurdly hushed conversation, Wesley turned back to his girlfriend and her ex-fiancé with a sly grin. "Congratulations, Derek. You've been reassigned."

"Reassigned?" Peyton asked, angrier than before. "Wesley Todd, what did you do?"

Wesley walked into the kitchen, putting himself between Peyton and Derek, once again, as he took her hands in his own. "We don't need him, Peyton. I'm going to protect you, just like I promised."

"And where am I going?" Derek asked, trying hard to ignore the pain vibrating off Peyton's skin at Wesley's touch.

"You'll be with Peyton's sister, Skyelar. You remember her, don't you?" Wesley smirked as his inner glee shone through his eyes.

As it turned out, Derek was a blessing in disguise after all. Now, Wesley was free to watch over Peyton, uninhibited, and he found the protection he owed to

Skyelar. That should keep Elias off his back for a while. It should also give Wesley Time to work out the kinks in his little project with Kaylee. A special gift for Peyton that would solve all of their woes. Yes, this would be better for all of them in the end.

"Sure. Skyelar." Derek shrugged. He struggled to recall much about Skyelar aside from what he overheard between Kordelia and Kaylee in recent years, but, after what he went through with the Conquisitors, Derek just assumed there was a lot he didn't remember about his Life before—well, before he was taken.

"If that's what Sebastian wants, then I'll go. But, Wesley, I don't appreciate you overreacting."

"And I don't appreciate you showing up like you never left," Wesley retorted.

Derek wanted to respond, but he kept quiet for Peyton's sake. The last thing he wanted on his first day back was to start a fight and hurt someone she might actually love—though he had his doubts about that. So he squeezed Peyton's arm and walked out of her house. Out of her Life. Again.

In utter disbelief over her boyfriend's jealous actions, Peyton slipped her sandals on, grabbed her keys and phone, and stormed out after Derek. If it was a fight Wesley wanted, then it was a fight he would get. They really couldn't just sit and be peaceful with each other, could they? Wesley always had to start something. Sure, he would be apologetic later, but it might be too late by then. Peyton wasn't so sure she could let this one go.

As much as she wanted to follow Derek just to spite her boyfriend, that wouldn't bode well for her later. If she wasn't going to forgive Wesley for this, she had to know for sure. Seeing Derek gave her butterflies and made her long for the past. But, now that his arrival in Murlance was sinking in, Peyton wondered if she could even forgive him either.

He left her. It was a screwed up love triangle that Peyton never wanted to be in. She stood at the driver's side door to her own car, watching her almost-husband drive away. She could follow him, but that would be a rash decision. Something she would do simply to spite Wesley and his childish fit. So she refused herself the opportunity, desiring to soothe the shock to her system first.

In that moment, Peyton recalled telling her sister how much she loved Wesley. Oh, how quickly feelings could change. Or was it that they were not even real to begin with? Was that even possible? She needed someone else to help her sort this out. Someone with a bold and objective opinion because she was too close to it to think clearly.

As Peyton climbed into her car, the sting in her left side returned to remind her that there were other things more detrimental than this. She really needed to have that injury looked at. Might as well kill two birds with one stone, she thought, starting the engine.

"Peyton, stop!" Wesley ordered, running after her. "Where are you going?"

"Away from you!" Peyton snarled out her window. "And don't you *dare* follow me."

CHAPTER 7

THE BACK-UP PLAN

The news droned on from the living room while Elias sipped his spiked coffee at the small round table in the kitchen. Staring into his phone, Elias barely heard the reporter half-heartedly joke about a pet dog turning to a Lycanthrope.

Two weeks. It had been two weeks since he last saw Skyelar. He could feel her everywhere; he could sense her thoughts always bent on him. He just lacked the courage to go to her right now. He couldn't bear the thought of getting shot down. Of coming in second place to the Sanguis.

Seeing Aezra interact with Skyelar at The Devil's Fountain made his skin crawl and his chest ache. The way she let him touch her back and kiss her cheek was equivalent to a bullet being fired. Wondering if she met up with the bastard Sanguis afterward was too much to bear.

Nothing about the interaction breached his agreement with Aezra, but Elias wished so many times that it had. He'd imagined the different ways he could finally cash in all the debts Aezra owed. Many of which included killing the wretched son of a bitch once and for all. Who would miss him?

Well, his sister, for one. Why that woman still harbored any kindness toward Aezra, Elias would never understand. It was a great point of contention between them. Not their reason for being so estranged after all these centuries, but it was in the top three worst conflicts they ever had.

As much as Elias hated to admit it, Skyelar would also likely miss Aezra. Whether it was genuine or just old habits, Elias could not be certain. And he was not eager to find out.

Still, Elias wanted nothing more than a reason to step in and stop this gut-twisting feeling he carried. Because he could not interfere with Skyelar's Life, he took a step back. She had to choose her own path, and he had to prepare himself for whatever, and whomever, her choice might be. Being centuries removed from the way things used to be, Elias could not bet his Life that Skyelar would choose him. Not at this stage. Not with his limited permissible involvement. They were simply too different.

Damn his sister.

Damn Aezra.

Damn himself.

Cowardice.

That was what it boiled down to. In all the years, all the centuries he'd existed, Elias considered himself a lot of things, but never a coward. Particularly as it pertained to Skyelar. He huffed through his nose and closed his eyes. There was a first Time for everything, he supposed...

Then, his ears picked up the sound of the reporter discussing an attack on campers at Freedom Park that morning. What the Hell? Elias rolled his eyes and sighed. Something was happening with the Creatures of this city and Elias had a hunch that the culprit was closer to home than he had the patience to deal with.

Right on cue, Lilith came into the kitchen, yawning. Her wild hair was pulled into a messy bun atop her head. She wore a red cotton tank top that hugged her silhouette a little too tight so her breasts could almost be seen as if she wore nothing at all. The tiny white shorts she wore in conjunction didn't leave much more to the imagination.

With her back to him, Elias could see half of her backside hanging out of the bottom of the shorts as she reached for a mug. All he could do was shake his head.

"Late night?" he asked, returning his gaze to the last text conversation he had with Skyelar.

Lilith turned with a smile, sipping her hot coffee with heavy eyes. He would judge her for sleeping in so late, but what else did she have to do today? Hell, he was dressed in his jeans and a button-down shirt as if he was ready to go to work, yet he was home. Clearly, he had nothing to do either, but everything on his mind.

"Nights with Aezra are always late," Lilith shrugged, taking a few steps forward so she could lean on the counter.

When was the last Time she saw him so sad? Her long memory struggled to answer. Not even when his sister royally fucked up everything did Elias allow a frown to form on his ruggedly handsome face. Back in those days, he just got vengeful, claiming sadness was a pointless emotion. Anger, vengeance, bitterness. Those were useful emotions. They prompted action and swifter satisfaction.

Lilith was used to seeing Elias' eyes shine like sharp venomous daggers, dark and foreboding. He was always thinking, always contemplating how to get what he wanted. Fuck what everyone else wanted. That was his motto for as long as she knew him, which was basically her entire existence. Sure, he would give someone what they wanted as long as he got something out of it. And it was never exactly as they wanted, was it?

Briefly, Lilith wondered about the gift he had given her. The gift of Aezra. Reuniting them was a calculated risk, Lilith understood that from the beginning. But it was not calculated for her; it was calculated for Elias and for Aezra. Lilith was just caught in the cross-fire.

If he had Aezra right where he wanted him, Lilith wondered what was making his eyes so soft and glum. For the first Time in her Life, she felt a small piece of her heart break for him. Her dear friend was in so much pain. Something she was only versed in when she was the one inflicting it.

"I'm glad you mentioned Aezra," Elias said, finally putting his phone down.

Lilith blinked a few times, startled by his sudden words. As he put the phone down, she caught a glimpse of what had held his attention. Skyelar's text messages. Pursing her lips and straightening a little, Lilith rolled her eyes. She might have known that was the cause of his odd demeanor.

Upon first coming to Murlance, Lilith had no reason to dislike Skyelar. Having never met the woman before, Lilith was willing to play nice. But the longer Lilith bore witness to Elias' uncharacteristic confusion and longing, the more she resented the stupid Creature for doing it to him.

If Skyelar was going to be with Elias, then she should just do it! Quit dragging him around and making him miserable because it was really making Lilith's job difficult.

On second thought, most of it was probably Elias' own fault. Lilith knew him well enough to know how easily he self-sabotaged anything he enjoyed. His ignorant slut of a sister had him convinced he did not deserve happiness. That he was unworthy of love.

Yeah, well, Lilith had a few choice words for Jenny, if Elias would allow it.

To Lilith's recollection, Elias had only been in love once before, but Lilith never met the woman. All Elias would say was he screwed up. Big Time. Now, Lilith was certain he was on his way to repeating the past. And for what? Just so he could stop feeling the heavy emotions that hurt him so long ago? After all, wasn't it better to be numb than to be in pain?

Gun shy. That's what he was. Lilith understood his plight. She was equally terrified of screwing things up with Aezra again, but she persisted, anyway. Why should Elias not do the same? He would need to address his fears eventually or he would sabotage whatever this was with Skyelar before it even started.

"What's wrong with Aezra now?" Lilith asked with a sigh. She really wanted to ask about Skyelar, but refrained. He would tell her when he was ready.

"Nothing specific. You've just been enjoying him so much lately that I think we need some help around here."

"Help?" Lilith chuckled into her coffee. "Like a maid for the house?"

Elias chuckled at her attempt to lighten his mood. "You know that's not necessary."

She shrugged. "Worth a shot."

"No, I'm talking about help for you," Elias continued. "It's come to my attention that you're a bit distracted, albeit appreciative of my kindness. But I think it would benefit us both if I called—"

"No." Putting down her coffee on the counter, Lilith shook her head. She needn't hear anymore about who he would call; she already knew.

"No?" Elias chuckled, shaking his own head. "I'm not giving you a choice in this. You're working for me, and I think you're overloaded."

"Elias, you know I am eternally loyal to you and what you need. I've never doubted you, even from the beginning when I had no idea what I was in for. I chose sides when I probably shouldn't have, and it was your side. It always will be. That said, I have to draw the line here. With all due respect, of course."

"You always were good at flattery." Sitting back in his chair, Elias folded his arms and smiled. He was amused, which was a nice aside from his self-afflicted pity party. "Alright. Plead your case, if you have one."

"Are you kidding?" Lilith laughed, leaning back against the counter behind her. "The others hate me because you chose me first. They don't think I have seniority to travel with you like this. Bringing them here will make my Life absolutely miserable."

"I am aware of all that," Elias agreed, "but you have to trust that I will protect you from them. You are the captain of this ship. They will follow your lead, or, I promise, they will walk the plank."

Lilith shook her head and rubbed her temples. It was entirely too early for this shit. Who was she kidding? No Time was a good Time to think about bringing in her colleagues. No matter what Elias said, he couldn't protect her from the wrath of those she once called friends. Being Elias' closest confidant tended to make others jealous.

It just so happened the others were more ruthless than almost anyone in Murlance. And they only listened to Elias.

"Thank you for that vote of confidence," Lilith sighed, "but I still object to this. I promise you I have it all under control."

"Is that so?" Elias wondered with a smirk. "Where's Ava, then?"

"Oh, come on. You know last night was the full moon." Lilith waved her hand at him as she took another sip of her coffee and folded her arms beneath her voluptuous breasts. "Ava went hunting like the rest of the Lycans. I'm picking her up later this afternoon."

"Interesting." Elias rubbed his hand over his dark beard, kept closely shaved against his jawline. "Since she hunts in Liberty Forest, I wonder if she has anything to do with the attacks this morning."

"I doubt it," Lilith responded quickly. She was trying to dispel her own worries just as much as his.

"I don't," he insisted. "I know what kind of control you have over her beast. It may be natural for her species, but it's not for ours. I've told you before this relationship is a bad idea. You're walking a fine line, Lilith. I'm not sure you can handle how tight the rope is going to get if you keep this up."

Lilith heard what he was saying, but she refused to listen. She bonded with Ava from the moment they met. It was so rare for someone like Lilith to have that strong of a connection to anyone at all. Elias knew that better than anyone, yet here he was chastising her for it.

As if she would let anything bad happen to her darling Ava pet. That was simply absurd. It didn't matter that she was still trying to sort out all the feelings she had toward Aezra and his Life-Blood sickness. Ava and her beast were the one thing that calmed Lilith's heart right now.

If Elias really wanted to, he could read into her mind and learn all her deepest fears, but he wouldn't do that, she knew. Just like she knew most of her fears were related to Aezra, and what he had been forced to become.

Worst of all, it was evident from looking at her. Elias could feel just enough pain radiating from her that he wanted to lighten her burden with the suggestion for more help. As much as she appreciated it, she had to do all of this herself.

"You know my relationship with Ava is true," Lilith said, finally. "I didn't use any magic to make that happen. We're bonded, Elias. I can't just let her go."

Elias nodded, but kept his dark green eyes sharp and steadily serious. "You're bonded her way, not ours. With everything happening, I don't need her to get hurt. You need to break the bond and set Ava free or I'll do it for you."

CHAPTER 8

WAX AND WANE

This Mortal was being difficult. Hope had never encountered a Mortal willing to put up so much resistance. The bond was there, but it was weak. Hope's magic was weak. What was going on?

To struggle so much in a simple mind bond with a Mortal was almost unheard of! If it did happen, no one talked about it. There was a reason Angels attempted the relationship with the mind first: it was easy. Or, it was supposed to be. Most Mortals had no way to guard their mind from the magic of the other Realms. That's what made many of them so susceptible to the dark powers of Hell.

Hope spent centuries stealing Mortals back from Dark Angels. She took pride in it, actually. Combatting them was a fun past-Time that always made her feel like a queen. The queen she longed to be.

Never before had she faced such a struggle when trying to reach inside the Mortal's mind. Hope briefly considered just going down to Earth to take the woman by force, but that would be dangerous. She could lose everything if she did that.

As badly as she wanted—no, needed—to take the Wielder of Fate throne, Hope had to play the game Fate's way..

After several days of struggle, Hope finally made headway and bound herself to the Mortal in question by a very long and thin mental tether. A glowing pink tightrope that risked snapping if the wind blew too hard. With previous bonds, whatever the Mortal felt, Hope would feel, too. She was meant to guide the Mortal's decisions as objectively as possible to ensure a better, more Heavenly path.

With this Mortal, however, Hope barely felt anything close to that. Perhaps this Mortal was strong and didn't need that much guidance. It was known to happen on occasion. So Hope did what she always did after bonding with a Mortals' mind: she took a break. The woman would be fine for a while without her. What was the worst she could do?

Besides, Hope needed a bit of rest before she attempted to bond with the Mortal's body. That was always a little more work, emotionally and physically.

Her unusually weak link to a Mortal further emphasized her own lack of bond with *The Hand*. Was Fate really rejecting her? Hope shook her head as she stretched out on her long, high-backed couch in the Observatory of her Guardian castle. Her soft pink gown draped over it, delicately, and sparkled in the light of the day.

There was no way *The Hand* could reject her. Never in Heavenly history did a potential Wielder of Fate not claim the throne. Hope always wanted to go down in Heavenly history for something, but this was not going to be her something.

She needed to clear her mind, that was all. Remembering what Patrise told her about focusing on the Mortal, Hope begrudgingly decided she had to make her mental tether stronger. The body bond would not form if the mental bond was too weak or broke.

With a heavy sigh, Hope wished Jaxsen were there. This would all be so much easier if she could consume some of his magic so she could obtain what she needed. Stupid Angels of Wisdom. Stupid Pied Piper. If they hadn't taken him away, she wouldn't be in this mess right now.

Suddenly, an idea struck her. Hope realized she did not need Jaxsen to be in her castle to consume some of his power. She could just go to him.

Swiftly, Hope flew to the Castle of Wisdom in Ecstasy. She carefully flew around the back of the castle to avoid the Defenders at the front door. The last thing she needed was more Defender blood to clean. No one could know she was there.

She searched the windows as stealthily as she could, barely risking a hair from her shining blonde head to be seen. There were not many windows, though, and she was left sorely disappointed. The only real windows in the castle were to the chambers of the Angels of Wisdom or their common areas. Damn!

Rounding the castle in more frustration than when she got there, Hope caught a glimpse of an Angel in white wandering the courtyard. As Theo turned his head to glance over his shoulder, Hope gasped and darted back around, praying she was unseen. For a moment, she just breathed and contemplated returning to her own castle in Grace. This was too risky. She would just take the Mortal by force and be done with it.

A flutter in her heart gave her pause. She put a hand to her chest, trying to calm herself. What now? Hope peered around the side of the golden Castle of Wisdom only to discover Theo leaning heavily against the Tree of Life. His head hung low and his right hand braced his stance against the Tree while his left clung to his chest. Hope felt a weight being placed on her own chest.

How odd, she thought. She had never felt such a sensation before. Angels did not typically bond to each other unless they were lovers. Even then, it required the entire Trinity of mind, body, and soul before this type of sensation was felt.

Curious, Hope decided to investigate further. Theo could be her ticket to see Jaxsen, after all.

Flying back around the front of the Castle of Wisdom, Hope smiled at the Defenders and landed softly behind Theo. She was certain to clear her throat softly so that she made a noise to alert him to her presence.

"Theo, are you okay?" She asked, placing a hand on his back gingerly.

Theo turned and smiled at her. "I thought that was you I felt lingering nearby."

"Really?" Hope was worried now. "I thought only souls who are bonded can feel each other."

"Oh, Angelic magic is a fickle thing, Hope," Theo half-smirked. "Fate affects us all in varying ways. But not having a Wielder to control it tends to encourage more sorrow and worry. Your struggles have been weighing on my heart, I suppose."

Theo pushed himself away from the Tree of Life with great effort. Slowly, he dragged his feet toward the small stone bench in front of the Tree and sat to catch his breath. Only when he appeared content did Hope dare to follow. Glancing at the Tree of Life, her eye caught a glimpse of a heart-shaped carving in the bark of the Tree's trunk.

Hope's eyes widened in sheer disbelief. That was impossible. She would have known it was the Tree of Life before making her stupid, defiant carving. That had to be a different tree. A standard Garden tree.

Yet, the more she replayed that afternoon in her mind, the more she could only recall that particular Tree. The stupid Tree of Life. Oh, Hell. Fright clouded her mind, forgetting all other woes. The punishment she would suffer if anyone found out would most certainly be the end of her existence. This was so bad! How could she have been so careless?

"Hope, is anything wrong?" Theo asked. "You seem quite troubled."

Hope tried to adjust her attitude, but she just could not step away from the Tree. Shaking her head, forcing a smile, Hope realized she had to move away or she would arouse suspicion. Quickly, she moved to sit next to Theo on his bench, ensuring her body blocked his view of the Tree of Life.

"I'm fine, Theo. I assure you."

"No, you must be worried about Fate," Theo presumed, shaking his head at her. "Its stubbornness to bond with you must be frustrating."

Continuing to hold her fake smile, Hope felt herself falter only a little at his insight. "How did you know?"

"I live with two women. Nothing is ever really 'fine'." Theo chuckled. "And I will confess, we're all frustrated as well."

Hope frowned for a moment, surprised at her desire to be vulnerable with Theo. "Do you ever feel...weak sometimes? Like you have so much knowledge and power, but it's just not enough?"

Theo took Hope's hand and squeezed it softly, smiling at her face. "As a matter of fact, I do feel that way right now. It's normal, Hope. Confidence, much like power, waxes and wanes with the seasons. You just have to remember this is all interwoven in the same tapestry. If just one thread frays, we all risk falling apart."

A silence lingered between them for a moment and Hope contemplated Theo's words. In her mind, Theo was implying she needed to bond with her Mortal completely. That would fix everything. Just strengthening the tether to the mind was not going to be enough to achieve her goal. Of course, a complete bond was not easy, but she had done it once before.

Then, if she completed the Mortal bond, she could consume the power of her Mortal and take what she wanted by force. *The Hand* would be powerless against her. She would be the only one who could rule it.

"Thank you, Theo," Hope smiled, sincerely. "That really was helpful."

As Hope rose to leave, Theo leaned forward in a coughing fit. She was startled and her white wings folded around her involuntarily. She knelt in front of him and attempted to help, but his Defender quickly flew over to take him away.

"Do not fear, Hope," Theo said in a choked voice. "I'm fine. I just want you to remember what I said. Your path to *The Hand* affects more than just you."

Theo's Defender took him into the great golden castle and Hope found herself more determined than ever to do this. She may have hated the Angels of Wisdom, but she always had a soft spot for Theo.

CHAPTER 9

THE DOUBLE AGENT

Patience was not one of her virtues, lately, and she feared she was going to be stood up. Although it wouldn't surprise her in the least. The woman in pastel blue wished she could be at the same cafe she always went to in Downtown Murlance for these meetings, but plans changed. In changing those plans, she was not waiting for Lola to show up in her matching pink shirt, hat, and sunglasses.

This Time, the woman in blue waited on Wesley Todd, Junior Pastor of the Church of Life.

Wasn't that something? Never in two hundred years would she have suspected her big brother of being a pastor. He never was very spiritual, in any sense of the word. Yet, that was precisely what he was doing. Why he was doing it, she had yet to determine.

His call to her was so rushed that she had no choice but to meet him in the open of Freedom Park. At least her outfit would blend in with the crowd since it was the peak of summer. Wesley made it sound important on the phone. Something big was happening. Of course, that was something big by Wesley's standards.

By comparison to her own chaotic standards, Wesley lived in a secure little bubble of love and joy.

Trying not to look inconspicuous, the woman in blue focused on reading her bible as she sat at a bench. All around her, children ran and screamed, playing their youthful games; adults laid out blankets and cooked on the provided grills; some even played frisbee or tossed a ball with a dog. The park was lively today and it made for good cover for their meeting.

The woman in blue had to be patient. He would be there soon enough.

And Wesley was there. He had just pulled into the parking lot next to the park. Before getting out of his car, he decided to try to locate Peyton once more. Since their fight that morning, she had not bothered to call or text. And now she turned off her phone's location settings, making her impossible to track, electronically. Sure, he could track her the old fashioned way, but that was a huge risk that he could not afford.

Wesley tried to control his anger, but he had to slam his hands on the steering wheel a few times just to get some of the frustration out.

The woman in blue glanced up when she heard a few beeps of a horn. Blocking her clear line of sight to the parking lot was a grinning redhead approaching her. The wind caught her bright, curly hair and blew it around her face in small tendrils. Her long, pale legs were made to look even longer in the tiny denim shorts she wore. At the base of those lean legs were bold red sneakers as if she had just stollen them from the wicked witch.

The woman in blue chuckled to herself. No, this was the wicked witch approaching. She tried not to judge her impending guest, but that low cut baby blue tank top did not leave much to the imagination. The closer she got, the more clearly the woman in blue could see the lace outline of the red bra underneath. Much to her dismay, even in dark sunglasses, the two women still managed to lock eyes. Damn it.

Lilith took a seat at the picnic table across from the woman in blue without being asked. She didn't need an invitation. This was a public place and it would have been rude to walk by without saying hello to someone she knew.

"Boy, you guys really love your bible stories around here, don't you?" Lilith asked.

She reached over to tilt the bible downward so she could see the book the woman was reading. Revelations, Lilith mused. How on-the-nose.

"What can I do for you, Lilith?" The woman in blue asked, closing her book, and pulling it closer to her body.

The woman glanced around the park and caught a momentary glimpse of Wesley at the top of the stairs. But, in a flash, he was gone. Likely scared away by the intruder at their table. This was why the woman hated meeting on this side of town. There was bound to be someone she knew at every turn. And she knew a lot of people.

"Oh, nothing, really," Lilith said. "Why? Were you here for someone else?"

The woman in blue shook her head. "No. I was just enjoying the fresh air."

"I can tell," Lilith said with a sarcastic laugh. "I hope you weren't trying to hide from someone. Did I blow your cover?"

Beneath her large glasses, the woman in blue rolled her eyes. "No. I'm actually just leaving. It was good seeing you."

As the woman in blue swung her legs around the bench to rise, a frisbee was sent flying straight for her face. Without thinking, the woman reached in front of her face, palm out like a stop sign. The disc halted in mid-air before sailing back to the group of teenagers across the park with nothing more than a flick of the woman's wrist. No one seemed to notice or care that she did not once lay a finger on the frisbee.

No one except Lilith.

By the Time it occurred to the woman what she had done, she could feel Lilith grinning behind her. She turned to look at the gorgeous redhead with the perfectly pale and made up face. Seeing Lilith stare at her expectantly with her hands folded beneath her chin, the woman wondered if she could still flee without further questions.

"Oh, I think you'd better sit here and talk with me for a minute," Lilith said, reading the woman's mind without her knowledge or permission. This woman was weak. For someone two hundred and fifty years old, Lilith thought she should have been experienced enough to feel when another force entered her mind. Obviously, the last two hundred of those years had not been good to her.

Or was it the last four years that really weighed on her? Yes, Lilith knew a lot more than these idiots of Murlance gave her credit for.

Obediently, not looking for trouble with a full-blooded Mythic, the woman rotated her body so she faced Lilith once more. She had a feeling her days of flying under the radar were about to end. "Elias told you I could do that, didn't he?"

"Oh, Harper," Lilith grinned. She stretched her arms out in front of her to be closer to the mayor's mistress. "He didn't have to. You're not as good at playing both sides as you think you are."

"Damn it, Lilith, can you not say my name out loud?" Harper scolded, pulling the brim of her hat down in an attempt to hide her face.

"Who are you hiding from?" Lilith laughed out loud, retracting her arms. "None of these people care. You're just the mayor's mistress, and nothing more. Practically invisible. Which is why your little scheme is *almost* perfect."

"Oh, people will care," Harper argued. "And if they find out I'm a double agent—"

Lilith held up a hand and shook her head. "Harper, I'm not here to rat you out. In fact, I'm here to make a deal with you. And I think you want to make this deal more than you're willing to admit."

Harper looked around. "Is this something from Elias?"

"Not exactly," Lilith shrugged. "More like something from me on behalf of Elias. Something Elias doesn't even know he needs in order to succeed."

Harper slowly brought her large sunglasses off her face to look Lilith in the eye. She was skeptical. When Elias said he was going to let Lilith take control of his campaign, all the Melatrommi were skeptical. No one knew her and they worried she wouldn't take their fight seriously.

"Lilith, I really think you should run things by Elias first," Harper encouraged. "He's the one running for office, after all."

Lilith shook her head slightly with pursed lips. "He prefers not to be bothered by such trivial things. His priorities are—elsewhere right now. But everything I do is to ensure his success...You *do* want to see him succeed, don't you, Harper?"

Without hesitation, and because she was backed into a corner, Harper nodded.

"Good," Lilith said, smiling. "Because I happen to know what you did to that little family you've grown so attached to, and I'll be sure to enlighten all of them if you don't cooperate."

"How?" Harper gulped. "You can't possibly know anything."

"You're right. How can I possibly know that you helped clean up a certain *Incident* four years ago by blaming it on some poor, innocent soul? Good job, calling my bluff."

"I—I don't know what you're—"

"Look, Harper, this little game of mind-warp magic might work on the Jerichos, but it won't work on me."

"I didn't do anything wrong."

Lilith belted out a laugh. "Oh, Harper. Who are you trying to convince?" She leaned forward on the table, her thin and chiseled face growing quite serious. "Because I happen to know that if Mayor Jericho finds out what you did, you'll be tossed out with yesterday's trash. And if he finds out what you really are—well, I don't think Dr. Danes will let you go free any Time soon."

Harper gaped, utterly floored with Lilith's miraculous insight. Even Elias did not know that information. How Lilith ascertained it was a mystery. If Harper was stronger, she could read it in Lilith's mind. As it was, Harper could only do what was best for maintaining her secret Life.

Clearly, feigning innocence wasn't going to work. Lilith had the ability to read into Harper's thoughts to decipher the truth. Something Harper suspected had just been done without her knowledge or approval. But that could not matter. Closing her mind off to Mythics like Lilith was not an option. She simply was not strong enough.

"Fine. What kind of deal do you want to make?"

"Meet me at The Devil's Playground tonight after sunset." Lilith reached over and took the large sunglasses away from Harper, putting them over her own eyes. "We're going to shake things up a bit."

With that, Lilith took Harper's sunglasses and rose from the table, leaving Harper alone to do as she pleased. Walking across the park in the direction of Liberty Forest, Lilith desired to investigate the area where the campers were attacked that morning. Before she could shake things up with Harper, she had to see for herself if her precious pet was, indeed, a menace or if she was in danger.

CHAPTER 10

THE OLD TREE HOUSE

After her brief—and surprisingly frightening—meeting with Lilith, Harper managed to catch up to Wesley. That he waited for her meant this was something serious. In the four years since the inception of their scheme, Wesley had never come to Harper for anything else. They would only see each other when the Jericho family held meetings, but it was never as cordial as Harper would have liked.

For the record, Harper had been against their plot from the beginning. Perhaps that was why Wesley did not acknowledge her as kindly or as frequently as she wished.

Wesley was a different Creature than the one she grew up with so long ago. The first fifty years or so of their lives were splendid. Sure, they were orphans, but they had each other. She even stood at her big brother's side when he found a woman who loved him for the Creature he was. That had been a beautiful day of sunshine, flowers, and celebration. Their legacy would have lived on through the family Wesley created even with the odds stacked against him.

But Time had not been kind to Harper and Wesley, and he was resentful for it. Harper could have felt the same. In fact, she had every reason to, but she dealt with their tragedy differently. Now, they were set on two separate paths. She wanted to ensure the safety of their kind, reuniting the various Creature species; all the while Wesley wanted to destroy everything they knew out of hatred and resentment.

At least he was willing to come home with her. Surely, that was a sign that things were starting to turn around. As they drove cautiously up the winding road, deep into Falshooke Mountain, Wesley managed a slight smile. The sight of the massive, hollowed out redwood tree filled his heart with sadness and his mind with memories. Most of them good; the few bad memories suffocated him like a viper.

"I can't believe this place is still standing," Wesley confessed as they got out of the car and climbed the ladder inside the massive trunk. They walked together to the edge of the cliff and stared at the old log house across the bridge. "I thought for sure it burned after The Great Extermination like all the others."

"I may be weak," Harper smiled, "but I can manage to keep this place alive."

They walked inside the same small cabin where Elias met Harper weeks ago. Home. That's what they used to call it. Hundreds of houses and hundreds of redwoods just like theirs once stood in a magical colony of Fairies. Unfortunately, all that changed when the Lycans wiped them out two hundred years ago.

Wesley had been right to assume the place was gone. That was what Harper wanted everyone to think. For two hundred years she lived a secret Life, often returning to this place for physical and spiritual healing. To her, it was a symbol of all Creatures and their ability to thrive in the face of adversity.

Looking around the old house, Wesley couldn't help but grin like the child he once was. The place was still lit by candles and solar lights. The furniture was still made of the same old tree roots that he remembered. And there were still old books on ancient Fairy lore, situated on a shelf in the common room.

"Damn. Do you remember the stories they told us about Lycans?" Wesley asked, thumbing through a book that was more truth than fable.

Harper nodded. "I seem to remember you wanted to be a Lycan more than anything. It scared the Fairies. You couldn't wait until the full moon."

"God, I was so ready to hunt," Wesley laughed. "And I *had* to take you with me. They wouldn't let me change unless I took care of you, too."

"It's been so long since I've fully changed, I don't know that I'd know how anymore."

"It hurts," Wesley said, sadly.

"So you do still do it," Harper wondered. "After all these years claiming you hated Lycans, you still change."

"I have to. This beast—it's not quiet. Not like the beast I used to be. It demands a lot." He shrugged and turned to face his little sister. Wesley took her hands and kissed her knuckles. "I'm not the same as I used to be, Harper. Letting those scientists fuck with my genes…"

"You can still set things right," Harper pleaded squeezing his hands. "If we work together, we can stop the Conquisitors from killing us and our Creature cousins. It worked four years ago."

"Yeah, but they'll keep trying," Wesley said, releasing her hands. "You know they'll keep trying. We stopped them for four solid years, but they're back at it again. Angrier and more determined than before."

"And you're helping them this Time," Harper added. She studied her brother for any sign of remorse, any sign of weakness that would tell her he wanted her to end this. Yet, she saw nothing save a black abyss that was a beast she no longer knew.

"I have to," Wesley said. "I'm a different kind of beast now. Not much Mythic magic left in me. You're probably stronger in that department. I just know I can't keep living this way, Harper. It's too painful. If I let it, the…thing that's inside me might take over. I can't let that happen."

Harper wiped a tear from her eyes and sat on the intricately woven tree-root couch. The leaves carefully laid overtop the roots were soft enough to provide cushion from the stiff bark.

"Why did you want to meet with me, Wes?" Harper wondered, leaning her elbows on her knees. "If you're not switching sides, you might as well leave. It's what you always do."

"That's not fair," Wesley snapped, turning on her with a growl. "I came to you because I was hoping you could help me with Derek. No matter what, you're still my sister. I thought you felt the same."

"*That's* why you called?" Harper laughed. She covered her face with her hands, unsure whether to be hysterical or upset. "Wesley, I can't help you with an unfixable problem. You have to realize Peyton's feelings toward you are a product of your magic. I told you when we were in that lab years ago that you would regret this."

"Impossible. There's no way my magic would entrance her this long. I'm not strong enough. Not like you. It's fading."

"And you want me to force her to love you?" Harper stared him straight in the eye, searching for a sign that he was joking. She wished he was joking. "Our combined magic is still active over everyone. No one suspects a thing, nor will they ever, unless we dispel the magic. The only difference with what you did to that poor Creature is Peyton's feelings for you required the absence of Derek. I'm sorry he's back, but that's not my choice...or yours."

Frowning, Wesley clenched his fists hard to keep the wild beast at bay. This was his little sister. The only real family he had left. He was not going to hurt her more than he already had. Although it was tempting just to get her out of his way.

It was a shame that she always seemed to be the one willing to tow the line. Willing to push the limits and try to fix the real issues at hand. Who knew she cared so much about being a Creature that she was willing to set the line on fire for once? To toss everything they worked for together out the window for her own salvation. That certainly changed things.

"Wesley, whatever you're thinking right now, don't do it."

Wesley chuckled and ran a hand through his hair. "And here I was thinking I could meet with you and persuade you to my side with the sorrows of my love Life."

Harper shrugged her shoulders and leaned back on the couch. "Looks like we were both wrong."

"You know, I'm still hurting from losing my own family," Wesley sniffled at the thought of his former wife and daughter. The gruesome way he was forced to watch the Lycans tear them apart. Tiny, delicate wings ripped to shreds, tossed into the air, catching fire from the embers of the destruction of their colony.

Wesley still had nightmares of it all. Every Time Peyton went out to that despicable club, he imagined losing her the same way. The beast within was meant to be stronger. It was meant to protect her from such dangers. Instead, he made himself a monster that she would never want to live with. Telling her the truth would be a worse demise than watching his tiny fairy daughter's bloody wings turn to ash. So he had to fix himself instead. And fix her. Being a Creature was a torturous way to live, and Wesley Todd had enough.

"Oh, Wes," Harper shook her head and winced. "Honey, we both lost family in The Great Extermination. But we have to keep pushing forward. We have to make their deaths mean something."

"Yeah, I know," Wesley sniffled again, wiping his eyes before the tears he held back plunged out onto his cheek. "That's why Peyton is so important to me. I finally found someone I love just as much…"

Harper just sat, letting him get out the pain in his heart. Whether he liked it or not, they were alone in this. No one else knew what it was like to go through that war, to lose everything. Every Creature they loved; every trace of magic that was gifted to them by the Fairies. Every ounce of the Creatures they once were.

Harper and Wesley were orphans on the run for one hundred and fifty years before they found the courage to return to Falshooke Mountain. Home. Now, it appeared both of them found their adoptive families. It was just a shame they didn't find families on the same side of the debate.

"Listen," Wesley said, kneeling down in front of her with his hands resting on her knees. "Kaylee and I are working on something big. It's going to change everything. James is going to make a big push for a cure once we're done. I think you should stay here. Maybe work on cloaking this place a little better."

"I appreciate your concern, but I can't," Harper shook her head. "I'm in this fight. I just wish it was the same side as you."

"Me, too, kid," Wesley said. He rose and leaned in to kiss her on the forehead. "No matter what happens, know that I love you."

Harper closed her eyes as he walked away. He always walked away. It was easier for him than staying and fighting the hard fight. He purposefully and strategically chose to side with the Conquisitors because it was easy. He could blame them if something went wrong. If he stuck with Harper, he would have no one to blame but himself.

Wesley never was good at admitting when he was to blame.

"Oh, and, Harper?" Wesley stopped in the front door, waiting for her to look at him. "You need to stop hunting for me in the forest. You're too weak to face me, even if you do find me."

CHAPTER 11

UN-HEALING

Ava was hurting more now than she had been that morning. Whatever that beast was that attacked her in Liberty Forest, it managed to get her good. Still, even with a bite from another Lycan, the water from Alchemic Falls should have healed her more than this. That she was still so injured is what made her unsure if it was another Lycan at all.

But what else could it be?

Damn her beast! If she hadn't been craving a post-full moon snack, she wouldn't have been attacked. Then there was the distraction of the wolf. The entire deck was stacked against her from the beginning, she supposed. Still, she could have taken that wolf. With Lilith's soft, calming voice whispering in her mind, Ava knew she could easily have killed that wolf and gotten her snack.

It made her wonder if that beast—God, please don't think the dreaded "f" word—was there to protect the wolf. That would be unusual unless they were mates. Sure, real wolves traveled in packs, but most Lycans just found a common hunting area and tolerated those who were there before and those who would come after.

The tragedy of The Great Extermination ensured Lycans were no longer interested in the hive-mindset. They might hunt together on the rare occasion if they knew each other well enough to be trusted. Husband and wife or parent and child were the primary "packs" of the modern world, but even that was reserved for larger prey.

Then, a low voice resonated in her head.

Hunt. Kill. Feast.

That was definitely not Lilith. All she could hear as she sat alone in her bathroom was a wild command to feast. She had to hunt, and she had to find something to rip apart, or she would die. That was a voice unlike any she had ever heard inside her own mind.

Ava was officially scared. She recalled what it was like for her cousin when that blood-sucking Sanguis took over her mind until there was almost nothing left. Ava didn't think she could handle it if the same thing was happening to her. She wasn't as strong as Skyelar. Even at Skyelar's weakest, Ava admired her for her resiliency and courage.

But who would be inside Ava's mind that wasn't Lilith? Ava didn't know anyone else. Unless...No. Stop almost thinking it. Ava was not feral. She was not going to turn feral. She would feel differently if she was feral. She assumed so, anyway. Having never seen or known a feral firsthand, Ava didn't really know what to expect.

Hunt. Kill. Feast.

There it was again! Sitting in the middle of her bathroom floor, Ava held her knees close to her chest and put her hands over her ears. She closed her eyes tight, mentally willing the voice the stop. She was just sick and paranoid. That was all.

And where the Hell was Lilith?

Hunt. Kill. Feast.

Food was the last thing she actually wanted. Ava's stomach had been flipping in circles all day long. She lost count of the number of times she heaved up just about everything she ate in the last twenty-four hours. It was all over her nice bathroom, too. Just when she thought there was nothing left, she had to hurl all over again.

Thankfully, her body calmed down in the last thirty minutes. Ava knew she should have called her father, but that would mean explaining everything. No one in her family had really seen her in two weeks. Her father would want to know where she'd been and who she'd been with. Too many questions. Too much to explain that would worry everyone. The last thing Ava wanted to do was get Elias or Lilith in trouble with her stupid family.

Hunt. Kill. Feast.

Groaning, Ava rapped her head against the toilet bowl, begging for a little peace. She wondered again where Lilith was. She should have been here by now. It was the oddest sensation to desire someone so completely without restraint. Ava never relied on anyone the way she relied on Lilith. It was as though all she knew how to do was sit here and be sick until Lilith told her to do otherwise.

She should have known this would happen after drinking from *The Fountain*. Elias always said the price would be high, but the reward would be sweet. So was Lilith the reward or the price? Her heart sank to the pit of her stomach, making her gag again.

"Oh, God, please no more," she begged.

It was no use. She gripped the sides of her toilet bowl again and heaved what was left in her stomach into it. Flushing, she leaned her head against the cool porcelain for just a moment. This was getting dangerous. Maybe Skyelar would have something for her. It would certainly be easier than going to her father at the hospital.

Reaching on top of the sink for her phone, Ava intended to call her cousin. Hopefully, Skyelar would do a house call because Ava really didn't want to move. Before she could press Skyelar's name, however, her doorbell rang. Groaning again, Ava thought if she just stayed in the bathroom, they would go away.

Hunt. Kill. Feast.

When the doorbell sounded again, Ava knew she had no choice. She had to get up and answer the door if she wanted to save herself. Even if it meant she would vomit all over whomever was waiting for her.

Stumbling from the bathroom at the back of the small one-bedroom cottage, Ava's world spun. She clawed at the wall with her wolf paws, desperate for any kind of grip. Artwork fell off the walls, some of it hitting her arms on the way down. She ping-ponged from various points of contact, clutching the dining room table, the leather couch, and every wall she could sink her claws into.

Pulling the door open slowly, Ava smiled when she saw Lilith standing on the other side. She couldn't help it. Relief washed over her, assuming Lilith could save her. Although Ava had never seen Lilith save anyone or anything, she had every confidence her master, her lover, could do it. Even in the darkest hour yet of her illness, Ava's beast adored and submitted to the redhead beauty.

Being a Lycan sucked sometimes.

"Ava, precious, what is wrong with you?" Lilith asked, concerned for her pet.

She walked inside the recently built cottage and immediately noted the scratches along the walls and claw punctures in the furniture. She focused on Ava, studying her carefully. Making the move to the middle of the woods in Falshooke Mountain two weeks ago was not something Lilith liked at first. The condo Ava had on the park was closer to Elias' house. One look at

Ava's deathly pale face, however, and Lilith was suddenly very glad to be in the middle of no where.

Lilith didn't even have to remove Ava's shirt to see the deep, raw bite on her neck and shoulder. Upon inspection, the wound was not even close to healing. Shaking her head with a sigh, Lilith expected as much.

Walking the area of the Forest where the campers were attacked, she could smell the blood and the foul odor of a confused Creature. Something that was not normal. It had bitten Ava. Lilith had enough magic to see that in a living memory as she touched the ground where they fought.

Lilith feared the worst now because this was uncharted territory for her. Lilith had never healed anyone in her entire existence. Then again, she had never been given the opportunity. Who knew? She might have some untapped magic inside her that could help. It wasn't likely, but optimism was cheap. A Hell of a lot cheaper than the stone cold truth.

"Do you know what did this to you?" Lilith asked.

Ava shook her head. Her teeth chattered although her house was warm. Her skin was pale and glistening with sweat from her drastic heaving. "I've never seen anything like it. It just came out of no where."

"Come here," Lilith ordered, walking her pet to the leather couch with puncture marks in it. "Let me see if I can't clean that up for you."

Ava sat and obediently waited for her master to return. "I've tried everything, Lil. The only thing that worked was Alchemic Falls. Will you take me back there? Work a little magic with it?"

Lilith looked at her skeptically, although she knew too-well the magic that pool held. Some of her magic came from those very waters. It was a powerful place and it could heal a lot of wounds, but Lilith was finding optimism more costly than she expected. "I don't think that will work…"

"Please, Lil," Ava begged, wincing in pain as she moved her left arm. "Between your magic and the Falls' magic, I'm sure you can heal me."

Lilith pressed her bright red lips together until they turned white around the edges. Nerves were getting the better of her, which was an unnerving feeling in itself. If she tried and failed, Lilith was unsure how she would handle it. She had never lost a bond to Death before. Then again, she could succeed. She had magic on her side.

"Okay, my pet," Lilith said with forced confidence as she leaned over Ava and stroked her cheek with her hand. "If you think it will help, I'll try."

CHAPTER 12

THE KISS GOODBYE

Driving Ava's car, Lilith took her the relatively short distance to Alchemic Falls. Death weighed heavily on Lilith's heart. She wanted so badly to be able to save Ava and cut these ties with as little heartache possible. Breaking the bond was not ideal, but the last thing she wanted was for Elias to step in. His interference would prove too painful. Yet, with Ava this sick, Lilith was starting to doubt that was Fate's plan anyway.

Lilith parked the car on the dirt pull-off in front of the road entrance to Alchemic Falls. She walked over and opened the door for Ava, taking her right hand to help her out of the car. Throwing Ava's right arm around her shoulders, Lilith could feel just how sick Ava was. Her body was freezing and she was weak, dragging her feet as they walked. Lilith wrapped her left arm around Ava's waist and helped drag her down the dirt path to the pool of the Falls.

The water roared louder than usual in Ava's ears. It wasn't that loud just a few hours ago. Yet, somehow, it sounded muffled. Was that normal? Wasn't that something her father had said about low blood pressure? Oh, God! Ava's heart rate increased and her eyes widened as she feared she was dying.

Hunt.

Ava shook her head in an attempt to rattle the voice out through her ears. At least it was just the singular command. Encouragement dared to peer around the corner and shine a ray of light on Ava's ill face.

Lilith stopped walking in front of the rock ledge and sat Ava down on a large, flat rock. Putting a hand to Ava's heart, Lilith felt the rapid, out-of-Time beating. It wasn't the feeling or sound of a normal heart that was scared; this was something different. Something Ava had been too afraid to admit to herself. Lilith could see it clear as day as the wound on Ava's neck and shoulder throbbed steadily with every thud of her pulse.

When Lilith inhaled, it was a trembling breath that hitched on a stifled sob. Ava looked at her as if for the first Time and tilted her confused head. Her hand reached up to examine Lilith's face, but Lilith caught her, unwilling to risk the contagion.

Hunt.

The singular command echoed louder than any other thought in Ava's mind. As her eyes glazed over, Ava was more willing to succumb to forceful order of the unfamiliar voice. She tried to turn away from Lilith to do as her master commanded, but Lilith caught her chin, sharply, in her hand to keep her steady.

When Lilith met her darling pet's gaze, she knew the change was happening. Ava's eyes were glossy and the amber in them was fading away. Soon, it would make way for something much more dangerous. A black soot that filled the entire eye and sought only for blood and fresh flesh.

Hunt.

The word flashed in Lilith's mind for a split second as it attempted to command Ava. No, this was not the same Ava that Lilith boded with only weeks ago. This was a shell of the Ava that used to be and Lilith had to prevent it from becoming a monster that ripped this beautiful body apart. It was amazing how deep their bond was in just two short weeks.

Sometimes Fate wasn't the bitch everyone thought she was. Only sometimes.

Kill.

Unwillingly, a few tears slid down Lilith's cheek and she covered her mouth in a gasping cry. Ava continued to stare. Unfeeling and unconcerned with Lilith's emotional display. Deep inside, some part of Ava knew what was going on, but that part of her was helpless to do anything but stare as it was consumed by the sickness. Driven to madness by the echoing orders. Compelled to reach her hand out and rip Lilith's throat apart.

"Oh, Ava," Lilith whispered through her tears. "I'm so sorry. I'm sorry I have to do this, but I can't let you turn feral."

She leaned in, knowing her window of opportunity was waning, and kissed Ava's lips one last Time. As their lips met, a dark red swirl of magic started from Lilith's lips and bled onto Ava's paling face, dripping onto her lips like gloss. Ava inhaled deeply until the red swirl entered her mouth and slipped down her swollen throat to infect her lungs.

The process would start there with decreased breathing. Then, Ava's entire body would begin to numb as if turning to stone. Her lungs and heart would be the last things to harden, but they would slow just enough to help Ava slip into a dream-like state before the blood stopped flowing to her brain. It would be painful at first, but Lilith had a feeling nothing was more painful than turning feral. Thankfully, it was a fast process.

Kill.

When she saw Ava's eyes widen in confusion and pain, Lilith lifted Ava's body using only her magic and laid her gently in the pool of Alchemic Falls. She stood by the rock ledge, watching as her pet gasped for breath, but was unable to move to swim back to shore. Swiftly, as the paralysis took hold, Ava's body sank into the depths of the Falls, drowning her.

Lilith's heart ached and she put a hand to her chest as the magical Lycan bond between them broke just as abruptly as it formed. She cried as she turned away, leaving Ava's car on the side of the road. As much as she hated to do it, Lilith was in enough trouble with

Elias to let Ava run around feral. Her loyalty to him had to come first, and she knew this was one way to prove it.

Fortunately, for Murr County, Ava Jericho would not feast ever again.

CHAPTER 13

THE MORTALITY QUESTION

The last Time a Mortal was of such critical importance, he ended up crucified. Fate corrected everything, of course, but the damage had been done. Wars were started over that Mortal; politicians tried to use him as leverage in their debates. All because of a sibling squabble between Heaven and Hell.

That was what worried Bane about Samuel's plan. There were more questions than answers. Why would he ask a Dark Angel to break a Guardian's bond? Especially from the future Wielder of Fate. More importantly, how did Lucien not know about this Mortal already, if she was so important to Fate? Truthfully, Bane feared for the day Lucien did find out. He wasn't quite prepared for another war of historical proportions.

Still, Bane would do as he was asked. He could have found the mysterious Mortal before Samuel came to him, but Bane had not really tried very hard. At that point, he was more curious than he was determined. Now, he owed this favor to Samuel and he would oblige without complaint.

When it came down to it, Bane owed it to Eveylynne to fulfill the debt and succeed in this Divine favor. He could not risk sending Eveylynne to *The Hollow*. While falling in love with her was definitely a rookie mistake, Bane couldn't help it. He had loved her from the first moment he saw her on Earth. His master was kind enough to keep her safe from harm until Fate allowed him to dismiss her, freeing her into Bane's arms. Now, all Bane wanted was to see Eveylynne smile. Mischievous as that smile could be.

Although Eveylynne was a very difficult woman to love, and, although Bane understood why Lucien quite begrudgingly took her under his wing in the first place, Bane still adored her. He could only hope she loved him enough to appreciate what he was doing for her. The sacrifices he was making to keep her alive.

In the tallest tower of his castle made of bone and charred flesh was Bane's Observatory. As he entered the dark room with black stone floors, Bane lifted his hand ever so slightly and the pit in the middle flickered to life in orange and red. The black walls were cast in shadow as the flames danced along the emptiness.

The warmth soothed his chilled skin and Bane sat on the plush chair in front of the fire pit. Closing his eyes and hovering both hands over the flame, Bane pulled the white hot from the bottom of the pit until it rose to his level. The magic flowing through the fire caused it to change from orange and red to purple before settling on the most brilliant shade of sapphire blue.

Concentrating with all his energy, he located Hope in Heaven. In her Guardian castle in Grace, she felt distraught; angry, even. Her confidence was waning. Why did this Guardian have so much anger in her? So much doubt? If she was to be Wielder of Fate, Bane feared the Three Realms would disintegrate into *The Hollow* within a day.

Ignoring the concern in his gut, Bane searched the open air around Hope. He had to locate the tethers that bound her to her Earthly soul. Samuel's insistence that there was a bond to be broken led Bane to believe Hope would have the Trinity nearly complete. Expecting to feel no fewer than two of the three tethers clinging powerfully to Hope, confusion settled in the room around Bane when he only found one.

Now, that, was unusual. How had one measly tether gotten the Pied Piper in such desperation? Guess it was Bane's job to find out.

Bane gave the pink glittering tether a gentle tug to ensure it was secure. It was there, but it was incredibly loose. Stranger still, but he continued. Ties between an Angel and their Mortal were like fishing line cast into the ocean. If Bane wanted to see what Hope's catch of the day was, he just had to follow the line. And much like fishing line, the tightness of the tether was not critical. If it was properly hooked into the Mortal mind, body, or soul, the bond was nearly unbreakable.

Nearly.

Eyes still closed with his hands facing the fire, Bane gently wrapped himself around the pink line and followed it to Earth. Moving slowly, to avoid alerting Hope to his presence, Bane allowed his magic to guide him where he needed to go.

When he entered the Earth Realm, everything opened up to him all at once. Bane's eyes shot open to look into the white of the flame as he was shown Falshooke Mountain. Many long years had passed since he last saw that city. Centuries. The last Time he saw Alchemic Falls with the dramatic mountainous backdrop—well, bad things happened. Things that he was still atoning for.

Was that why the Pied Piper chose to call on Bane? Perhaps it had less to do with his magical abilities and more to do with his deep-rooted connection to the location. Whatever the real reason, the Mortal was here; Bane could feel her. So close. He just had to reach a little further...

That proved easier said than done. A great concentration of magic swallowed him, nearly knocking him off his course. So much raw power generated in this one town. Bane was inclined to believe this was the epicenter of an Earthquake, like all magic used across the world was drawn from Falshooke Mountain.

No wonder Hope chose this Mortal. Sure, Falshooke Mountain had a mighty magical history, but the Mortal in question dialed it up to eleven. Eagerness and anxiety waltzed inside Bane, unsure if he was really ready to meet this stronger-than-expected Mortal being.

A sudden surge of power leaked from deep in the woods of the Mountain. With little effort, Bane narrowed his eyes and his sight became clearer. There she was in an adorable little stone house. He could see it all inside the flame just as clearly as if he was walking in the very grass around her house.

The sheer amount of power radiating from the house alone was incredible. Bane didn't think any Mortal could have magic that strong. Pushing through the thick of it to get inside her house was like swimming in a pool of gelatin.

When Bane finally entered the house to see the Mortal for himself, he paused, awestruck at the Creature who could spook the Pied Piper. She was simply beautiful as her long ponytail swayed when she moved around what appeared to be a laboratory.

Bane could sense something surrounding her. Something more than Hope's shockingly weak bond with her mind. The closer he got to her, the more he felt something akin to a force field keeping him out. But that was impossible. No Mortal could share a bond with more than one Angel at once. Could she?

Abruptly, the Mortal turned to look over her shoulder, grey eyes narrowed, searching for something behind her.

Holy shit, were those eyes piercing!

Bane jumped in his seat in front of the fire. He could have sworn she was gazing right through the flame that separated them. Could she see him just as clearly as he saw her? No, he told himself. Again, that was impossible.

But when the force of her magic wrapped tighter around her body like a protective shield, Bane wondered if the impossible was probable, after all. Although it was said no Mortal could sense the Angelic bond, he had his doubts right now.

Then again, maybe it was all in his mind. It had been a very long Time since he formed an Angelic bond with a Mortal, so Bane admitted he might be a little rusty. Perhaps he was no longer as calming and suave as he used to be. Sure, that was it.

Still, Bane continued to watch this Mortal carefully as she studied her surroundings. The magic in her stare, alone, was hypnotizing, and Bane just wanted to drown in the grey of those eyes. Bane suspected those were not Human eyes. This Mortal was something else. Some kind of Creature, but what kind?

The longer he stared into the image in his fire, the more something tickled the back of Bane's mind, the hairs on the back of his neck standing on edge. This Mortal…there was something about her. Something almost otherworldly. Those storm-filled grey eyes held a mystery that Bane was suddenly eager to solve. All the while, that tickle in his mind gave Bane the irrational thought that he had the solution somewhere in his memory banks.

Her concentration broke when her phone buzzed, and she turned away to answer it. Her voice was lyrical, almost Angelic. Bane knew well what Angels in Heaven sounded like; this Mortal was something special. As she made plans to go out that night, Bane made the decision to follow her. He would sit in front of that flame for as long as it took to weaken Hope's grasp on her until it broke.

Bane couldn't quite place what it was about this Mortal that made her so special, but he knew he did not want Hope to have any part of her. Particularly if he was able to solve the mystery floundering around in his mind. And, just like that, Bane was very invested in Fate.

CHAPTER 14

THE CREATURE TAMER

The engineering department was considerably quieter than the rest of VerHum Labs. Walking there, however, left a mass of guilt and anger in the pit of Wesley's stomach. Passing through the halls of the infamously coined Death Lab was agonizing. Hearing the pathetic Creatures call out in pain and misery spoke to his own inner-beast, riling it up again.

The first few times he passed them by, he stopped to offer some Godly words of comfort as taught by Nole. The challenge was looking at the Creatures, watching them morph from Human to abhorrent beast. Controlling himself from cringing in front of the beasts proved the greatest challenge of all. So Wesley stopped looking at the Creatures altogether, if he could help it.

After a week of offering unsolicited comfort to his fellow Creatures, Wesley gladly wore the proverbial blinders and rushed by the wretches to and from the engineering lab. He was here to get rid of this disease, not have sympathy for it.

Badging himself into the engineering lab, all Wesley heard were low talking voices and the hum of machines. It was refreshing and much easier on his absurdly sensitive beast.

The engineers each had their own project to work on for the Conquisitors, assigned to them by Kaylee. This was her department and only those projects approved by Mayor James were allowed in the lab. Thankfully, Wesley's little brainstorm from a couple weeks ago was one of those eagerly approved by James. The shooting at Town Hall two weeks ago served as a reminder that the Creature issue was the only one that mattered. Needless to say, the mayor just as easily called for Wesley's ideas to be the top priority of the VerHum Labs engineering department.

Pride swelled through Wesley as he approached Kaylee, sitting at her metal bench at the other end of the room. She had obsessively studied the sketch she made based on Wesley's imaginative description. Many lines were faded, erased, and drawn over again as modifications were made to form something real. It was certainly one-of-a-kind and she hoped they could make it work. So far, all of their testing failed. Moreover, Kaylee was really worried about Wesley's ability to maintain control.

"How's it going today?" Wesley asked, unintentionally sneaking up on her.

Kaylee jumped and dropped the papers onto the floor. She let out a small yip as she turned with her hand pressed to her heart.

"Wesley, I swear, that's not funny," she smiled, thankful it was him...in Human form.

"I don't know," Wesley grinned. He walked to the other side of the table and sat down. "I think it gets funnier each Time. You scare so easy."

Kaylee rolled her eyes and gathered the papers that he simply walked passed without picking up. While Kaylee found Wesley's insight into some of her projects helpful, she never was sure what she thought of him as a person. Knowing, firsthand, what lurked inside him probably had a lot to do with her hesitation.

She remembered creating that beast; she knew what it could do. The damage it had done already was costly, but it was nothing her father wouldn't pay to cover. Of course. Because money made the world go round, didn't it?

Still, Kaylee always thought letting him leave Danes' Genetic Research Center back then was a mistake. A Creature that ruthless should not have been allowed to be free. He could hurt other Creatures and kill Humans without having much control over it. Regardless of how "fine" he insisted he was, Kaylee suspected a day would come when he would crack. When that day arrived, no one would be safe.

"So, I'm thinking we've almost got it," Kaylee said, stacking the papers back together in order. "This morning I modified some of the wiring."

"But is the electric pulse still there?" Wesley wondered.

He picked up a heavy metal cuff and examined it closely. The outside was polished to a mirror finish so he could see his reflection. The inside was sanded down as well, but not as smooth. The cuff had a thick width to it and a number of sturdy springs inside it in order to withstand the pressure of expansion.

More importantly, though, the inside of the cuff housed a small mechanism that would activate a tiny butterfly needle if pressure was applied. Once the needle was activated, the metal teeth from a taser would send a shockwave to whomever was fortunate enough to wear the cuff.

"Well, I assume so, but I'm not going to test it on myself," Kaylee laughed.

Wesley chuckled and looked up at her. "Good thing I'm here, then."

"Wesley, wait a second." Kaylee reached across the table and took the other cuff away from him. They were a working set and one would not work without the other. It was a failsafe in case a Human accidentally got caught in one of them by a wretched Creature.

"Are you sure you're up for this?" she asked. "You've been doing this for weeks."

"A little self-sacrifice goes a long way," Wesley smiled. He reached for the other cuff and put the pair on his wrists.

"Sure, but...I just don't want you to go full Creature on me and I can't get you back."

"Then stop filling these with saline."

"That's Delia's department, not mine."

Wesley shook his head and handed her the small remote, which also doubled as the key to free the wearer from the heavy bracelets. While the cuffs were programmed to work independently of any kind of remote control, Wesley insisted on having one anyway. Sometimes a little shock to the system would remind a disobedient Creature who was really in charge.

Waving off Kaylee's fears as irrational, Wesley went to the large pod behind them. Between her skills and his control, no one was going to get hurt.

The test pod was Kaylee's latest design. Walls thick enough to not only sustain the thrashing and banging of a strong Creature, but thick enough not to crack under the pressure of water. She designed it specifically for Subject Alpha, but Kordelia and James had yet to give the green light on that transfer.

Thus, it became the test pod for the engineers. Right now, Wesley did not need the water element, just a pod that would keep him inside if he managed to fully change. Throughout the course of this little experiment, Kaylee was proud of her sturdy design. Although he had not yet changed completely, Kaylee felt safer with that thick wall between them.

The door sealed closed with the push of a button, and Kaylee stood on the outside, looking in. She held the remote, but did not use it. They had to see if the cuffs would work on their own first. Ideally, the remote would never be needed unless the Creature in question was to be set free. But, if the cuffs failed, they needed something to halt Wesley's grizzly beast before it changed. Because once that thing took control, nothing else would work to calm it.

So far, each trial yielded mixed results. And Wesley had the gall to poke fun at Kaylee's anxiety…

Closing his eyes, Wesley's breathing increased as he allowed the feral beast living in his Human body to attempt to come forth. In fact, he dared it to. He wanted to stop this thing. He wanted to show his own Creature who was boss. He wanted to be the one who tamed all the unruly Life on this planet.

Painfully, Wesley's skin started to stretch and rip away from his arms. Kaylee grimaced and turned away. She never could watch a Lycanthrope change; it was repulsive. However, she did not look away for long. Where Wesley usually started to gurgle and howl, now he was just yelling. But it was his Human voice calling out as he fell to his knees.

Kaylee whipped her head back around to see Wesley still mostly in his Human form. She smiled and exhaled a sigh of relief, despite the disfigurement in his arms. She realized, now, that his yelling was from the injection and shock. Clearly, it was still working properly.

When Wesley was finally fully Human again, Kaylee opened the pod and used the remote to unlock the cuffs. She took them from him and put them on the table to inspect for damage.

"That hurt like Hell," Wesley said, rubbing his wrists where he was punctured. "A little heads-up that you replaced the saline would have been nice."

Payback, Kaylee smirked, proudly. "CJ was working on something for Subject Zeta and I thought I'd try it."

"I think it was a little too slow for my system, but it worked." Wesley sat down across from her once again. He folded his arms in an effort to keep them steady as they continued to vibrate from the shock. "Just a few more tweaks and we should be ready to use this bad boy."

"Do you know who the lucky victim is?" Kaylee wondered, helping Wesley disassemble the cuffs to make the adjustments.

"No one's told me anything," Wesley admitted. "But, if it's all the same to you, I think I know the perfect candidate."

CHAPTER 15

A LITTLE MERMAID

Making her way into the experimentation lab —Chloey Jo didn't care what everyone else called it, this was *not* a Death Lab—she checked on Julia McCoy. What was left of her. According to the overnight notes, Subject Alpha was no longer responding to the medications given to her while on dialysis. Looking up into the pod, Chloey Jo understood what the notes meant.

Dialysis had helped Julia as much as it could. At least it cleared her of whatever made her feral. That was a positive step for science, right? Well, it should have been. If only Creature genetics weren't so dominant. This specially modified dialysis machine was designed to cleanse Creature bodies of the unnatural elements in their blood.

Apparently, for a Creature, anything and everything about Humans was unnatural because it was cleansing Julia of her Humanity. Fast, too. Chloey Jo stood for a moment and watched as Julia's legs suctioned back together and a dry, scaly skin grew over them to bind them.

Swiping her badge to enter the pod, Chloey Jo turned off the dialysis machine in an effort to slow the process. Looking at the medications, she noted the only thing entering Julia's bloodstream was a saline solution. Curious, Chloey Jo stopped the saline drip to see what happened.

As the last of the saline traveled slowly down the tube into Julia's body, her breath quickened. Julia's chest heaved up and down in rapid pulses as if she was trying to catch her breath amid the fresh air around her. Thankfully, they had her sedated enough that she could not move. Chloey Jo didn't want to know what would happen if Julia woke up like this.

Then, Chloey Jo remembered the engineering lab where Kaylee worked. Getting another idea, she unlocked the mobile bed and pushed it out of the pod, ignoring the glare from the HPA on the corner. At the end of the rows of pods was a sharp right turn to another seemingly dead end hallway.

Chloey Jo swiped her badge on the blank, white wall and the door slid open. She pushed Julia into the quieter part of the lab where only Kaylee and a few other engineers worked. She was unsure exactly what they worked on in there, but Chloey Jo did know they had a special piece of equipment just for Subject Alpha.

Wesley's head perked up when his sharp ears picked up the sound of rubber rolling over tile. That was unusual. Garnering Kaylee's attention, he nodded behind her so she could see the Conquisitor pushing a patient into their work space.

"CJ, what are you doing in here?" Kaylee asked, rising from the metal table. "And what are you doing with Subject Alpha?"

"I'd like to put her in the tank," Chloey Jo stated, matter of factly. "I don't think we're ever going to make headway with her if she's not in her full form."

Kaylee folded her arms and narrowed her brows. "Did Delia give you clearance for this?"

"If it worries you that much, I'll take the blame."

"That's not what worries me," Kaylee admitted. "We're using this pod for our own experiments."

"I guess we could trade pods," Wesley suggested. Admittedly, he was just as curious as Chloey Jo.

"See?" Chloey Jo said. "Problem solved. Now, will you please help me get this set up?"

"Oh, for crying out loud," Kaylee rolled her eyes.

She led the way to the pod and opened it. Helping Chloey Jo push the bed inside and secure it, they both stepped out. This pod had never really been tested before with a Mermaid inside, but she supposed they couldn't do more damage than had already been done to Subject Alpha.

Once they were both out of the pod, Kaylee pressed the green button on the control panel to seal it tightly. Kaylee stared for a moment with her hands on her hips, expectantly. The women glanced at each other, worry written all over their faces. If this failed and Kordelia found out, they knew there would be Hell to pay.

Kaylee took a deep breath and pressed the blue button so a vat opened in the ceiling and water flooded the pod. It hit Julia's body hard and bounced off her, causing her to heave and gasp violently. For a moment, Chloey Jo considered stopping the experiment, but she kept her composure and waited to see what happened. Curious, Wesley approached them and watched from behind, not eager to get too close just in case.

When the water level rose above the bed, Julia's body was unmoved. Instead of floating, she remained prostrate on the bed, her hair flowing around her gently. The heavy breathing and heaving subsided to the point that none of the Conquisitors in the room could tell if she was breathing at all.

Just when Chloey Jo feared she had killed Subject Alpha after all, Julia's eyes fluttered open. Looking around, frantically, Julia gasped for breath, reaching for her throat.

"Oh, God, Kaylee, drain it!" Chloey Jo panicked.

Kaylee mirrored her panic and started punching in the code to drain the tank. Before she pressed the last digit, she glanced up as Julia freed herself from her hospital gown. The Creature known as Subject Alpha writhed gracefully to wiggle out of the ties and other restraints. Using her arms to propel her, Julia swam upward. Her legs were fully seamed together in one long, opaque fish tail.

Julia swam around easily and freely, breathing as if she had scuba gear. The Conquisitors marveled at the sight. None of them had ever seen a Mermaid up close before. Not even Wesley had been so close to one in his two hundred and fifty year existence. They remained some of the most elusive Creatures, quite particular about who they trusted on the surface.

This transformation was a miraculous revelation. The others might have been star-struck with Subject Alpha's natural form but Chloey Jo was enamored with other things. The quick regenerative properties that this Mermaid seemed to possess gave Chloey Jo hope that she could find a cure for her father. Perhaps within Julia herself.

Cautiously walking up to the glass, Chloey Jo tapped on it to get Julia's attention. "How are you breathing?"

Julia smiled, but could not hear due to the thickness of the glass between them. Instead of responding, Julia simply shrugged and swam to the other side of the tank to examine her new cage. She was sad to see none of her books had been brought over with her. Not that they would survive the water anyway.

"You didn't think to install a microphone in here, did you?" Chloey Jo asked, turning back to Kaylee.

"No, but she is literate, you know," Kaylee retorted. "Just write it down."

Smiling, Chloey Jo turned to the metal table to snag a pencil and what she hoped was scrap paper. Scribbling her inquiry about breathing, Chloey Jo pressed the paper to the glass for Julia to read. When Julia swam back over to the glass, she smiled and nodded. Lifting her left arm to reveal the side of her bare chest, Julia revealed five slats in her skin, rippling in the water between five of her ribs.

"Are those gils?" Kaylee asked, stepping toward the glass to take a closer look.

"Yes," Chloey Jo said, amazed. "I think they are."

CHAPTER 16

PIECES OF THE PUZZLE

Skyelar was alone in her lab. It hadn't felt that way a few hours ago, but she was certain she was alone now. It was strange. For a while, she almost felt like someone was watching her. Like they were inside her lab behind her, waiting to tap her on the shoulder. But she saw no one. A ghost, maybe?

Chuckling to herself, Skyelar shook her head. A lot of magic existed on Earth, but not ghosts. They were parlor tricks used by Humans who wished they had magic like a Mythic. Everyone knew that.

It helped that Aezra called when he did. At least it seemed to scare the invisible intruder away. Oh, who was she kidding? There was nothing invisible about the intruder. He wasn't even intruding on her. Just weighing heavily on her. Yes, Elias Luck was real and he was invading her mind and heart.

In the two weeks since she'd last seen him, Skyelar lived more in her own daydreams about him than in her sad reality. She tried to call him, but he still refused to answer. The most she got from him was a text to let her know he was alive. That was good. She was glad for that. Relieved even. She drafted a text asking him to come over so they could talk about their future. It was a bold move, but after that near-Death scare, Skyelar didn't want to waste any more Time.

Before she could press "send," her message screen pinged with another message from Elias. He told her he saw her with Peyton. And with Aezra. Elias knew how difficult it could be to end a chapter, so he wanted to keep his distance while she worked things out.

Two weeks later, Skyelar still did not know how to respond to him.

His words weighed on her. Caused her sleepless nights. A boulder in the pit of her stomach would have been lighter than the guilt she carried over letting Aezra get within fifty feet of her. Moreover, that was the part that made her angry. Furious, even. She had nothing to figure out. Nothing was going on with Aezra.

Absently fingering the emerald around her neck, Skyelar held back tears. None of this made sense. Elias promised he would always be there for her. Why would he just casually step aside and let Aezra weasel his way in again?

There she was, lying to herself again. Skyelar knew damn well Aezra wasn't weaseling his way in without her help. If she didn't need Time to work things out, she would have sent her pre-drafted message right away. She would have told Elias right then and there that she was done with Aezra for good and she wanted a future with him.

But she didn't.

Why didn't she? Probably because she was angry at Elias for even making the suggestion. His inability to stand in the way was wearing her thin and she was sick of it.

So why didn't she send that text to Elias? Well, it was probably also because she was angry with Aezra for being so damn manipulative all the Time. Damn it all and their hot-blooded history. All she wanted was to make sure he didn't starve to Death. The bleeding heart mixture was supposed to last him months at a Time, but he kept coming back for more, sooner than she expected. At least it kept him from biting her.

But he knew too well how to push her buttons and make her weak for him. That was against the rules.

Really, if Skyelar wanted to face facts, she never responded to Elias because she was pissed at herself. After spending so much Time and energy being angry at Aezra, Skyelar realized she never truly reconciled her feelings for him. It was selfish of her to let that history continually creep up in her Life. It put Elias in the same awkward spot they were a year ago: the rebound guy. And Skyelar knew Elias didn't want to be the rebound; he wanted to be the one.

Shit. It had been a year hadn't it? A full year to the day since she was supposed to marry Aezra, but struck him down with lightning instead. Maybe that was why she was more emotional than usual. Remembering the way Elias carried her into his home and let her use his black and gold dress shirt in place of the destroyed wedding gown…Never mind that the gown was her mother's. Yet another reason for Kordelia to hate her.

Skyelar had to snap out of her daydreaming sooner than later. She cared too much about Elias to keep him in the deadly "other guy" zone.

That was it, she decided, suddenly. When she saw Aezra later that night, she would end things…Again. But for good! He could have her entire bleeding heart supply if he wanted, but he couldn't have her.

Skyelar was done. She had to be.

Resolute with her decision, Skyelar went back to her work. She twisted her hair around the base of her ponytail to wrap it in a bun. It was too hot to have it touching her back right now. Even if she was likely only sweating out of nervousness.

Wiping her hands on her shorts, Skyelar forced herself to concentrate on those conspiracy theories her sister mentioned. With a freeze-frame of her DNA and Peyton's side by side on her projector, Skyelar perused some of the websites Peyton sent her.

While most of the theories were just amusing trash, others actually caught her attention. One blog, in particular, speculated that the Jericho family had secrets so deep that no one really knew the truth anymore. While Skyelar was sure that was true, that wasn't the part of the blog that interested her.

Rather, Skyelar was interested in this person's theory that she wasn't a biological Jericho in the first place. Taken aback by the outlandish claim, Skyelar dug deeper, only to find a small community of support for it. Most people believed Skyelar simply manifested into existence four years ago when *The Incident* occurred. It made her chuckle until she started compiling evidence for it.

Numerous phone calls, searches through her own home, and hacker-style internet research later, Skyelar was despondent to come up empty. No birth certificate was on file for her. In any state. No record of attendance at any of the schools she remembered. And, most of all, no evidence that she set Danes' Genetic Research Center on fire. Well, all of that certainly explained the lack of genetic similarity between the samples on her projector.

Sadly, Skyelar could believe the lack of relation with Peyton. It was rare enough that two pure Humans gave birth to a Lycan. It was damn near impossible for the same pure Humans to, then, give birth to a Mythic.

It sent chills down Skyelar's spine and scared her. If there was no record of any of the Life she remembered —including nothing about her involvement in *The Incident*—why did the entire Jericho family remember it? Even Wesley and Harper remembered it, and they weren't part of the Jericho family. Not by blood relation, at least.

Skyelar was up to five bloggers now who agreed with the initial post sent from Peyton, yet she remained skeptical. Skyelar distinctly remembered fighting with her mother—or the woman she called "mother"—years ago in the old DGRC. Kordelia had the biggest breakthrough of her career. She had legitimately perfected how to cure Creatures. The long-sought after cure actually existed four years ago. But Skyelar got upset.

Kordelia wanted to use that cure on Peyton in an effort to cure Peyton, and, well, Skyelar couldn't let that happen. She did the only thing she could do to end it all: she set the whole building on fire. Nearly every bit of research was utterly destroyed, except for a journal or two that Kordelia might have saved. Moreover, it all but ruined Kordelia's entire career.

Skyelar's magic had always been wild and untamed. Like a Lycan not permitted to change at will. She had no idea what she was capable of four long years ago in a fit of rage. Her magic was simply unpredictable. Weak. Yet, somehow, she managed to break four of Kordelia's ribs, burn nearly every record, and take a Life all in the name of protecting Peyton. She did it with nothing more than the magic in her own hands and the hatred in her heart.

That was how it happened. Skyelar knew that without a shadow of a doubt. She was there; how could she not remember it?

Yet, these six bloggers insisted nothing about the traumatic event was as it seemed. Skyelar laughed in nervous disbelief when the primary blogger went as far as to suggest Skyelar had even been treated in Healing Hands Hospital for smoke inhalation and a concussion.

Smoke inhalation? Concussion? That was impossible. Skyelar set fire to the building from the outside. She wouldn't be stupid enough to remain inside while she did it unless she had a Death wish—which she most certainly did not! Still, the blogger had the hospital record scanned in as proof. There it was in black and white: Skyelar Jericho was treated for smoke inhalation, a concussion, and a few minor scrapes and bruises at Healing Hands Hospital. The treating physician being none other than her Uncle Reygal.

Who was this blogger that seemed to have all the answers? Inhaling on a long breath and exhaling again, Skyelar wondered if any of this was even possible. Was it even worthwhile to continue researching? The way the bloggers viewed it, the entire fire was a cover-up for something bigger and Skyelar was the scapegoat. Mayor James was the master of scheming, wasn't he?

Since there was no proof that Skyelar was adopted by the Jerichos before *The Incident,* she was inclined to think the seemingly conspiratorial bloggers were actually onto some truth.

Shaking her head, Skyelar knew that meant someone had infiltrated her mind to plant the memory there. And not just her mind, but everyone else involved with the Jerichos on that fateful day four years ago. It was the only thing that made sense. From the beginning, she knew Peyton was right; Skyelar just didn't want her to be quite so right. It was too scary to think about the level of magic that was required to pull off a grand scheme like this. And for so many years.

There was no question that a Creature was involved. It had to be a Mythic or a Sanguis. Someone with strong mind abilities and even stronger magic. After all, magic was fluid and Skyelar was not as strong back then. Four years or forty years, it didn't matter. Skyelar had only really come into her true power this year.

Come to think of it, four years ago, Skyelar met a couple Creatures who happened to fit the bill for a plot like this.

Finishing the entry from the primary blogger with all the sources and documented evidence, Skyelar's heart skipped a beat when the writer claimed Skyelar could not be involved in something so horrific. She was innocent as an "Angel."

Immediately, Skyelar knew who the author was and she had so many more questions.

CHAPTER 17

SIGNATURE LIFE

Try as she might, Kordelia could not seem to get Nole to leave her alone. Signing some stupid separation agreement might have been important to him, but that was the very last thing on Kordelia's lengthy list. In fact, she would do the next to last thing and still probably find something more important to do before she considered signing those papers.

Still, Nole persisted. He followed her around the entire Lab, learning too much classified information for her liking. By the Time she was ready to go into the experimental lab to check on the subjects, Kordelia knew she had to humor her husband for a few minutes if she was to get any real work done.

She led him into the conference room across from the main research lab, where most of the genetic compounds were kept. Nole walked into the room and sat on one side of the table. Kordelia closed the door without locking it and sat on the other side. They were silent for a few minutes, waiting for the other one to speak.

She placed her hands on the table, palms down and drummed her perfectly manicured nails on the pressed and polished wood. Her white lab coat was unbuttoned and she wore a pretty orange pencil dress with black kitten heels. Naturally, her hair was in a bun on top of her head like a ballerina. Kordelia would have it no other way.

Staring at her from across the table, Nole thought about how perfect she looked. Kordelia always looked so damn perfect. Flawless. It was the most aggravating thing about her. Nothing could be out of place. Even Nole and the girls always had to be impeccable.

They were the perfect illusion, Nole and Kordelia. That was when Nole realized why his father liked her so much. She was so good at creating the illusion of exquisiteness and having it all together that she made even Mayor James look like a victim of his own crimes.

Hell, Kordelia's actions made Nole wonder why Harper was the family publicist.

For the first Time in their marriage, Nole sat across from his wife less than perfect. His white polo with a gold cross on the breast was slightly wrinkled and he wore it untucked with his jeans. He knew it bothered Kordelia and he was glad for it. For once, Nole could be comfortable with himself. Now if she would just sign the damn agreement!

"Nole, honestly, if we're just going to sit here and stare at each other, we can do that at home," Kordelia said.

Nole shook his head. "That's not your home anymore, Delia. Just sign this so we can both move on. I know you're tired of having me hang over you about this."

When Nole pushed the tan envelope in front of her, Kordelia continued to stare. She had been served with the initial petition by the new Sheriff of Murr County. Inside the envelope was a copy of the separation agreement. An offer at a civil ending.

Well, that little show was certainly something not worth reliving. While she appreciated Nole's attempt to spare her any further embarrassment, Kordelia still refused to remove the papers from the envelope for perusal.

The truth was Kordelia was not ready to be without him. How many times had they discussed divorce in the past? She always said he would never go through with it. What made him all of a sudden decide he had the gall? It frightened her, but she would never say so.

Here she was on the verge of the second biggest breakthrough in her entire career and he was threatening to cave the entire house in on her.

"Kordelia, please," Nole said, rubbing his hands over his face, "We don't need to drag this out. We've been doing that for thirty years."

"I need Time to read them," Kordelia complained. "I'm just too busy right now to deal with another one of your flighty little whims."

Nole snatched the envelope and removed the documents, tossing them in front of her with a sharp thud.

"Let me break it down for you, Dr. Danes," Nole snapped, uncharacteristically. It was enough to widen Kordelia's eyes and stiffen her back even more, if that was possible. "We have irreconcilable differences in that you want to murder our daughter and I do not."

"Is this a joke to you?" Kordelia asked, offended at his tone and implications.

"Not at all, but I'm starting to think it is to you," Nole bit back. "I have all your things boxed up in the garage right now. I'm telling you, if you don't come get them this weekend, it's all going to charity."

"Nole!" Kordelia gasped.

Nole's face wrinkled and he shook his head in confusion. "Oh, don't act surprised. I've been telling you about this for weeks."

With a light tap on the thick wood door, Skyelar walked in. Oh, good. She loved walking in on her parents when they argued. What kid didn't? Feigning a smile, Skyelar closed the door behind her and stared awkwardly at her parents. At least, who she thought were her parents.

"Skyelar," Kordelia said, surprised, "what are you doing here?"

"I actually came to see Dad." She pointed at Nole and shoved her hands in her pockets. "But I guess I can meet you at your house when you're done here…"

Nole shook his head. "You might as well take a seat, Angel, because I won't leave until your mother signs everything."

"Then you're in for a long night, Pastor," Kordelia scoffed, "because I am not signing anything."

"Are you serious right now?" Skyelar groaned. "Quit acting like a child, Doctor Danes. There are more important things going on right now."

With a flick of her wrist, Skyelar lifted the pages of the stapled packet to each place where a signature or initials was required. She twisted her hand in a few loops and forged Kordelia's signature on each and every blank. Her father was getting his divorce whether Kordelia wanted it or not. He deserved to be free of her. They all did.

Kordelia gaped at her daughter. Clearly, Skyelar earned her courage from her father because that was a bold move, even for the Jerichos.

"I don't know why you did that," Kordelia said, turning her nose up at her daughter. "It'll never hold up in court."

"You know, I've got a really loyal notary at the church who would beg to differ," Nole smiled. "And don't forget that I'm good friends with Judge Ashford." He sat back in his chair and folded his arms, proudly.

Skyelar finally sat down next to her father, facing her mother. "Why are you even so upset about this, Mother? You hate him. Just get the divorce and move on."

"If you must know, *Skyelar*," Kordelia snapped. "I've never hated your father. I've only ever hated you. And you just gave me another reason why."

Skyelar laughed and shrugged. "Well, the feeling's mutual."

Nole reached across the table to secure the papers back in their tan folder. He held them close on his side of the table and stared. Without thinking about it, he reached over and squeezed Skyelar's hand, thanking her for the assist. He really did feel better already, even if it wasn't Kordelia's real signature.

"Well, since you're still sitting here, Delia," Nole said, breaking the thick silence, "our daughter had some questions about *The Incident*."

"No." Delia pushed away from the table. "No, I won't relive that tragedy while I'm in the midst of a new one."

"Yeah, I know," Skyelar said, lifting her hands to stop Kordelia. "But can you at least try? After all the shit we've put each other through, don't we deserve a little closure?"

Kordelia sighed and folded her arms on the table. She hated reliving the memory, and she hated admitting when Skyelar was right, but it appeared both were her best option right now. If she was really going to divorce Nole, she might as well get closure for *The Incident* and divorce Skyelar, too. Maybe they could figure out some unanswered questions together.

"Well, what about it?" Kordelia questioned.

Skyelar opened her mouth to speak, but hesitated, blurting out the awkward inquiry. "I mean, did it really happen the way we remember it?"

"What a ridiculous question!" Kordelia exclaimed, rising from her chair. "How could I ever mistake the the feeling of being crushed beneath flaming debris, Skyelar? You did that. You destroyed everything I worked so hard for and nearly took me and your sister with it." Running her fingertips along the edge of the table, Kordelia stared at her shoes. "Some days, when I think about that baby, I wish you had."

There was nothing Skyelar could say to change her mother's way of thinking. Clearly, Kordelia had been holding on to this for some Time. The question was how much more beyond *The Incident* was she holding onto? There had to be something Skyelar was missing. After the conspiracies she uncovered an hour ago, Skyelar wouldn't be surprised if she was missing an entire lifetime of pieces to Kordelia's puzzle. But she wasn't going to get her answers from the woman that was supposed to be her mother.

"Delia, settle down," Nole said, sternly. "We're not placing blame; we're just clearing up some fuzzy memories. Is that right, Skye?"

Skyelar nodded, but Kordelia continued to pout and they let her. With a huff and heave that started to turn into a sob, Kordelia covered her mouth with her hand and stomped her heels out of the conference room. After slamming the door behind her, Kordelia leaned against the wall next to the door to catch her breath.

The tears came without her permission. The memory of losing everything in that fire was still too fresh. It still weighed on her heart like it happened just yesterday. Although she might have learned a few things that changed her perspective of *The Incident,* Kordelia's emotions would not let her forget what it felt like to lose a Life in such a tragic way.

Skyelar might have been right about closure, but Kordelia knew this was not how she would get it.

The kind of closure Kordelia needed was not for the Death of the unborn child. Life ebbed and flowed. Some lived; some died. It was science. What upset Kordelia more than anything was losing all of the research, the cure. In all the years since *The Incident* she had never been able to replicate anything she researched.

Until last year, Kordelia presumed all of her useful methodology from the DGRC was dust in the wind. Watching Skyelar, examining the Jericho family bloodline a bit closer, and Kordelia wondered if she simply did not want to shatter the Utopian illusion she had created.

With another heaving inhale and focused exhale, Kordelia slowly realized a window in her house of perfection had a brick thrown in it. And it came from the inside. Would she engineer a fix for it so no one could see? Or would she begin chipping away at the fragments to let the air inside? It was getting awfully stale in there.

With a week and a half until the Independence Day festivities, there was no telling what the correct choice was anymore.

CHAPTER 18

LIFE IMITATING ART

Nole waited for Kordelia to leave before he smiled at his daughter. They could hear Kordelia crying outside in the hallway, but they ignored her. Melodrama was her strong suit when things weren't going her way. That was one of the reasons Nole was glad to divorce her.

"So...Peyton sent me some blogs..." Skyelar said slowly. "One of them had some pretty interesting things in it..."

"I'm sure you found a lot of interesting things," Nole continued to smile. "The internet is a strange place."

"Okay, be honest with me," Skyelar said, surprisingly nervous.

Nole reached over and took her hand, rubbing her knuckles with his thumb. "You know I always am."

"You wrote a blog about me, didn't you?"

He laughed and sat back in his chair again with a new light in his soft brown eyes. "I did. About six months ago. I was hoping you'd find it one day."

"Why wouldn't you just tell me?" Skyelar sat back, mirroring his pose. "I don't know if I ever would have found it on my own. And I really want to know how you have a different memory from the rest of us."

"One question at a Time. First of all, when *The Incident* happened, Delia and I were separated," he reminisced, unenthusiastically. "But when your uncle called to say Delia was having surgery and her lab burned down, I was in this sort of haze. It's like the Life I had before that phone call was just a dream. A movie I saw or something."

"Yeah, I know how that goes," Skyelar said, sadly, recalling her fabricated relationship with Aezra.

Nole frowned with his eyes and shook his head. "Well, when Reygal said your name and that it was your fault, the Life I had before just became only memories with you. You and Peyton growing up together; you and Delia butting heads. And all this tension that would lead to an implosion like that."

Skyelar narrowed her brows and tilted her head. Her right hand came up to the jewel hanging around her neck and rubbed it for comfort. "But the hospital record you posted—it said Reygal treated me for smoke inhalation and a concussion or something."

Nole nodded, refusing to deny anything he knew anymore. "He did. He doesn't remember that he did, but the records say so. I found those in an old rusty filing cabinet we forgot all about. It was with the police report about the fire. You were in there, Skye, and you got injured from it. I don't quite remember why, but I'll bet your mother does."

Nole paused and stared at the wedding band on his finger. As the film of his old Life flickered in the forefront of his mind, Nole recalled desiring this divorce for years. Long before Kordelia dared to experiment on a fetus. Nole could not stand behind her as she changed God's will like that.

Now, he could be free. He removed the wedding band and set it on top of the tan envelope with resolution. Like a weight too heavy for him to carry anymore.

"Anyway," he resumed, "when you figured out Aezra was in your head last year, that's what got me started thinking about *The Incident* all over again. Maybe that movie I thought I saw was real and everything else was made up. Then I found the police report last month and, well, it all made a Hell of a lot more sense than what the rest of the family believes."

"Why didn't you tell me?" Skyelar wondered again, a little hurt that he would keep something so big from her. He was the only member of the Jericho family she really trusted.

"Because, Angel, I don't have anything else to give you." Nole rubbed his ring finger in the spot where the wedding band used to be. The skin was soft and smooth. "As far as I know, I'm making all this up because of the stress of the divorce."

"You're not crazy," Skyelar chuckled lightly. "Peyton and I aren't related. Not a single solitary piece of genetic info in common."

"Ah, so the cat's out of the bag," Nole smiled. "Related or not, you girls are so damn smart. I knew you'd figure it all out one way or another."

Skyelar shrugged with a half grin. "I guess. I mean, I feel like I'm an imposter now. Like I've been living someone else's Life. All I have left are questions that I guess can't be answered."

Leaning forward again, Nole took both of her hands in his like he would pray with her. "Angel, I may not know exactly why or how you came into our lives, but, to me, it's like you've been here all along."

Tugging her into him by her hands, Nole cuddled Skyelar against his chest and stroked her soft, dark hair. He had thought about that before writing the blog. Did he want to expose this truth and lose everything he believed? Once the veil was lifted, there was no putting it back down. Yet, Nole still pushed forward and he was glad for it. He knew he could love her more knowing that she was a gift for him and his family. Even if her Purpose was still a mystery, Nole knew she would do good.

Skyelar always did good in the end.

Nole felt her tears falling onto his chest and he tilted her head up to look at her in the eyes. He kissed her nose and she smiled. That was more like it. She had the most radiant smile he'd ever seen. Coupled with those murky grey eyes, she was a picture if he ever saw one.

"Now, you listen to me," Nole said, putting his pastor voice on. "I have all these memories of you etched right on my heart, and no one can take those away. Like all your fancy tattoos there."

Skyelar smiled at him and leaned her head on his shoulder. "I love you, Daddy."

"I love you, too," he said, softly. "And you have more than you think you do. Peyton still loves you. No matter what she says. And you've got a young man who gave you that necklace. That's not insignificant."

"That's the other thing," Skyelar said, sitting up to inhale deeply, forcing the rest of her tears to retreat. "I don't even think I have him anymore. My heart—it feels so...empty."

"Now, don't say that," Nole waved her off, brushing the tears from her cheek. "You guys have your whole lives ahead of you. These things take Time. You and him both know how to make it right. You just have to get up and do it."

Skyelar laughed, involuntarily, and almost hysterically. Clutching the gem around her neck tightly, her knuckles turned white. Her breath hitched on a hiccup, making her blush for her unusual emotional display.

"Dad, I don't think I have the energy to sort this out with Eli; figure out who the Hell I am; and sort through the shit the fucking Conquisitors are trying to do all at the same Time. Plus I've got this stupid new Creature I found—"

"Don't do all that, honey," Nole said, hurriedly. He smiled at her wide and proud. She was so much like Kordelia in spite of not being biologically related. They both had the worst habit of biting off more than they could chew, but they would never ask for help. They didn't like burdening anyone with their troubles, but when his little girl started to have a nervous breakdown in front of him, Nole knew it was no burden to help her.

"What?" Skyelar asked, trying to steady her breathing.

"Angel, no one said you have to do any of those things if you don't want to," Nole smiled. "Who cares about biology? You're my daughter; you're Peyton's little sister. There. Problem solved."

The corner of her mouth curved slightly at her father's overly-simplistic solution. "It's not that easy."

"Sure it is!" Nole insisted. "Skye, I can give you a simple solution to every single problem you listed, but the real solution here is to give it up to God. Let Him sort it out for you. If you listen real close, you can hear Him whisper to you. I hear Him every single day."

"I'm just so worried if I drop the ball on anything, I'll lose it all." Skyelar leaned forward and put her head in her hands. "I'm at such a loss, and...overwhelmed."

That may not have been easy for her to admit, but Nole was glad she was able to do it. Maybe having all those things on her plate gave her the confidence to stay grounded. He worried she might get flighty and do something drastic, so he showed her more affection than normal. Encouraged more than he normally felt was necessary. Anything to ensure Skyelar stayed the course.

She couldn't lose track of the light. If she did, that's when he knew she would travel down the path of no return. He watched it happen with Kordelia. While Nole had no way of knowing what that path was, he knew Skyelar Jericho was a gift from God, and he would be damned if anyone would ruin her mission. Including herself!

"You know, Angel, I can sit here and tell you everything's going to be fine all night, and I'll keep doing it if you need me to. But if it were me with that long list of grievances, I'd say nothing is more important than the man who's clearly got a piece of your heart."

Skyelar looked up at him, tears staining her face and washing the grey out of her eyes. Still, she smiled. He was right; everything else she had to do was just busy work. Speed bumps to slow her down from what she really wanted. Regardless of who her family was, Skyelar knew she did not want to live any kind of Life without Elias.

CHAPTER 19

A WOMAN SCORNED

Kordelia wanted to go back inside to finish their conversation. After calming herself and touching up her makeup in her office, the director thought it only logical to understand Skyelar's motives. Perchance, mend a few fences.

Contradictory to her standard rational nature, Kordelia's emotions got the better of her when it came to Skyelar. In four years, that little brat had not offered to discuss the heartache of *The Incident* once. It was almost as though Skyelar didn't go through the same trauma. Well, Kordelia certainly would believe that Skyelar didn't face the same emotional turmoil; she always was a jealous little Creature.

Just as she decided to go back into the conference room, Kordelia happened to glance through the blinds to see Nole holding Skyelar lovingly against his chest. The devotion of her husband toward the girl shattered Kordelia's heart. There never was enough love to go around in their little family, no matter how he tried to preach it in his sermons.

The thought did cross her mind that she was the jealous one, not Skyelar. It wasn't the first Time that thought occurred to her, but she refuted it with hard evidence. Namely, the evidence that Nole always willingly made exceptions for Skyelar while letting the rest of them fall into the mud and the muck. And now he was divorcing Kordelia because of it.

Well, that stopped now. Kordelia would be Nole's victim no longer!

Swiping her badge on the keypad across the hall, Kordelia entered the small research office. Thankfully, Chloey Jo was on duty for the next couple of days. As fond as Kordelia was of Peyton, she knew the bond her daughters shared was stronger than either of them were willing to admit. Peyton was weak for her little sister, and Kordelia had to do damage prevention before it was too late.

"Dr. Danes," Chloey Jo said, seemingly exhausted already. "What can I do for you?"

"I need you to work on the Omega Project," Kordelia ordered.

She attempted to remain stoic as she said it, but her bitterness and anger bled through. Running a hand over her hair, Kordelia adjusted her glasses and cleared her throat. She had to maintain control. Getting upset would only give Skyelar more power. And that little bitch had enough power as it was.

"My pleasure!" Chloey Jo perked up, instantly ceasing all other activity. It was no secret Chloey Jo had been dying to get her hands on the Omega Project for weeks. She firmly believed giving it to Peyton was a terrible mistake. The Jericho sisters were up to something; Chloey Jo just knew it. Now, it seemed Kordelia was finally inclined to agree with her.

"Can I ask why?" Chloey Jo asked, attempting to sound innocent enough.

"No, you may not," Kordelia stated, regaining her composure. "You may think you've done well with your little experiment of Subject Alpha, but I promise you, this is not a reward."

"Dr. Danes, I'm sure she's more useful to us this way than in a medically induced coma."

"Well, we'll see, won't we?"

Kordelia went to Peyton's half of the office where the small refrigerator sat beneath a shelf. Inside were all the Jericho samples Peyton was assigned to decipher and attempt to cure. Skyelar's specimen was not difficult to find as it was the only one that glowed in its eery fashion. The vile was warm, too, in spite of being in the fridge at a low temperature.

Using one of the empty tubes on Peyton's desk, Kordelia poured half of the glowing specimen into it. When she put the other one back in the fridge, Kordelia marched over to Chloey Jo's bench and gave her the impossibly small sample. It was the closest thing to a cure that they had, so it had to be used sparingly.

"What's this?" Chloey Jo asked, confused.

"The Omega Project, Dr. Johnson. It has come to my attention that none of you are taking this matter as seriously as it is. As such, you'll be competing against Peyton to find a cure."

"Well, that hardly seems fair," Chloey Jo complained. "There's only a week and a half left. How can you expect me to give you a cure when I'm already behind?"

Kordelia put the glowing tube in a wooden holder and went to the sink to wash her hands. "Because the stakes are incredibly high, Doctor. I agreed to bring Jared to the Lab for the safety of the county, but, if you fail me, I will ensure he's properly exterminated."

Chloey Jo's jaw dropped to the floor and her heart splashed into the acid of her stomach. "You can't do that."

Kordelia finished drying her hands and spun on her heel to face her subordinate. "Do you really want to risk that I can't? He's a danger to himself and others, Chloey Jo."

Chloey Jo gulped and shook her head. She knew how serious Kordelia could be when it came to her work. Everyone knew the VerHum Labs director was a powerful woman, but Chloey Jo doubted anyone suspected she had the ability to kill an innocent being. Something about the shadows floating in her honey brown eyes warned the young Conquisitor that Kordelia's power was stronger than anyone knew.

Regardless of what Jared was, he was still Chloey Jo's father. The mayor may think he needed this cure for the general Creature populous, but Chloey Jo was suddenly acutely aware that her father had to be her top priority. If he could not be cured soon, all of Murr County would take this political deal as an opportunity to destroy what they truly feared.

Days like today, concerns such as these, were shining examples of why Chloey Jo had no Life outside of Jared. He needed her more than he knew, and she refused to let him down now. If Kordelia's aim was to make her Conquisitors more ruthless, like her, then Chloey Jo had to be up for the challenge.

"What about Peyton?" Chloey Jo dared to ask. "What happens if she fails?"

"That's not your concern. You just focus on keeping your father alive and giving me that cure." Kordelia started for the door, keying her badge to slide it open again. Before she stepped into the hall, she turned to Chloey Jo again. "Oh, and, CJ? I mean for you to get that cure by any means necessary."

CHAPTER 20

FLESH WOUND

Shortly after arriving home from VerHum Labs, Skyelar's magical alarm system alerted her that Peyton crossed into the border of her property. Nothing resounded around her to inform her of her sister's presence. Instead, it was a soft tickle on the back of Skyelar's neck, raising the hairs ever so slightly. It was a gentle warming of her blood that someone familiar was approaching. The very aura that Peyton carried with her stretched out and knocked on Skyelar's door long before Peyton's car pulled up next to the house.

It was good timing, too, because Skyelar was getting anxious for an update on the Conquisitor's progress. The last thing she heard from her sister was that no one was even close to a cure. While that pleased Skyelar, she also worried her mother would start to get desperate. Ten days until the picnic was not a long Time, but Skyelar knew better than to underestimated Kordelia Danes.

Here was hoping their little disagreement back at VerHum Labs did not add more kerosene to the fire.

Skyelar inhaled a deep breath, recalling Nole's words of encouragement. Focus on one thing at a Time. One solution would lead to the next. When she wasn't so worried about it all falling apart, she would be able to put the pieces into place. While she planned to focus on her situation with Elias first, Skyelar still wanted to know what was happening with the Conquisitors. Even if she paused her own research for a while.

So she left the door open behind her and sat on a stool at her work bench, waiting for her sister to enter. When Peyton screeched to a halt in the front yard, Skyelar slid, cautiously, off her stool to walk to the doorway. Angry Peyton was dangerous. Peering around the doorjam, Skyelar worried who was going to come crashing in: the Human or the wolf? As a precaution, she waved her hand in a minuscule movement to open the door to the cage on the other side of the room.

Better safe than bloody with a destroyed lab.

Peyton stomped into the lab, eyes ablaze with amber and the threat of changing, but Skyelar breathed a sigh of relief that she was still Human right now. Human Peyton was someone Skyelar could tame. Wolf Peyton, Skyelar would have to fight to throw in that cage.

"He's fucking alive *and* in town!" Peyton announced, slamming the door to the lab closed behind her. The walls rattled with the force of her anger. Skyelar's magic bled off the worried walls, encircling her in an invisible force field until she knew she was in the clear.

"Okay..." Skyelar exhaled, leaning against one of her stools to stay out of the way. "Who are we talking about, again?"

"Oh, no one special," Peyton laughed, throwing her hands into the air. "Just Derek-fucking-Noble!"

Skyelar was left speechless for a moment. Derek Noble was definitely the last name Skyelar expected to hear her sister say at all, let alone to say he was in town. So many questions ran through her mind, but she had no idea where to begin.

"I know what you're thinking," Peyton grumbled, seeing the wheels turning in Skyelar's head. "I have absolutely zero answers. Only these weird mixed feelings that I don't feel like dealing with right now."

Gaping at Peyton's rare emotional honesty, Skyelar simply nodded. She could not help the surprised look on her face. There was no way Peyton could spring that kind of news on her and not expect her to be involuntarily shocked.

Not quite ready to calm down, Peyton stomped her way over to the small greenhouse where Skyelar kept her marijuana. She needed something to release this tension. Driving aimlessly for a couple hours did her absolutely no good. It only served to bring her disorientation to a fiery rolling boil.

Tugging at the handle to the four-foot marijuana habitat, Peyton hoped Skyelar had something strong. Something that would wipe her brain clean of that morning. She didn't care if she was drooling in the corner of the couch. As long as she didn't have to feel whatever this was. But Peyton only got angrier when she tried to pull the handle to open it and it wouldn't budge. Using all her strength, Peyton yanked on the handle, nearly shattering the entire greenhouse to pieces.

With a quick flick of two fingers upward, Skyelar unlocked the greenhouse so Peyton could help herself. She just stood back and smiled when Peyton turned to glare at her for helping. Peyton didn't want help right now, but there were limitations to what the poor Creature could do. Watching her sister sloppily roll a terribly packed joint, Skyelar decided this was one of those limitations.

"Just go sit down, okay?" Skyelar said, taking the paper and ground plant from her. "I've got this."

Without using her magic, Skyelar rolled a tight and neat joint, even lighting it for Peyton to avoid further hassle. She intended to just let her sister have the entire thing, but seeing her so uptight made Skyelar nervous. And she had to take a quick hit before handing it over.

Grateful, Peyton accepted the joint with trembling hands. She inhaled and exhaled once before putting it up to her lips with measured movements. Mid-inhale,

Peyton winced, suddenly remembering the real reason she was there. Not yet, she thought. She needed to calm down a little more before letting Skyelar do her work. Still, she switched hands and leaned on the non-injured side, hoping Skyelar wouldn't notice.

That was absurd because, of course, Skyelar noticed. Skyelar noticed everything about Peyton. Unobtrusively as possible, she moved to the coffee table and sat in front of her sister.

"Take off your shirt," Skyelar ordered, albeit gingerly. "Please."

"Fuck off." Peyton laughed and blew a smoke cloud in her face. "Please."

Skyelar chuckled and inhaled some of the smoke. "Peyton, I can do this the easy way or the hard way. I really don't care."

"That's fine. No one seems to care about my feelings anyway." Peyton handed the joint to Skyelar for only a moment so she could remove her oversized tee shirt. She used her left arm to cover her bare breasts. It was just as well; it helped keep her arm out of Skyelar's way.

When Peyton was comfortable and puffing on the joint again, Skyelar was surprised for the second Time since Peyton's arrival. The inflamed and infected wound in Peyton's side visibly throbbed over her ribs. Pieces of Peyton's muscle and tissue were exposed.

"How are you not dying on the floor right now?" Skyelar wondered.

Peyton shrugged. "The wolf, I guess. Sometimes it takes most of the heat. You know, so I can feel all these wonderful Human emotions instead."

Skyelar ignored her sister's angst and held her hands over the wound. Heat radiated from it like hot coals were placed directly inside the flesh. When she touched it, Peyton growled, low and threatening.

"Can you not put me in even more pain?" Peyton grumbled.

Skyelar shook her head and laughed. "Oh, is this not enough of a distraction from your emotional turmoil?"

Peyton allowed herself to snicker. "I don't think I'll ever be free of it."

As Skyelar rose to go to her medicinal greenhouse, she pulled a rolling cart with her. Just a few mixing tools were all she needed. Anything surgical could be done with magic and leave Peyton in less pain in the end.

"So what made Derek come back?" Skyelar dared to ask, since it seemed her sister wanted to talk about it.

"You'll never believe this." Peyton took another hit off the joint as it shrunk down in size. "He's an HPA."

"And let me guess, he's yours?" Skyelar shook her head, amused at the irony of it all.

Derek abandoned Peyton four years ago, and Wesley swooped in like the cowardly opportunist he was. Skyelar knew Wesley was convinced he could protect Peyton, but she also knew Wesley didn't have what it took. Evidently, Skyelar wasn't the only one with that insight. It seemed Derek was brought back specifically for the woman he abandoned in the first place.

That was the precise reason Skyelar wanted to start creating her own Fate. Sometimes Life was too unpredictable and got too out of hand. Her father was right; she had to take control of things before someone else took control of her…again. Quite frankly, so did Peyton. Derek was back for a reason and Skyelar doubted it was just because Sebastian needed more guys for the Human Protection Agency.

Shaking her head with a knowing grin, Skyelar mixed together some of her most fragrant flowers, including rose petals, marigold, and a touch of lavender to help ease Peyton's anxiety.

"Well, he was," Peyton laughed. "But Wes lost his shit the minute he showed up. Now he's yours."

"Excuse me?" Skyelar paused in her work to stare at her sister. She really wished no more ambushes would creep into her Life today. That was three at once just from Peyton alone! Including the little discovery of being something short of an imaginary friend, Skyelar was neck deep in surprises and she was waving the white flag. This was getting to be too much.

Peyton put the joint back up to her lips and toked until it was nothing but a nub of ash. She eyed Skyelar with pursed lips, holding in the smoke, refusing to let it go just yet, and shrugged.

Turning back to her work, Skyelar shook her head, fervently. "Why the Hell would anyone assign me an HPA at all? Let alone Derek Noble."

"Well, that, my darling baby sister, was all Wesley Todd's idea."

"You're high," Skyelar laughed, returning to her with the topical ointment.

"Getting there," Peyton closed her eyes to let the warmth of the high creep over her body.

"Seriously, Peyton. There's no way Wesley would care about my safety. I can take care of myself."

"Oh, I know you can!" Peyton agreed, opening her eyes wide. She lifted her arm off her breast another two inches so Skyelar could get to the entire wound. Prepared for it to sting, Peyton was thankful when the ointment was soothing and cool on her skin. Either that or the THC was kicking in. "As much as I hate this, Skye, I am glad you're getting protection."

Stoned or not, Peyton did want to make sure her sister was safe. She had no idea what kind of chaos reigned in VerHum Labs. Peyton would sleep betting knowing Skyelar would not become a victim to all the threats she heard from the other Conquisitors.

"I'm worried since Elias hasn't been around," Peyton stated after a pause.

Skyelar gulped down the lump rising in her throat, threatening to choke her, and tried to smile. She was going to take care of that, but she wasn't ready to talk about it again. The way she broke down in front of Nole was unlike her. Skyelar usually didn't get bothered so deeply, and she definitely didn't need more advice on it. Especially from Peyton. As much as she loved her faux big sister, Peyton was a mess.

Instead of responding, Skyelar simply poured all her efforts into rubbing all of the ointment on her sister's wound. It was unusual that she wasn't healing and Skyelar wanted to know why.

Using a cotton swab, she rubbed it gently on the edge of the wound. Still refusing to comment because she felt the tears too close to her eyes, Skyelar took the swab to her work bench and extracted the specimen from it with a quick wave of her hand. In the next moment, the specimen was on the projector for them to see.

While Skyelar worked, Peyton put her shirt back on and watched her sister, closely. At the mention of Elias' name, she saw the very same look in Skyelar's eyes that she herself always had for Derek. It was a faraway look that made her eyes glitter and shine. It was a look that came from the heart. A look that said she knew she could live without him, but she didn't want to try.

Shit. This was bad.

"Skye," Peyton started as she gently pushed herself off the couch. "Why don't you just tell Elias how you feel?"

Skyelar heard her sister's question, but refused to answer. It was better to concentrate on the work in front of her. She could do this and not risk crying. She could do this and not miss Elias so much.

Staring into the microscope allowed Skyelar to ignore Peyton's incessant badgering. Oh, how the tables had turned! Not very long ago, Peyton couldn't stand Elias. Now, she was concerned for Skyelar's feelings? This whole Anomaly thing really had changed their entire dynamic.

In the tiny slide under the closely zoomed microscope, Skyelar studied the mutation of the specimen. She immediately recognized Peyton's genetics; she had seen it enough to know the general pattern. Then there was this other thing. What was that?

Zooming in as much as she could, Skyelar stared at this strange infection. It was twisted and tangled and looked nothing like a normal Creature. Then again...Hadn't she seen this before? Or something like it? It just looked too familiar.

Jumping off the stool, Skyelar snagged one of her journals from the shelf next to the bench to flip through it. She knew she sketched something like this not too long ago. Where was it? Thumbing through the thick white pages, she finally found it.

Wait, what? Glancing back and forth between the drawing and the live mutation on the projector, Skyelar was in denial. There was no way. Was it actually possible that this was the same species of Creature that attacked Peyton last month? She went to her black fridge and removed a vial that only had a small amount of an unknown specimen left. Taking one drop in the smallest size she could manage, Skyelar dropped it on a new slide and put the two next to each other.

"I'll be damned," Skyelar said, staring at her projector screen.

"What?" Peyton asked, leaning over the microscope for a closer look. "What'd you find?"

"Peyton, this is almost the same thing that attacked you last month."

"Holy shit, it is." Peyton glided over to the screen to look closer at it, her shadow covering the image only slightly. "But this new one, it's distorted. You don't think it's feral, do you?"

Skyelar shrugged because she wasn't entirely sure. She had only studied feral genes in college, but this was close enough to what all the textbooks showed. "I'm pretty sure it is."

"Oh, God!" Peyton turned to her sister, suddenly very sober and fearing the worst. "Am I feral now?"

"Don't be stupid," Skyelar said, shaking her head. "Since it was just a scratch, you're fine. It's going to take a few days for you to heal, probably, but ferals don't transmit that way."

"Yeah, but I should be healing already, shouldn't I?" Peyton asked, highly concerned. "Maybe we should run some more tests to be sure."

"Peyton, you are actively fighting this as we speak. I could see a difference even as I put the ointment on. We don't have to do more than we already have." Skyelar put a hand on her sister's shoulder and laughed. "But if it'll make you feel better, you can come back tomorrow and I'll put some more on."

"Yeah, let's do that."

"I mean, if you really want to come over just to see Derek, you don't have to lie about it," Skyelar teased, sensing her sister was more relaxed. "I won't judge your affair as long as you clean up after. No miscellaneous DNA in my lab."

Peyton slapped her sister on the arm playfully. The weight of a feral beast lurking in Murr County was heavy enough for them to bear. Hell, even the weight of the race for a cure was enough to wear someone out. Through all that, though, Peyton could see something even more heavy holding Skyelar down and dragging her around by the heart.

Still, she wouldn't force her sister to talk about it. Peyton would never force Skyelar to tell her anything that weighed her down. All the times Peyton just wanted to get upset, Skyelar always let her without question. Just like this afternoon. Peyton supposed she owed Skyelar one, especially for healing her so well.

"So what do you think it is?" Peyton asked, eyeing the specimen on the screen. "The beast didn't look like anything I'd ever seen before, but it definitely had a stink to it."

"Honestly, I have no idea," Skyelar shrugged. "But I'm going to work on figuring it out. We can't have a feral on the loose."

Peyton nodded. "I can stay if you want and we can work on it together. And those theories, while we're at it. Have you had a chance to look at any of those sites? I'd really like to talk about them."

"Yeah, I did. They were—well, they were eye-opening." Skyelar knew Peyton already had all the answers. She may not have gone to Nole to get them, but she suspected just as much as Skyelar probably knew. They each had their own way of doing things, but it yielded the same results in the end. Yes, Skyelar would talk about this with Peyton, but not tonight. Not when there were more pressing issues for Skyelar to tend to.

"Okay, so I'll stay over. We can go through all this together." Peyton smiled, excited to have a night away from Wesley.

"Actually, I do have plans tonight." Skyelar turned all the way around in her seat to face her sister. "Rain check?"

Opening her mouth to inquire about her sister's plans, Peyton decided it was none of her business right now. Of course, she had her suspicions. Just as she had with the news of the fabricated facts of *The Incident,* Peyton would make her way to the same answer with her own methods. If Skyelar wanted her to know right now, she would have been more specific. As long as she stayed safe, Peyton didn't feel it was her right to pry. Not about this. Not after seeing the look in Skyelar's heart-melting grey eyes.

"Sure," Peyton decided with a soft smile. "I'll call you tomorrow. And, uh, thanks for letting me vent and healing me and shit."

"Love you, too," Skyelar laughed as she watched Peyton leave.

Her palms were sweaty when she finally exhaled the breath she forgot she was holding. She would dig deeper into this specimen all right. Something out there was hunting Peyton. Biological sister or not, Skyelar loved Peyton and she was going to make sure the mystery beast was stopped.

But, first, she had a food supply to cut off.

CHAPTER 21

THE OTHER WOMAN

Lilith spent all her tears on the walk from Alchemic Falls back to Ava's house to retrieve her own car. She thought she would feel more pain since she was bonded with Ava. Wasn't that how this usually worked? Yet, by the Time she got to Aezra's apartment, Lilith was simply sad. No dramatics; no physical heart-breaking. Just mild sadness. The Lycan bond sure was different than what she was used to.

She missed Ava, for sure. The Human was sweet and bubbly and loved to party, but the beast—that was what really hooked Lilith. The loyalty and control the beast gave to her was unlike anything she had ever felt before. Lilith was so used to being the one that was told what to do and how to do it. Getting the opportunity to exert a little authority over someone else for a change was exhilarating.

Now that Ava was dead, there was no one for Lilith to control. That rush was gone. A strange melancholy filled her heart in the place where Ava used to be. It wasn't permanent, by any means, but it was there for now. She had hoped to come to Aezra's to find she could replace the melancholy with a new, more invigorating rush. After all, they were ancient lovers. They were destined to be together.

If that was true, why the Hell was he currently getting an outfit ready for a date with another woman?

"Aezra, are you even paying attention to me?" Lilith complained.

She was sprawled across his bed in all her naked glory. Blood still stained her neck and breasts from his feeding. Her body still tingled from the pleasure of the sex. Yet, her post-sex high was gone. As soon as Aezra was finished, he started preparing for his date later that night. A date that was not with her.

"I'm sorry, Lily," Aezra said, turning to face her. He put his lounging basketball shorts on as he searched through the closet to find something to wear. "I just need to get another fix, you know? I can feel it leaving me and it's like part of my soul goes with it."

Lilith sat up in bed and dangled her long, thin legs over the edge. "Aezra, I swear, if you don't quit seeing her, I'm going to lose it."

Aezra walked over to her and took her hands in his, attempting to control his trembling. A clear sign of his dependency on his Life-Blood. It drove both of them to the brink of insanity, and he was worried Lilith would be the first to snap. If Aezra lost control first, he would just perish. But if Lilith lost control, as she threatened to do, he was in for serious trouble.

"Lily, please don't get this way," Aezra begged, kissing her knuckles.

"Get like what, Aezra? How am I getting?" She recoiled her hand, hoping he would say something stupid so she could slap the shit out of him. That was what he really needed. All this Time alone to do as he pleased had him hallucinating that he was indestructible. If he wasn't careful, Lilith knew someone who would eagerly prove otherwise.

Uh-oh, he thought. He was backing himself into a corner with her and he could not see the way out. He was no longer experienced in balancing a relationship with her to remember how to keep her from biting his head off at every turn. Even if he did remember, he was sure her needs had evolved with Time just as his had.

Whether she wanted to admit it or not, Aezra and Lilith were two different Creatures from when they last saw each other thousands of years ago.

"That's not what I meant," Aezra said, trying to back-track.

"Then tell me what you did mean," Lilith demanded. She jumped off the bed and covered herself in his sheet.

"I just don't like to see you upset, is all." Aezra sat on the bed now. He felt a little light-headed, but he had to keep his strength up.

"Maybe I wouldn't be so upset if you'd quit seeing Skyelar!"

"She's my Life-Blood, Lily. I don't know what you expect. I didn't ask for this curse, but I can break it, if you'll be patient with me."

Lilith rounded on him so fast he almost forgot she wasn't a Sanguis. She could move quickly when she wanted to.

"I have been patient with you, Aezra!" Lilith exclaimed, throwing her arms in the air. "I've waited for eternity for you to figure your shit out so you can come home. How do you think it makes me feel to see you like this? Like you haven't even tried at all."

"You don't think I've tried? I just found Skye—what?—three, four years ago? It took me two years just to get her to date me. I mean, I know we were supposed to get married six months later, but she ran! I'm sorry she's a little bit of a challenge."

"And that's another thing!"

Lilith stopped herself before she could say too much. This was already getting out of hand when she really just wanted confirmation that he was done playing games. She could not allow Elias to be right. Lilith knew Aezra was her Purpose; there was no way his Purpose was anyone but her.

"Do you love her?" Lilith asked, finally, voice hushed.

She wanted him to listen to her. She wanted him to really take the Time to think about the question. If Aezra had real feelings for this stupid little Mortal Mythic, then Elias was going to have a real problem on his hands because Lilith was not going down without a fight.

"What?" Aezra responded, completely caught off guard. "Lily, please, I was only trying to marry her so she would let me do the Blood-Lust ceremony and I could come home. That's all."

"Cut the bullshit, Aezra."

In an instant, Lilith lifted her right arm, curling her fingers and wrist and quickly extending them again. As she did, a small dagger emerged out of the tattoo on the inside of her forearm. The ruby in the hilt of it glinted in the light of the bedroom while the sharp, venomous point of it barely tapped Aezra's throat, careful not to cut him until she was ready.

"I'm stronger than I was when we first got together," Lilith said, exuding confidence from every pore, refusing to waver in her control of the blade. "If you dare to make me the other woman again I will send you straight into *The Hollow*."

Aezra gulped, but not too hard. He didn't want to accidentally get pierced by that blade because he knew what was coating it. Seeing that she was truly serious, Aezra knew he had no choice but to obey. Lilith was, indeed, stronger than him. She had thousands of years to hone her craft.

On the other hand, Aezra had thousands of years to find a Life-Blood that he didn't think existed. Now that he thought her found her, he could not easily let her go. Just as Lilith could not so easily cease using the magic she obtained. The difference was Aezra just needed a chance to regain his old strength before things could change.

"Okay, Lily, you win." Aezra held his hands up in surrender. "Just give me one shot. One chance to get what I need so I can heal. Then you'll never be the other woman again."

"Do you swear?" she asked through gritted teeth.

"Yes! Yes, on my treacherous soul, I swear."

Lilith finally pulled the blade back into its tattoo on her arm where the ruby found a home in a gold bracelet on her wrist. Aezra took a deep breath and blinked hard, twice. Of all the close calls he'd ever had, that was by far one of the most frightening.

"Tonight, when I meet with her, I'll take what I need and I'm all yours."

Dropping the sheet so he could stare once again at her naked body, Lillith straddled her lover on his bed. She presented the throbbing veins in her neck for him as a pre-game feast. It was her intent that he should remember not to bite the hand that fed him because Lilith would not hesitate to bite back.

"You better not lie to me, Aezra," Lilith said as he kissed and teased her neck, pulling her body against his.

Abruptly, as soon as she felt the fangs brush against her skin, Lilith pushed him, prostrate onto the bed and climbed off of him. She gathered her clothes and put them on, intending to leave before the fight could rekindle, as she was sure it would. Their fights had a magical way of never completely resolving.

"What are you doing?" Aezra asked, eyes black with desire. "Where are you going?"

"I have work to do for Elias," Lilith said. "But I expect you to keep your word so I can see you in the morning."

"Oh, you can count on it, babe," Aezra grinned a toothy grin. "I'll even come to your place to celebrate."

CHAPTER 22

OUT OF LOVE

This is so nice," Sylvia smiled as she sat to the left of James at their dining room table. "I'm so glad you guys decided to do this."

It was the first Time in a month that Sylvia was genuinely happy. Since the formation of the Human Protection Agency, James invited Kaylee and Sebastian to come back home until things settled down. It was a pleasant surprise, and Sylvia spent all day getting Kaylee's old room ready at the end of the upstairs hall.

Living with her mother again was not ideal, particularly because of Harper, but Kaylee was willing to do it for her husband and father. They were concerned for her safety. She was the mechanical engineer responsible for most of the equipment used at VerHum Labs, so they couldn't risk letting her get hurt.

It was temporary, though. Dear God, it had to be. Sebastian promised her as much. After the Independence Day picnic, everything could go back to normal, and no one would be on high alert. Still, Kaylee couldn't help but wonder if her father would still be at risk for assassination attempts after he won the election. Creatures could be vicious. And, now, they knew just how scared the Humans were.

Sitting next to her mother, across from her husband, Kaylee spooned a helping of potatoes onto her plate. She stared, waiting while everyone else got what they wanted so they could say Grace before eating. She couldn't help but notice Harper barely put anything on her plate. Maybe it was how she always was, but Kaylee thought she saw the home-wrecker trembling a little.

"Harper, is everything alright?" Kaylee asked after her father concluded the prayer. "You look like you've got something on your mind."

"Leave her alone, Kaylee," James insisted. He leaned over to his right and kissed his mistress lovingly on the lips. "This race has everyone on edge."

Kaylee simply nodded and took a sip of her wine. Seeing her father's affection for Harper made her lose her appetite. She glanced at Sebastian and he shrugged at her. What could they do? They were guests in James' house. Both of them knew he was not going to stop having an affair just because Kaylee was uncomfortable.

"Well, Mayor," Sebastian said, breaking the silence. "The HPA has official jurisdiction and policing authority in Murlance, so that's one less thing to worry about."

"Excellent work, Sebastian," James commended between bites of his steak. "So will you take over the investigation for all these killings? Even the ones from a couple weeks ago?"

Sebastian nodded and opened his mouth to speak, but Harper cut him off. "What about Falshooke Mountain? Does the HPA operate there?"

"Sweetheart, remember, the Mountain is populated by Creatures," James said, smiling. "The HPA are for Humans and Jericho family members only."

"To her point, James," Sylvia interjected, "You do have two granddaughters who live in the Mountain. I'm sure they would appreciate the protection."

"Oh, that reminds me," Sebastian said, sipping some of his beer first. "Wesley called today. He's volunteered to join us and watch over Peyton."

"What about Derek?" Kaylee wondered, innocently.

"Derek?" James asked, brows narrowed, as he propped his elbows on the table. "The guy that was supposed to marry Peyton?"

"The very same, Mayor," Sebastian said. "We, uh, we got him out of his contract early. I thought he would be the perfect Agent for Peyton, but Wesley asked to have him reassigned…to Skyelar."

James tilted his chin toward the ceiling in contemplation for a moment. He had not planned on giving Skyelar any kind of protection. In fact, she was most of the reason he wanted protection for the rest of the family. The closer they got to a cure, the more he feared she would lash out. While she had yet to do so, he still feared it would happen.

Then again, it would look good for him to send Agents to those Creatures he was related to in the Mountain. Not as much for protection as for monitoring. It might even show the rest of the Creatures that those miscreants weren't to be trusted, but they could always count on their mayor to keep them safe. James smiled as he ate another bite of potato and decided he would have to thank Wesley for his suggestion tomorrow.

"That will work out fine, son," James said. "That way we can keep an eye on her without being too much of a threat."

Sylvia rolled her eyes and put her fork on her plate firmly. "James, really! When are you going to stop this?"

"Mom, remember what Skyelar can do," Kaylee defended. "I think we ought to keep an eye on her before she tries to kill someone."

"On that note, Sebastian," James said, declaring the previous debate over with his simple change of subject. "Are you ready to bring in the next subject?"

Sebastian nodded his head. "I've actually got guys on it tonight."

"Wait," Harper looked around, worried she'd missed something. "What's going on tonight?"

James patted her hand. "Nothing you need to worry about, sweetheart."

"No, Dad, she's right," Kaylee interjected, dropping her fork less delicately than her mother. Although she supported her father's regime, she still felt uneasy about Subject Beta. Instead, she wished they could wait until they had more than blind experiments before they brought him in. "Tell Harper what you plan on doing to our family. I'm curious how she's going to spin this one."

"Kaylee, I understand your concern," Sebastian stepped in, authoritatively. "But in your dad's defense, we have to move quickly if we're going to beat the competition."

James followed suit and put his silverware down. If they were going to debate instead of eat, then he would debate them all. It didn't matter because he was determined to win. He was the mayor of Murr County; a Jericho. He always won.

"That's right, Sebastian. And I'm quite concerned with Elias lately. The Melatrommi are loud, but they're a nuisance that we can deal with. They've yet to produce anything against us. Elias, on the other hand...he's been too quiet."

"Well, if it's a big stir you want, Mayor, I think bringing in Subject Beta is the right thing."

"Subject Beta?" Harper asked. "Will someone please tell me what the Hell is going on?"

Sylvia slammed her fist on the table and rose. For once she was in the know and Harper was not and she hated it. Knowing who Subject Beta was and knowing that James was fine with the entire experiment was simply abhorrent. Without a word, she stalked up the stairs to her bedroom to collect herself in peace.

Everyone left at the table stared at James. His marriage had not been strong for a long Time, but, lately, it seemed to be hanging on by a thread. Even Harper was unsure how to keep them looking good for the public anymore. James just kept digging deeper and deeper and she was running out of believable cover stories.

Shaking her head, Harper stared at James. Being kept in the dark was not ideal and she was not going to sit around and be patronized, only to have to clean up another mess later on.

Suddenly, Harper rose from the table. She had an appointment to keep and it was more and more tempting to go along with whatever Lilith wanted after sitting at this table tonight.

"Sweetheart, where are you going?" James asked, dryly, frustrated with the women in his Life.

"I have a meeting with another client," Harper spat.

"This late? It's after eight!"

"James, you're not the only one I work for." Harper grabbed her purse off the hook and turned back to face him. "Go check on your wife like a decent husband."

When Harper slammed the door behind her, James rolled his eyes and sighed. Excusing himself from his daughter and son-in-law, James took his Time going up the stairs. For years, when Sylvia would have her tantrums, he would just let her go to her room and do what she needed to do. There was never any need for him to chase after her. In fact, he made it very clear he was not the type that liked the chase.

Still, Harper was right. Subject Beta was a sensitive topic and Sylvia had promised to support him through all these sensitive and difficult things. He supposed she would have no incentive to support him if he didn't make the effort to return the favor to her in whatever it was she thought she needed.

He knocked on Sylvia's bedroom door and creaked it open slowly. She sat on the foot of her bed, staring at a picture of Reygal. Shuffling inside the room, James sat on the side of the bed. The side he used to sleep on before he invited Harper into their lives.

"Sylvia, honey, I know this is hard—"

"No you don't," she interrupted. "You have no idea how hard this is for me. You don't love them like I do. You don't even love them at all."

"Love who? Our children?" James asked, confused. "Of course I do!"

Sylvia turned to face him, still clutching the picture of Reygal to her chest. "You tolerate the Human children, James. You treat them like staff. But you go out of your way to de-Humanize our first born. My perfect little boy."

"Darling, that little boy isn't Human. He's a terror who kills Humans for nourishment." James dared to scoot a little closer in an attempt to show concern for his wife's well-being. "He's less your little boy, now, than he was when he was born."

"*Our* little boy, James," Sylvia sobbed. She pushed the picture into his hands so he was forced to look at the man he called a monster. "*You* are his father. Don't you dare forget that."

Hesitating to speak, James pushed the photo away from his face gently. "Sylvia, I'm just trying to help get him under control before someone gets hurt."

"Listen to yourself, James," Sylvia demanded, rising from the bed to pace. "Reygal isn't out of control. You are! Creatures aren't circus acts. They're people with lives just like us."

Rising from the bed, James closed the gap between them and took the picture away from her. He set it on her dresser before taking her hands in his. For the first Time in a long Time, James looked at Sylvia and wanted her trust as his wife. He didn't want her to resent him for the choices he made to better their family. There was a Time when he knew she would have given that trust gladly. What the Hell happened to them?

"Please, Sylvia," he begged, kissing her knuckles. "You have to believe I love our family. I'm just trying to protect them. That's all."

Under any other circumstance, Sylvia would have melted at his touch, at his kiss. Not tonight. Tonight, he showed his true colors. She finally saw him for the monster that he truly was, and she made it a point to clear monsters out of her closet.

"And does part of that protection include replacing me with your little slut?" Sylvia asked, bitterly.

James was floored and tilted his head in question. "I thought you liked Harper...I mean, we both agreed to this arrangement..."

"Oh, she's a sweet girl," Sylvia said as she removed her hands from his and turned to the mirror on top of her dresser. "But she's the cause of this disconnect between us. For years, now, I've put up with your insane affair. Watching as she takes you away from me, piece-by-piece. Now, you expect me to let you take my kids and grandkids away, too?"

"Where the Hell is this coming from, Sylvia?"

Sylvia turned to him, then, with eyes dry as the desert. "From fifty years of neglect, James. Fifty years of battling other women to get you to love me. I'm always last in line after them and your career."

"Oh, so, now, you decide you're unhappy?"

"I haven't been happy for twenty years, James. But you've been too preoccupied to notice."

"Yet, here you are, still married to me. Still living in my house. Still begging me to love you." James stared at Sylvia for a beat, chest heaving, eyes soft and shamefully fearful. "I don't know what else you want from me."

"My freedom, Mayor Jericho," she retorted, coolly. "I want a divorce."

CHAPTER 23

UNLIKELY ALLIANCE

Standing in the woods outside of Elias Luck's house in the dark was just as scary as she presumed it would be. She was like a criminal stalking the richest houses on the block. It would have made her less uncomfortable if she was already inside the club, but the doors wouldn't open to her. Of course they wouldn't. She just had to be early, didn't she?

From her Creature sources in the Melatrommi, Harper learned The Devil's Playground was very literally a basement club that Elias operated. It was something he did for those Creatures who needed a darker, more solitary outlet. A place where they could commit their vile deeds without the fear of being judged or caught by Humans. Evidently, only the Creatures who drank from *The Fountain* were privy to the club. There was no rule of secrecy; yet, Harper knew, firsthand, that the Humans had no idea this place existed.

It begged the question: what was going on in there? She shivered and her jaw clenched at the thought of finding out.

The fact that she even decided to come to this demented place was clinically insane. Then again, Lilith was Elias' most trusted ally, though no one in the Melatrommi knew anything about her. Rumors told of a hellacious type of power that she possessed. Speculators claimed she was one of the original Mythics from before The Great Extermination. Others claimed she was stronger than Elias, as if she was the Devil in disguise.

Honestly, Harper thought, trying to calm the goosebumps grazing her skin. Who came up with such ridiculous speculation? Most Mythics from The Great Extermination had gone into hiding. Everyone knew that. They were afraid to use their magic, so it was lost to them, leaving them nothing but their Humanity.

Now, Skyelar might have a little more insight into the whole Lilith mystery, but Harper was not exactly in the position to just sit down and have a margarita with Skyelar to talk about Lilith. Hell, she did not even know if Skyelar liked margaritas. Then again, she didn't think Lilith was in the position to persuade Harper to come to the club tonight, yet here she was.

Okay, so maybe Harper felt a little bullied into coming to this meeting. She feared what Lilith would do if Harper skipped it because she didn't want to help. Then, there was James. More and more, lately, Harper was being pushed to her moral limit. Not that she could share that with her brazen lover—as much as she wished she could. If he knew what she was...Well, her Life expectancy would decrease drastically.

So she had to work with Lilith. The lesser of two evils; wasn't that what they said? Rationalizing it as a means to help the entire Creature race, Harper forced herself to stand outside the external basement doors. She tried, again, pulling on the serpentine handles, but they wouldn't budge. Their gold, glowing eyes just stared at her, shining in the growing moonlight.

"I knew you'd come," Lilith grinned, approaching from behind. "Sorry I'm a little late."

"Oh, that's okay," Harper said. "I couldn't remember when you said we were meeting so..."

When Harper turned to see Lilith in the light of the rising moon, she saw the blood staining her flesh. Chilled fingertips traced over Harper's skin as the dew began to settle over the foliage. Sure, she had magic, but it was old and out of practice. If Lilith or any other Creature in that club decided to do anything to her, Harper would be the easiest prey alive.

Seeing Harper's gaze wander to the blood, Lilith smiled and shrugged. "Ugh. I'm not usually so unprofessional! I'm sorry about all this. Got a little distracted from Sanguis sex. You know how that goes."

Harper shook her head with wide eyes. "No...No, I'm afraid I don't."

As Lilith led Harper down the staircase into the depths of the Earth, she chuckled. Of course, she didn't know what it was like. Lilith was willing to bet

Harper had no idea what it was like to be anything but a false Human. Maybe once, a long Time ago, she was free to be herself, but not anymore. Life had moved on without her and she was stuck trying to figure out how to cope. Poor thing.

"Well, if you ever get the chance, I highly recommend it," Lilith said. "You won't regret it."

They walked through two heavy black curtains meant to muffle sounds before they entered a common area with a wall full of liquor and doors on either side of a lounge. Creatures were drinking and feasting and walking around in all their nude glory right in front of Harper's eyes. She'd never seen anything like it!

"It's great, isn't it?" Lilith asked, leading Harper to a couch in the corner. She wanted them to sit and talk, but still be able to see what Creatures had to do to thrive right now.

"I don't know if I'd call it 'great'," Harper confessed. "But it's something."

"Yes, it is something," Lilith nodded, soberly. "It's all some Creatures have until they're not hunted like criminals anymore."

Harper managed to pull her eyes away from the sex and flesh ripping in front of her to stare at Lilith. While the red hair was curling everywhere, her brown eyes were tame and calm. No obvious signs of dangerous intentions.

"Lilith, I'm the founder of the Melatrommi," Harper said, offended at the insinuation. "You, clearly, know my history. So you should know I'm all for the freedom of Creatures."

"I know you are, but you aren't doing enough." Lilith lifted her hand and summoned a glass of white wine to her. "Want anything? It's on the house."

Harper held up a hand. "Uh, no thanks."

"This little oasis, here, is Elias' way of providing shelter from the cruelty of Humans," Lilith explained, taking a sip of her beverage. "You dabble too much in politics, forcing Creatures to wait and see what happens. Meanwhile, you know, in your heart, what's going to happen. You know better than anyone what Mayor Jericho will do in the end."

Sighing, Harper nodded her head. Lilith was right. No matter what she did to try to keep James from hurting the Creatures of Murr County, she knew he would prevail because, in his heart, Elias did not really want to help them. He only wanted to help one of them, and that was not enough. If it came down to it, Harper could not say for certain that Elias would step up and take control from James.

Then, all the Creatures would die.

"Look, I know what you're saying," Harper said at last. "But there's not much else I can do. I'm too close to the other side."

"None of them know about you, do they?" Lilith asked into her wine.

"No, I don't think so. Well, they took a sample of my blood last month, but I haven't heard if they've checked it."

Lilith waved her off. "They won't. You and I both know they wouldn't dare question their fearless leader's choice of a mistress."

"Girlfriend," Harper corrected, defensively.

"Oh, excuse me," Lilith laughed. "Regardless, you're still undetected. And I know you still have a beast crawling around inside you somewhere. Even if it is old and tired."

Now Harper laughed. "You know how long it's been since I changed? I was too scared to when I was kid, so I don't know if I could do it now."

"And that's precisely why I need you," Lilith smiled. "You and your brother are the only successful cross-breeds in existence—"

"Just me," Harper said, sadly. "It's just me now. Wes has been feral since the Conquisitors got to him."

That put a little hitch in her plan, but Lilith figured everything could still work so long as Harper was agreeable to it. She would just have to tweak things a little. "Well, that's all the more reason for you to help. You can avenge your brother."

Harper thought about it for a moment. Her brother was too far gone, and he was her back-up plan. She had everything in her heart pinned on the thought that sibling love could persuade him to help her fight against Humans. Now that they were clearly on opposing sides, Harper figured she could use all the help she could get.

If it meant she had to pull out some old tricks from her bag, then she supposed it was a sacrifice for the greater good. Wasn't that was Nole always said?

"Well, then I guess tell me what you have in mind," Harper agreed.

"I just need you to be my decoy," Lilith grinned deviously as she explained how Harper was to help her. "You're going to help free some of the Creatures in the Death Lab. And, at the picnic next week, I'll do the rest."

"Now, wait, what will you do to them?" Harper wondered, worried.

"Let's just say you and your brother aren't the only ones who know how to work a crowd."

CHAPTER 24

HEARTACHE

Elias drank alone at The Devil's Fountain because he wanted it that way. Since the attack at Skyelar's house a couple weeks ago, he was preoccupied in his efforts to ensure her safety. Those efforts changed when he saw her with Aezra. The shadow of memory that washed over her face that night was just strong enough that Elias knew she was not quite ready to move on.

And Elias was not allowed to stand in the way. It went against the rules. The fucking rules.

He hated those fucking rules. Wanting nothing more than to spend all of his Time with Skyelar, Elias was tempted to intervene. If he put a stop to this now, it wouldn't be too late. He could salvage some of the Time he'd lost.

Yet, instead of getting up and taking a stand for what he wanted, Elias sat at his bar drinking alone. He promised he wouldn't interfere even if he could because *he* wanted to be Skyelar's choice. He wanted to be her willing choice. Not the one she felt obligated to.

Looking back through history, Elias did not care about being the first choice for anyone. In fact, he had a unique talent for being the last person anyone wanted to see. For Skyelar to have noticed him in the first place, was a blessing. For Aezra to stand in the way was routine. Frustrating and rage-inducing, but routine.

Well, not any longer. Elias had to take a stand and fight for what he wanted. There could be no consequence greater than what he'd already suffered, right? The problem was that annoying little voice that sang in the back of his mind. The voice was sweet, but it sang a psalm of darkness, fear, and pain.

What hurt the most was Elias understood Aezra's appeal. Aezra could kiss her, touch her, love her up close and personal. All Elias could do was dote on her. After a while, that simply wasn't enough, but it was all he had, for now. Until the future came to claim what it wanted. Lately, Elias wished the future would just rip the damn bandage off already. He hated sitting in this limbo, making friends with pain and doubt.

A long Time ago, in the deep caverns of Elias' memory, he let the pain shatter him. Break him down until there was nothing left. It proved unproductive. Before it could destroy him from the inside out, Elias banished the beast.

Moving through Time without burden, Elias learned it was easier to transmit his anger, his hatred, and his pain to those who sought to take advantage of him. He was the very disease James feared; the pinnacle of suffering.

Along came Skyelar, when he least expected her, and his whole world was suddenly flipped upside down. Existing for too long as the monster under the bed, Elias realized he didn't want to trek that path anymore. Not if it meant he would lose Skyelar.

Fate was such a cruel and ironic bitch sometimes.

He couldn't lose Skyelar again. Not to the likes of Aezra. That Sanguis truly was the bane of his existence. How was it Elias was bound by all these senseless rules of magic and Fate, but Aezra could move freely as he wished? Wasn't this Life supposed to be Aezra's punishment? Instead, it turned out Elias was stuck in his own personal Hell while Aezra faced no consequences for breaking all the rules.

If Skyelar had married Aezra last year, he wouldn't be in this predicament. Then again, everything would be entirely different. Elias might be on a darker course. He might have left town, and who's to say he wouldn't be covered in blood as a result of it all?

He gulped down the last of his bourbon—his fifth glass. While most Humans would be in a bit of an alcohol haze at this point, Elias was starting to see things clearer. In the amber tint of his freshly poured sixth drink, the ice cubes were grayed in hue. He closed his eyes and winced, reaching for the onyx around his neck to keep him grounded.

Those eyes. Skyelar's grey eyes haunted him, and Elias never used to believe in ghosts. In the foggy clarity of his drink, Elias knew he had to do something. He couldn't live, haunted this way. Haunted by thousands of lifetimes of pain and loneliness. Haunted by old rivalries and faded tattoos. Haunted by a glimpse of the past that brought a future he was helpless to stop.

This was not who Elias Luck was. Elias Luck was a businessman. Ruthless toward his enemies and giving toward his friends. Shrugging his shoulders as he took another sip, Elias noted it was getting more difficult to discern the line between those two parties anymore. Not that it mattered. He was becoming monomaniacal like his sister. Consumed in something so precious that he allowed everything around him to pass in a blur.

Twisting the onyx thoughtfully in his fingers, Elias wondered if Skyelar felt the same. If he hadn't doused the heat with fire last year—if he had kissed her deeper and let the situation escalate, where would they be tonight?

He remembered that kiss like it was yesterday. In fact, it was exactly a year ago yesterday. Oh, that sweet taste of rum and soda on her lips. The feel of the voluptuous curves of her body. Thinking on it now, Elias would give anything to relive that moment. To whisk her away and start a new Life as if they had nothing to lose. Wasn't that how he lived his Life for the last five hundred or so years?

All of a sudden, Elias' lifestyle was altered. Now, he had everything to lose. None of this was planned, and he hated when things didn't go according to plan. Everything just happened because of Fate, and Elias was left moping like a heartbroken cowboy because of it.

Reuniting Aezra and Lilith should have given the Sanguis ample opportunity to move on. Had Elias observed Aezra a little closer, he might have realized the Life-Blood already had its hold on the wretched Creature. It was only a matter of Time before Aezra went to extremes to obtain what he thought he needed to survive. Blind by the curse placed upon him all those centuries ago.

Elias kicked himself for not piecing it all together quicker. He should have known nothing could be civil or simple when it came to Aezra, but he was distracted. Chasing his own desires. Of course, that led to a serious problem—bigger than the Conquisitors—and he had to fix it. But where to begin...

Then, he felt it. The only presence on Earth that could overwhelm him to the point of sweaty palms and a rapid heartbeat. He was so overwhelmed that he almost fell off his bar stool like a drunken frat boy.

Feeling her so unexpectedly before he even saw her, Elias turned toward the door awaiting that first seemingly slow motion entrance after two weeks of absence.

The black door opened to let the moonlight in and their eyes met, instantly. Gazing into those grey eyes was like gazing into the eyes of an Angel. Elias did not feel worthy, and, yet, he knew that gaze was all for him. He knew because Time slowed down. As her heart pounded against her chest, he could feel it in his own. Almost hear it in his ears.

Two weeks was entirely too long. After seeing her now, Elias knew he couldn't go two more minutes without her.

Skyelar quickly closed the gap while trying not to seem too eager. He avoided her for a reason. If she ran to him now, she might scare him away again. She could not risk scaring him away again.

Her palms were sweaty. Why had that been happening all day? With her heart was thundering so loud, she felt the blood rushing to her ears. Elias was quite a sight for her incredibly sore eyes. Every night for two weeks, Skyelar came to the bar just hoping to feel him there. Usually, she missed him. But, tonight, someone above was smiling down on her. And now that he was in front of her, all she wanted to do was run into his arms.

Instead, she walked to him in fast, measured steps. Every step was another slam of her heart into her chest. Before she knew it, she was pulling him into *Focus*. Skyelar couldn't help it. When she locked eyes with Elias, nothing else in the world seemed to matter. Everything around them faded away like a muffled voice after a gun firing right next to the ear. The bar patrons were low murmurs, invisible to the two of them. No one else on Earth existed; no one else on Earth mattered, in that moment, but the two of them.

Skyelar stood in front of Elias in her capris and black Converse. Her black tee shirt, decorated with a golden skyline, fell off of her left shoulder. Tips of a pair of pink wings and the smiling head of a small and glittering green dragon peered above the fabric. A bundle of snapdragon flowers dangled above its head as it investigated the flora.

Skyelar's makeup was soft and natural with a pale pink lip. Cascading down her neck and back was her thick black and purple hair in a feathery curled ponytail. She was simply radiant, as if he was seeing her for the very first Time.

When her heart finally steadied, Skyelar stared at Elias, wondering how he could possibly be more handsome than she remembered. Two weeks. That's all the Time that passed between them. Yet, they studied each other as if it was more akin to two years.

Elias' beard seemed fuller now, she mused, pleased to see growing. Although he still kept it cut close to his jaw with his mustache close to his tasty, moist lips. His hair flowed loosely around his face, and Skyelar wanted nothing more than to run her hands through it. She smirked at his jeans and red tee shirt that blended in with the bar staff.

As they looked each other over, Elias grinned at the emerald necklace she still wore. Following his gaze with her hand, she held the emerald tightly as a show of affection and faith. Unable to restrain himself any longer, Elias reached for her hand. As soon as their flesh touched, a small spark shot between them like static electricity.

Skyelar ignored it, delighting in the feel of something so hot and unexpected after two weeks of being consumed by worry and fear. Determined to remain in this moment as if there would be no others, Skyelar let Elias hold her hand. They interlaced their fingers, and Elias dared to pull her even closer. He would pull her into his being if he could. Skyelar did not resist, slipping into his seductive orbit.

Tears quickly formed at the edge of her eyelids. God, she missed him so damn much! If he would just give her something, anything, so she knew where they stood. Where she belonged.

Until then, Skyelar was a lost soul trapped in Purgatory.

He heard her longing for him in her mind, felt it in the heat of her touch. Although he should have known better, Elias let his emotions, his heart, get the better of him. He pulled her closer, still, and put his free hand on her cheek. She leaned into his touch, standing between his legs as he sat on his stool, and sighed a shaky, nervous breath. This was it. This was what they both wanted. What they needed.

They closed their eyes and let their foreheads touch first. This was one of the few moments they were nearly the same height, and the corner of Skyelar's mouth lifted. The heat flowed between them in their own private bubble, and Elias tilted his face up so the tips of their noses kissed. He felt her smile; he knew, then, he was going to be in big trouble, but it would be worth it for this one stolen moment...

A cold sensation abruptly clawed up Skyelar's spine and her eyes opened in aggravation. That wasn't Elias. No, he wasn't cold like that. At last, it was Skyelar's turn to pull her face away. Tempting as it was to stay this way, she had to stop before it went too far. Quickly, their protective bubble slipped away, revealing the rest of the world spinning busily around them.

"Not this asshole," Elias mumbled low when he saw Aezra.

Skyelar heard him and smiled somberly, whispering her apology in his mind so only he could hear. Reluctantly, he released her, taking his hands back into his own gravity as she took a step away to increase the distance between them.

Seeing Elias at the bar, Aezra put on his best smile as he approached. Why shouldn't he be happy? He won, after all. Granted, seeing Skyelar stand so close to Elias put him on edge, but he tried to remain positive. Calm. Determined to complete his mission.

Skyelar chose Aezra once again, and there was nothing Elias Luck could do. Literally nothing.

To drive his point home, Aezra grabbed Skyelar's hand as it dangled by her side and yanked her around for a messy kiss. He pressed hard against her and felt her hands pushing away against his immovable chest, but he wasn't quite ready to let go yet. Elias needed to know, without a shadow of a doubt, who the victor was.

Watching the absurd display, Elias grumbled, gagged, and took another large gulp of his bourbon. He knew exactly what Aezra was doing. It was a damn shame it was working, too. To retaliate, Elias glanced at the couple out of his periphery and slowly crept into Aezra's mind. Without moving a muscle, Elias' mental fingers reached into that vulnerable opening while Aezra was distracted and tightened around him like a python suffocating its prey. Every single thought, all the intimate memories Aezra had about Skyelar only made Elias clench tighter.

Aezra grimaced mid-kiss, feeling the pressure on his brain like a tumor growing rapidly larger. Shoving Skyelar away from him so she smacked against the bar, Aezra hissed, opening his mouth in an attempt to alleviate the pain. His upper lip retracted, displaying those sharp and deadly incisors.

Elias willingly relinquished the hold on Aezra's mind, smirking into his bottomless seventh glass of bourbon. "Well, you seem to be feeling better."

"Fresh food will do that." Aezra clamped his jaw shut as if that would banish Elias from getting to him again. Reaching for Skyelar's hand, he pulled her back to him as he straightened and regained his composure.

With an antagonistic wink, Aezra put his hand on Skyelar's back, possessively, and escorted her out of the bar before Elias could try anything else. Aezra was a Sanguis on a mission. He made a promise to his lover and nothing would force him to break it now.

Skyelar glanced over her shoulder at Elias with regret and longing swimming laps in her soft grey eyes. She maintained eye-contact with him until Aezra escorted her out the black door and into the moonlit night. Before she could turn her head back around, she stumbled into Aezra as he stopped mid-step. He caught her quicker than she could blink without even trying.

"Hey, Aezra!" Chloey Jo said, approaching them from the parking lot. "I was hoping to find you here."

"I'm not sure why," Aezra laughed. "I thought I made myself pretty clear last Time you came to see me."

Glowering at her ex-boyfriend's arm around the likes of Skyelar, Chloey Jo's fists clenched and opened again. First, some long-lost lover returned to end things between them, and, now, Skyelar was back in his Life. How did this man always manage to have his cake and eat it, too? And what did that make her?

Anger boiled hot in the pit of her stomach. She wanted to punch Skyelar right here, so that she landed face first onto the pavement. If only she knew Skyelar wouldn't deflect her so effortlessly with her damned magic.

"Aezra, please, I just want to talk about what happened," Chloey Jo said, struggling to be civil. "You know, the whole infection thing…"

Aezra held up a hand to stop her. "We are not talking about that, Chloey. If you're starting to feel the ill effects, it's your own fault. I never intended to do that to you."

With a pout, Chloey Jo put her hands on her hips. "Now that's not fair, Aezra. We both participated in that act. Besides, you owe me for saving you after this bitch dumped you."

"Wow, okay…Look, if you guys need to work this out—" Skyelar said, pulling away from Aezra uncomfortably. "I'll just go."

Aezra grabbed her by the arm. It looked like a soft grip, but he held her in place, firmly. Damn him and his unholy Sanguis strength.

"You don't have to go alone," Aezra insisted. "Chloey, if you'll excuse us, we have plans."

"Aezra, wait!" Chloey Jo called after him. "Aezra, you can't turn your back on me like this."

"Chloey, I don't know what you thought this was, but I'm not interested anymore. Thank you for feeding me when you could."

As Chloey Jo watched Skyelar get into Aezra's sleek white car, she was devastated. A part of her hoped that their fight last week was just a show in front of Lilith. Like a secret code between them. Now, she saw that Aezra was serious and wanted nothing more to do with her. But what happened to the love they shared? She thought they had something.

Well, now that she knew where she stood, Chloey Jo was determined to show him. She would show Skyelar, too. And all the Jerichos. No one ever thought Chloey Jo Johnson was capable of much, but they would see. Before anyone could suspect, Chloey Jo would have a cure. When everyone came crawling to her for help with their loved ones, she would turn them all away.

Except Aezra and Skyelar. Chloey Jo had a special plan for them, and she hoped her father was hungry.

CHAPTER 25

BITE ME

Chloey Jo was the least of Skyelar's worries. She couldn't care less about the sad little Human and her feelings or whatever it was she bitched about. Especially not after that stunt she pulled a year ago to try to steal Aezra from Skyelar in the first place. It might have worked out for Chloey Jo this long, but Skyelar knew better.

Aezra only used people to get what he wanted; both she and Chloey Jo were no exception. He was a monster. Not like the monster hiding under the bed. No, Aezra was the monster that haunted dreams and altered realities to get what he wanted at the expense of everyone else.

He was the scariest kind of monster because he took the very essence of Life from his victims until they were empty. Not dead; that would be a blessing. Instead, he left his victims vacant with nothing else to do except pine for him and the day he returned a little of what he took.

At first, Skyelar had been sad for Chloey Jo, but not anymore. The dunce could break down genetics of Creatures, but she couldn't see when she was being used. Now, apparently, she was becoming a Creature herself. Served her right, Skyelar thought, smugly. Perhaps it would teach the Conquisitors a thing or two.

Not likely, but, hey, a girl could dream.

What wasn't a dream was her close encounter with Elias. She had him; he had her. They were in each other's grasp and all they had to do was reach out and pull each other into their mutual gravity. Thanks to Aezra, Skyelar had to reject Elias. That hurt. She was so close to finally working on her own happy ending and then Aezra entered the room. It shouldn't have come as a surprise. Aezra had a knack for ruining a good Time.

God, she resented him with every fiber of her being.

Interesting that she chose resentment over hatred. She considered that on the quiet drive back to his place. Yes, it really was resentment. Hatred took far too much energy, and Skyelar did not want to expel all that effort on someone who was not worth it anymore. That was why she had to end things. It had to be done tonight so she could seize her happy ending once and for all.

At the very least, Skyelar wanted to know if she would even find a happy ending with Elias. Her heart screamed that he was "the one," but her brain was skeptical until they gave it a real shot.

For now, she was stuck trying to figure out how to break up with this damn Sanguis after he all but declared their fictional love to Chloey Jo. Not only did that make the situation more complicated, but it made Skyelar's heart shrivel up and twist around itself, cold and unwilling to beat at all if it must beat for him. What was more, Skyelar was not in a position where she could so easily escape if he handled this badly—as she suspected he would.

This entire recipe would broil into trouble.

The ride back to Murlance was relatively quiet as a result of the impending trouble they both knew they were in. Although Aezra was upset with Chloey Jo as well, he was more upset with Elias. He tried his best to showcase his authority and power at the bar, hoping it would get under Elias' skin. As it turned out, Elias was quite good at getting under Aezra's skin. Too good.

Although Aezra was wild about Lilith, he swore had that magical connection with Skyelar. She was his Life-Blood, wasn't she? The one who could break this curse so he could be free to be with Lilith the way he wanted. That was Skyelar.

Well, if that was true, why was he having such a difficult task getting her to believe it, too? Unwilling to consider anything else, Aezra blamed all of his challenges on Elias. The bastard could claim he was not using magic to entrance her, but Aezra was skeptical.

Ignore it, Aezra coached himself. Elias couldn't do shit; they both knew that much. The curse Aezra was under freed him from the rules of old—the same rules that continued to thwart Elias' efforts. Thank goodness, too, or else this might prove an impossible feat.

Until Aezra got what he needed from Skyelar, she belonged to him. Until Aezra was able to cast her aside as easily as he had done to Chloey Jo, Skyelar was not up for grabs by anyone else. Even when he was finished with her, Aezra was acutely aware that Elias could never have her. A fact that Skyelar seemed to struggle to comprehend.

"Skye, what the fuck was happening with Elias when I got there?" Aezra asked, minding his temper.

He hadn't wanted to ask. He knew asking might open a version of Pandora's Box that he was not ready to tackle, but it was eating him alive. All that confidence he built up in himself and his Sanguis abilities cowered in the corner at the thought of his enemy being stronger.

How much resistance did Aezra face? Was there a way to combat it? Both not wanting to know the answer and needing the answer to his question was paramount in his plan. Tonight, Aezra was not going to pull any punches; he was determined to get what belonged to him. He promised Lilith as much, and he could not break that promise.

"I'm not talking about this, Aezra," Skyelar said, folding her arms across her chest.

Aezra scoffed in disbelief. "Yeah, well I am. I think I deserve to know."

Skyelar laughed, staring out the window at the darkness outside. "Don't try to pull that macho shit with me. You know how much I hate it."

"I'm not trying to do that, Skyelar," Aezra said, exasperated already. He just had to open the Box, didn't he? "I'm just trying to prove a point."

"You don't have any points to prove, let alone the right to even do it! Showboating the way you did was completely ridiculous."

"Was it?" Aezra wondered, temper flaring. "I'm just trying to look out for you. Elias is not the guy you think he is."

"Oh, you're one to talk!" Skyelar snapped, determined to defend Elias against this unwarranted attack.

Aezra came to a screeching halt in front of his building, jerking them forward in their seats. "Skye, you don't know Elias like I do."

With a hard roll of her eyes, Skyelar threw open her car door and climbed out. "You're right, Aezra, I know the real Elias. Not the villain you keep imagining."

Turning on her heel, Skyelar slammed the car door shut with only her magic. Aezra stumbled out of the driver's side and tried to follow her into the lobby of the building, but she threw up a fist as she walked and forced him back away from her. The pressure of the invisible wall keeping him away was intense and suffocating. His feet dragged against the concrete, heating the rubber soles of his shoes, forcing his leg muscles to work overtime just to put one foot in front of the other.

Unlike Skyelar, Aezra would waste precious energy on hatred, and he hated Skyelar for what she was doing to him. He hated the way she toyed with his heart; he hated thinking he never had her heart at all; he hated always getting so close to achieving his goal only to be blocked by Elias Luck.

This ended now. Tonight. Aezra was done playing her games. Tonight, she was his, and he would ensure she was helpless to stop him.

By the Time he was free, Skyelar was already in an elevator heading to the top of the building for his condo. Aezra tried hitting the button for the second elevator, but none of them would come to him. Of course, she used her magic to stall the elevators. Why wouldn't she?

Her tantrums were worse, now, than they used to be. It crossed his mind that she was just frustrated, and the corner of his mouth lifted. He would be more than happy to alleviate some of that frustration. After he climbed the damn stairs, it appeared. Forty flights of stairs to be exact.

Oh, he would climb them all right. Instead of cooling him down as he was sure Skyelar intended, the climb to the top only infuriated him more. Each step, another layer of that hatred that felt so good in his heart. Burning with rage so palpable by the Time he got to his floor that he was sure the air behind him was on fire, Aezra dashed to his condo front door.

He had to stop himself from questioning what the Hell was wrong with her tonight. He knew what was wrong, and he would take care of that, too. One thing at a Time. Right now, he wanted to focus on Skyelar and what he wanted from her.

Did she even remember tonight would have been their first wedding anniversary? Aezra hoped to memorialize it differently—with more affection—but it appeared she was empty. Fighting with her like this was so far beyond what he hoped for that Aezra was unsure if he could calm down.

Then he saw his front door wide open. Son of a—. He knew damn well Skyelar did not need a key or lock-picking tool to get inside. She had some serious guts tonight to use her magic to break into his house like she owned the place.

Striding inside, bringing the flame of his anger with him, Aezra slammed the door closed. Skyelar turned at the sound, opening her mouth to gasp. He darted toward her with a flash of nearly invisible movement. Prepared for his predictable attack, Skyelar held out both hands to stop him dead in his tracks.

The invisible forcefield that boomed out of her hands and shoved him back once more truly startled him. Caught him completely off guard. Aezra despised working so hard for a good meal.

She was certainly stronger than he remembered, but she was worth the fight. Her resistance only added kerosene to the fire of his rage. When he pushed against her invisible force, trying to break it down, Skyelar pushed back, harder this Time, gritting her teeth as she was determined to keep him farther than arm's length.

With a great shove, Skyelar sent Aezra flying backwards. He landed on his back with an incredible crack. The coffee table that attempted to break his fall shattered into a dozen dangerously sharp and jagged stakes of wood upon impact.

"All I wanted to do was help you, Aezra!" Skyelar shouted. "I didn't ask for anything in return. I just didn't want you to be the monster I almost killed a year ago. But, no! You just had to let that monster creep out again, didn't you?"

Aezra coughed, trying to catch his breath as he pushed himself carefully off the debris. She did *not* almost kill him! Why did everyone keep saying that? Standing on his feet again, albeit a little wobbly, Aezra examined himself. No major damage. His arm bled a little, but was fine. As long as nothing broke through his chest cavity, he was still alive.

"As I recall," he started, staring at her dark grey eyes as his grew black, "there was a Time when the monster turned you on."

Skyelar laughed, heartily, and put a hand on her stomach. "Oh, I just dare you to try that again, asshole. I have no problem leaving right now."

Aezra took a step closer with a laughing snarl that curled his lip so one of his fangs poked out like a wink. "See, I don't think you're going anywhere or you wouldn't have come here at all."

Rolling her eyes, Skyelar started to flick her wrist dismissively to move him out of her way. She was going to leave all right, and then he would see. He would finally see that she meant it when she said she was done with him. But, before she could complete her motion, Aezra apprehended her.

"I dare *you* to try that again," he whispered, his voice like a snake hissing in her ear.

Grabbing her around the waist, Aezra jerked her against him, forcing her body to feel his. Need driving into repressed need. Anger tangling with confused anger. Aezra looked at her lips and whetted his own with his slippery tongue. He could smell the blood rapidly pumping through her veins, encouraging him to pull her harder against him; closer, so neither of their bodies could breathe on their own.

Skyelar didn't fight him. She was furious with his behavior, and she could break his arm right now, if she really want to. Her dilemma was that she just didn't want to. They were both frustrated in similar ways. Knowing each other as they did, it would be easy to slip into the comfort of one another to alleviate the frustration. While Skyelar hated Aezra's possessive nature, she was willing to overlook it for some villainous release. After her close encounter with Elias, she was a dam about to burst. Physicality was a language they both spoke so well.

Naturally, that only made her more upset. Skyelar was supposed to dump Aezra tonight. Let him crawl into a hole somewhere and starve at her memory. Why, then, was she about to dive headfirst into a Sanguis affair instead of running back to Elias?

Rejection.

The thought of being so close and then rejected, yet again, was too much for her handle right now. Her heart would shatter irreparably and probably kill her if Elias turned her down again. So her heart remained in its igloo, shivering, yearning for warmth, but alive nonetheless. Feeling nothing for Aezra would be easy. Allowing her body the release it so desperately craved at the mere thought of Elias' bearded face kissing her body would be a guilty pleasure.

This thing elaborate dance of wills with Aezra? Well, that was punishment. It was messy and complicated things more than she intended. Entirely too much energy would be wasted hating herself after it was done. But she had to be punished. Elias had to be punished.

He left her alone. He had the nerve to step aside in spite of declaring affection for her. Instead of communicating with Elias like an adult, Skyelar chose to punish them both for opening herself to him. Trusting him to take care of her. Believing that he was different.

Elias always talked about the consequences of their would-be relationship. Well, here they were! And they were, damn sure, going to be ugly in the morning.

With Aezra's other hand, he grabbed the back of her head and smashed their lips together. She was a pot of hot water boiling over; he could feel it seeping out of every pore. Decidedly, Skyelar mirrored him and wrapped her free hand around his neck and held on for dear Life. This was going to be a rough ride. Might as well welcome it.

Relenting to him at last, Aezra tugged at her shirt, tossing it aside. Kissing her neck while he removed her bra, his hands roamed freely on her soft, porcelain skin. Aezra used to view Skyelar as a breakable doll, a collector's item that he couldn't remove from the packaging.

Now, seeing the power she had in her veins, Aezra knew she was far less fragile than he recalled. And he was eager to push the limits tonight. He wanted her to break; he needed to feel her crumble in his hands, giving him every piece of her that he always desired.

He would ensure there was nothing left for Elias. No way for his old friend to put Skyelar back together.

Then, Elias would finally know how it felt to lose everything.

He kissed down her neck toward her shoulder and the small gold chain brushed under his lips. It burned on the sensitive skin of his mouth and he clenched his jaw, trying not to overreact. Aezra wanted nothing more than to rip the chain off and toss it into the fires of Hell, but he refrained for the sake of just getting what he wanted. So, he moved to her shoulder.

Out of habit, when Skyelar felt the necklace move, she reached up to touch it to ensure it was still in place. The chain remained around her neck and the gem caged inside it swung close to her heart in spite of Aezra's attempts to push it away. She might have been mad at Elias tonight, but she refused to let him go so easily.

Certain the emerald wasn't going anywhere, Skyelar reached down and ripped off Aezra's shirt before she could change her mind. She ran her hands over his strong, rippling muscles. Feeling her way down his back and around to his toned stomach, Skyelar found the waist of his pants. Aezra pressed his hungry lips to hers again, entwining their tongues together while she unbuttoned his jeans.

Lifting her into his arms with little effort, Aezra put her on top of his dining table. Pressing his hard, impossibly immovable body on top of hers, Skyelar was pinned. He enjoyed the feeling of her bare breasts against his chest as he continued to grope and feel his way around her body, reminding himself of every curve she had. Even if those curves were tainted now by her affections for another man.

In this moment, she belonged to him. He was going to break her once and for all.

Skyelar wrapped her legs around his waist as he trailed kisses, suckling and teasing her nipples. Aezra took one of her hands and kissed her arm from her shoulder to her wrist. Testing his limits, Aezra pulled back his top lip ever so slightly and let his fangs softly brush against the delicate skin of her inner wrist.

"Happy anniversary, babe," Aezra said, looking up at her with a wink and a glint on his fangs.

The words slapped her in the face, confusing her in the midst of the pleasure she didn't want, but knew she needed. By the Time Skyelar's foggy eyes showed her brain what Aezra had planned, she knew she would move too slow to resist. In such a vulnerable state, she could never be faster than a hungry Sanguis. Left with no choice but to hold on for the ride, Skyelar held fast to Aezra's neck while his fangs extended and pierced the soft flesh on her wrist.

Skyelar winced in pain, opening her mouth in a silent cry, as Aezra sucked the blood from her body. Squeezing her arm hard, the blood was pumped to the bite wound faster with a stronger flow. It hurt, sure, but there was a sharper knife slicing her heart in two as realization suddenly slapped her across the face.

What had she done?

Tears crawled their way to the edge of her eyelids, daring her to blink so they could fall, but she refused. This was her punishment. If she was going to pass on a rare opportunity to be with Elias, then she deserved nothing less than the pain Aezra brought with him.

When he glanced back up at her while feeding, Aezra's eyes were coated in black as they all but rolled into the back of his head. Pure ecstasy. Finally! After searching more lifetimes than he could recall, Aezra tasted the fresh nutrients of his hopeful Life-Blood. No more magic and medicines. This was unadulterated, unfiltered Skyelar Jericho, and he could drown it in if he wasn't careful.

Every nerve in his body sparked back to Life, returning some of his old strength, reminding him just how powerful he once was. Thank God, too, because that mixture she kept giving him was losing its potency. He had to take it easy, though. If he drank too quickly, Aezra risked killing her. There was also the creeping thought that he might get sick from this afterward, but Aezra brushed it off as irrational.

With a mouth full of blood and eyes blacker than the night outside, Aezra leaned in to kiss Skyelar again. The bright red Life that flowed within her dripped and smeared all over her topless body in a darker hue that seemed to glow like a black light, but neither of them noticed. Aezra just knew he wanted more. Had to have more than this.

Violently stripping her of her pants, Aezra yanked off his own, and pressed his bare need against hers. Reaching for her other hand, Aezra did not hesitate to clamp his fangs down into her, releasing another river of blood into his mouth, dripping down onto their naked bodies. Penetrating her simultaneously, a sharp sensation of pleasure to danced with the pain that shot up her body and made her shiver.

Skyelar gasped as a soft moan growled out of her throat. Succumbing to his will in that moment, Skyelar ignored the blood dripping everywhere. If she thought about it, she would panic. Right now, she just wanted to enjoy the numbness in the pleasure. It would take her mind off of Elias, if only for a minute. And, in that minute, she wouldn't want to cry, thinking about how she wished she was with him instead.

Besides, those bites from Aezra would start to heal the moment Aezra lifted his fangs. Eager to feel anything but the pain squeezing her heart like a vice, Skyelar just let Aezra hold her steady with his Sanguis strength, and rode the pleasure wave until she almost fainted from the blood loss.

CHAPTER 26

LOOSE TETHER

Absolutely perfect. This was working out better than she thought it would. As the walls in Skyelar's mind crumbled and a bit of sunlight poked through, Hope knew this was her chance. He was breaking her, and Hope had to seize the opportunity. Instead of fighting for a way to bond with Skyelar's body, Hope could now just walk right in and plant her flag. But she had to move fast. The doorway to the body bond was narrow, even if it was open.

As Skyelar gave in to Aezra's physical desires, Hope sat in front of the Orb in her Observatory, eyes closed, and separated her mind's eye from her body. Hope carefully walked the fragile pink tightrope of Skyelar's mind as she made her way to Earth without ever leaving the safety of her castle.

This mental bond was embarrassingly weak, but it was there. That's what mattered. She couldn't latch the body tether if the mental one wasn't there. It was an unconscious acceptance by the Mortal. They had to be open and receptive to it before Hope could do anything.

Sure, Skyelar was only receptive to what Aezra was doing because she was punishing herself, but it was all the same to Hope! There was no Time to be picky and follow Divine Rule to the letter. If she wanted to bond with Fate, Hope had to be willing to exploit some weaknesses. Thankfully, Aezra was of the same mind.

Briefly, Hope reflected on that name as she made her way into Skyelar's mind. Why did Aezra sound so familiar? Perhaps she watched over him as a Shepherd. Sure. That was probably it. Shrugging, Hope knew she didn't have Time to reflect on her studies. All Hope had Time to do was complete the Divine Trifecta of mind, body, and soul. Then, she would be home free.

Two out of three was major progress, she reminded herself. Not enough for what she wanted, but it was more than she had before.

Concentrating hard as she opened her eyes and looked into the glowing light of her Orb, Hope attached another thick pink tether to the anchor in Skyelar's mind. With slow and gentle movements, Hope danced the invisible thread around Skyelar's body, wrapping her in it like a mummy. Skyelar wouldn't feel it happening, if it was done correctly, but she would feel a greater sense of calm once it was complete.

The poor thing would probably need it after being ravaged like this.

Wrapping Hope's protective threads around Skyelar was easier said than done in this case, though. With Aezra's body entwined with Skyelar's, Hope had to be cautious. She did not want to disturb this moment by linking with him instead. Threading herself carefully between their bloody bodies like a secret agent weaving through a laser maze, Hope started at Skyelar's toes and managed to wrap the Mortal up to her shoulders before she stopped and stared at Aezra.

Watching Aezra consume Skyelar's blood, Hope wondered if he would absorb some of her power as well. Was that possible? Hope should know the answer, but she hadn't paid too much attention when she studied the various Creatures of Earth. Oops. Guess that was a flaw in her remarkable resumé.

That begged the question of whether or not Hope should stop him. On the one hand, Hope needed all the power she could get from Skyelar. On the other hand, Aezra was strong. Could she even stop him if she tried?

Still holding on to the glowing rope that would bind her with her Mortal's body, Hope held a hand out over Skyelar's body. If Hope could feel Skyelar's magic flowing through her veins, surely she could discern Aezra's intentions. A Guardian should know if her Mortal was threatened, shouldn't she? If she really had to, Hope could take it back. But that was a lot of extra work she hadn't intended on doing...

Hold on. What was this?

Moving her hand over Skyelar's heart, Hope was halted in her tracks. Something embraced Skyelar—some kind of force field of magic barricaded her heart from intruders. Hope narrowed her eyes, contemplating, drumming her fingers on her lap.

Unusual as it was, this Mortal was more magically inclined than others. A purebred Mythic, Hope supposed. They were rumored to be some of the most powerful beings in the Earth Realm. Wasn't that why Fate introduced them? Wasn't that the entire point of Hope forming this tedious bond in the first place? Otherwise, Hope would not have wasted her Time with such trivial things. She would have went for the jugular by now to steal Skyelar's magic by force.

Deciding the protection within Skyelar was merely another extension of her guardedness, Hope ignored the force field around the Mortal's heart. It was limiting the amount of power Aezra stole to sustain his existence, and Hope was just fine with that. Less effort on her part! Although Hope did acknowledge Skyelar's scrupulous guarding of her own being could weaken the Angelic bond. If Hope wasn't careful, anyway.

Slowly, lines formed in Hope's forehead and around the corners of her mouth as she meditated on this discovery. Was it possible Skyelar was already bonded with someone else? Placing a hand over Skyelar's mind to examine the tether once more, Hope refused to allow irrational fears to become reality.

Yet, something was there, lurking inside her mind. Cloaking her in a stone house so no wolf could blow it down. Allowing the magic to wash over her own mind, Hope's legs began to bounce as her confidence was shaken. What was initially considered Mortal stubbornness was quickly warping into a magical skill set that Hope was unaware any Mortal could possess. It begged the question if someone else was in there, too, staking their own claim over this highly valuable soul.

Shaking her head, Hope was cognizant of such an impossibility. No one would dare to interfere with a Wielder of Fate bond. Not when the Wielder was as strong as Hope.

Unfortunately, Hope's monomania with power blinded her to her own weakness. Vanity and over-confidence refused to let her believe she was the one intruding on the other bond. Ignorance to the situation refused to let her acknowledge how weak and unprepared for Fate Hope truly was. If only she knew the truth; the Divine Truth...

Deciding this strange force was nothing of great concern, Hope attempted to resume wrapping the tether of the body around Skyelar. It would be loose, similar to the mental tether, but it would exist. In spite of Skyelar's efforts, Hope would complete the Divine Trifecta. She had no other choice.

Before she could continue, however, the mental tether suddenly snapped like a rope holding a prize that was too heavy. It frayed until there were only a few small strands maintaining the weakest bond. The frayed edges spiraled away from Skyelar and back toward Hope through the Orb, hitting her like a migraine pounding in her head.

What on Earth? Now, Hope knew that was simply impossible! The tether might have been weak, but there was no way for it to snap apart like that. Quickly, Hope dropped the body ligature and attempted to repair the mental cord by wrapping inside Skyelar's mind. Preoccupied with the mind, the body cord fell loose and began to unravel until it was in a glowing pool on the floor of Aezra's dining room for only Hope to see.

In the safety of her castle, Hope leaned toward her Orb to thoroughly inspect her Mortal. A dark cloud of smoke seeped through the floorboards of Aezra's dining room and enveloped Skyelar, shrouding her from view. Engrossed by their sexual appetites, the rising smoke was quite unapparent to the Mortals. But Hope could see it lucidly. It swallowed the glowing rope on the floor, preventing Hope from completing the bond, discouraging her from even trying.

Curious, Hope reached out toward the Orb, and her Earthly spirit mirrored her action. The heat rising from the floorboards and into the cloud made her palms sweat. It grew thicker the closer she got to touching it until she thought it would consume her as well.

Anxious, Hope backed away. There was no way for her to safely push through that smoke to bond with her Mortal. Not without losing herself in the fog as well.

Who in all the Three Realms would dare to block the Wielder's bond with a Mortal? Oh, Hope had an idea, and her face turned a light shade of pink with anger. All that hard work she put into securing these bonds and now she was right back to where she started. The mental tether was still there, albeit reluctantly. It was more loose than before thanks to that little snap. Now, Hope would have to spend precious Time repairing it before she could restart the wrap around Skyelar's body. Time she simply did not have.

Hope was no dolt. A Dark Angel of Hell was after her Mortal; that much was fact. Well, she would not stand for it. Did the Dark Angel even know he was screwing with the Wielder of Fate? If he did not, he was about to find out because Hope would not hesitate to reveal herself to her new nemesis. And when she found him, she would kill him.

CHAPTER 27

PAGING DR. JERICHO

In the late hours of the night, as the moon glowed high in the sky, Derek and Wesley were forced to work together. Sebastian claimed it was a critical mission that they could not fail, but Derek sooner be neutered than work with Wesley Todd.

"This is stupid," Wesley complained as they walked through Healing Hands Hospital. They wandered around corners, following arbitrary signs until they found the office for the Chief of Surgery in the Creature Division.

"No, it's civilized," Derek said. "Creatures deserve to be treated with dignity. Not taken in by force like wild animals."

"If you would just let me slap the cuffs on him, we could be done with this in five minutes."

"That's not how this works, Wesley. You may think you're in control here, but I can assure you, you're not. Which is why I'm holding the cuffs and not you."

Wesley rolled his eyes, and put on a smile when they got to the receptionist. They begged Captain Martin to determine who was in charge of this mission. When he declined, they argued the entire way to the hospital until Wesley, reluctantly, gave in to Derek. He supposed it was the right thing to do. If he wanted to stay on Peyton's good side, he had to let Derek take the lead and make all the mistakes.

If Derek continued to berate Wesley, however, Wesley just might have to punch him. It would be easy to claim as an accident. There was no way they were leaving this hospital without some kind of physical fight.

"Hi, there," Derek grinned when they stopped at a desk. The receptionist immediately beamed a smile back at him. "We're with the Human Protection Agency. Mayor Jericho sent us here for his son."

"I've been expecting you," the smiling receptionist said. She rose and unlocked the door to Reygal's office. "Go ahead and wait inside. I'll page him for you."

Derek thanked the nice girl, clearly on the Conquisitor's payroll. Without their little spies planted everywhere, gaining access to Reygal's office would have been damn near impossible. Derek felt despicable about the whole thing, but he was hired for a job, and he intended to do that job. If he could stick it out long enough, his debt to the Conquisitors would be paid and he would be free of them for good.

"I'm trusting you, Noble," Wesley scowled when they were alone in the office. He sat in one of the plush chairs. "Don't try anything funny."

Derek perused the family photographs on the bookshelves. "The only thing funny here is the lie you're clearly living. Why haven't you told Peyton?"

Wesley aimed his gun filled with silver bullets at Derek and cocked it. He growled low when Derek did not even turn around. That Lycan sure had a pair that he loved to flaunt.

"Go ahead, Pastor Todd," Derek taunted with a grin to himself. "Shoot me. That'll really make Peyton glad she's with you and not someone who really loves her."

The announcement sounded over the hospital speakers for Dr. Jericho to meet visitors at his office. Shortly thereafter, the squeak of his sneakers could be heard across the floor. He must not have been far. Frustrated as Wesley was, he uncocked the gun and put it away. For now. He would be able to put Derek in his place soon enough without silver bullets. Right now, he needed him to fulfill a debt. Above all else, Wesley could not give Elias the upper hand.

Reygal peered into his office and smiled wide when he saw Derek standing at his bookshelf. He laughed and did not hesitate to give him a hearty handshake that led to a hug. Reygal always did like Derek. He was a kind man with excellent control over his beast. That was something Reygal respected in a young Lycan.

"Derek Noble," Reygal laughed. "How the Hell are you? Does Peyton know you're back?"

Ignoring the glare from Wesley, Derek grinned. "I saw her earlier. She seemed...relatively happy to see me."

"Well, I'm sure she has a lot of questions," Reygal said. "Maybe some unresolved emotional trauma. It was sudden, you bolting that way."

Derek ran a hand over his closely clipped hair and shook his head. "Yeah, I'm going to find a way to make it up to her."

"I'm sure you will." Reygal reached out and patted Derek on the shoulder. "So what brings you back?"

"Actually, we're here on a job for the HPA," Derek confessed, nodding toward Wesley.

Reygal turned around for the first Time and saw Wesley. He smelled him when he entered, heard him breathing heavily at the mention of Derek's history with Peyton. Reygal chose to ignore him. By comparison to Derek Noble, Wesley Todd was nothing more than a controlling ass. In Reygal's humble opinion, at least. He wished for better for his niece.

"You're kidding?" Reygal laughed, turning back to face Derek. "Isn't that a little counter-intuitive?"

Derek tilted his head to the side and shrugged in agreement. "It is, but I'm obligated for the Time being."

"I see. And who is your charge?"

"Skyelar," Derek laughed, still unsure why he could not recall much about her.

Reygal laughed with him. Skyelar did not need protection at all. If anyone else showed up at her door, she might rip them in half and deliver the pieces back to James. Since it was Derek, Reygal was sure she would go easy on him. He hoped, anyway. After the emotional suffering inflicted on Peyton, Reygal wasn't so sure Skyelar even liked Derek anymore.

"Dr. Jericho, you should know I'm not here for a social call," Derek said, finally getting to the point.

Reygal smirked and folded his arms, planting his feet firmly in place. "Did my father send you?"

"He did."

"I was wondering how long it would take the old bastard to get the courage to come after me." Reygal stared directly into Derek's eyes, amber reflecting amber as both beasts felt the tension rising in the room. "He doesn't really care about anyone, you know."

"Be that as it may, I care enough for our species to give you a chance to come willingly."

"I've always liked that about you, Derek. You respect what we are."

"Reygal, it really would be in your best interest to come with us on your own."

Reygal shook his head and waved a hand at Derek. "I appreciate your concern, but I have to decline your offer. My father will kill me if I go to him. Willingly or not."

Before Derek could say another word, Wesley finally rose from the seat in the corner. All these niceties were getting on his last damn nerve. Reygal never was so friendly with him and Wesley hated that it got under his skin.

"Derek may have the patience for your games, Doctor," Wesley said, drawing his gun again and aiming it at Reygal, "but I don't. You're coming with us one way or another."

"Wesley, do you remember what my beast is?" Reygal smirked, only turning his head toward Wesley.

"It's been a while." Wesley cocked the gun. "Why don't you refresh my memory?"

Derek took two long strides to put himself between them. Although he had faith Reygal would not risk endangering his hospital, Derek wasn't so sure. Wesley certainly knew how to push all the right buttons.

"Reygal Jericho, you're an abomination to God and a menace to society," Wesley commanded in his best preacher voice. "By order of the Human Protection Agency and the Mayor of Murlance, you are to surrender yourself, immediately, to VerHum Labs."

"Wesley, does Peyton know what you're doing right now?" Reygal asked, the brown in his eyes disappearing with the light amber.

Before anyone could say another word, Wesley fired his gun. Derek turned and tackled the doctor, barely missing the flying silver bullet. Scrambling to get up, Derek could feel Reygal's Human skin heating as it started pulling away from his muscles to make way for the massive bear within. This was not how this was supposed to go.

Rolling his eyes, Derek pulled out the gun on his left hip and aimed it at Reygal's neck. As the doctor's skin quivered with the release of the beast, Derek did not hesitate to pull the trigger so the tranquilizer dart stabbed Reygal in the neck.

Reygal reached up to pull it out of his neck, but Derek shot him again in the chest. Releasing a growl that made the hospital tremble around them, Reygal tried to change faster into his beast. If he could unleash the bear, they could not use their tranquilizers.

Derek knew that and, as much as he hated to do it, he shot Reygal twice more with the darts. As the medication finally took effect, Reygal's body calmed and remained Human. It was a shame to have to treat him that way, Derek thought. He was such a respected member of the Lycan species.

"Damn it, Wesley!" Derek said, shaking his head at the mess in the office. "We agreed I would wear him down."

"You were taking too long," Wesley snarled. "I don't have Time to listen to you gossip like girls."

"Fine. You want it your way? You get to carry him out."

Derek laughed and holstered his gun. He patted the cuffs and double-checked the fastener. Wesley desired those cuffs. He was itching to use them to control the Creatures of Murr County. Well, that was not going to happen on Derek's watch. There was a new authority in town—one with a score to settle. As far as Derek was concerned, Wesley better watch his back. The only Creature that posed a threat to Murr County was that accursed thing living inside Wesley.

Walking by Wesley, out of the office, Derek hoped Reygal proved stronger than the medicine and woke up while Wesley carried him. It sure would make things a lot easier. However the likelihood of that happening was slim. So Derek continued walking to the car where he waited for the junior pastor to lug the heavy Creature doctor all on his own.

CHAPTER 28

HITTING HOME

Today was going to be a good day. Chloey Jo could feel it in the air around her. In spite of her wild nerves making her tremble and shake her leg at the breakfast table, she knew everything was going to work out just fine.

This would be the last breakfast they had this way. After today, her father would not have to eat ground organs with blood for breakfast. He could eat waffles with her. Or eggs and bacon. Chloey Jo was willing to bet Jared would love the taste of cooked bacon. Pig organs were one of his favorite snacks.

God, to not have to worry about keeping that stupid red cooler around anymore! Chloey Jo was almost giddy with excitement. It made her anger from the night before less palpable. She would deal with Skyelar and Aezra, but this was more important.

When Jared agreed to come in for experimentation, Chloey Jo was wild with excitement. And maybe a little fear. Kordelia wanted him in there as a reminder of what Chloey Jo had to lose, but this was definitely a win. Now, all the guesswork was removed. Chloey Jo should be able to cure her father in no Time!

The day before, she went to all the pods in the lab to find the quietest and cleanest one and decorated it just for him. It would be like he was in his bedroom here at home. Since she was working so much, they would really get to spend more Time together.

Then, she could walk out with him healed. The first Zombie to ever be returned to his Human state. Permanently. Wouldn't that be fantastic?

Jared sat across from his daughter at the table, sipping his blood and liver smoothie. He reached for the plate of raw food in front of him and gnawed on a sausage roll. He was nervous, but not for the experiments. Jared was nervous to fail his daughter.

"It's going to be so nice when we can cook that sausage for you," Chloey Jo smiled, taking her plate to the sink.

Jared rose and put the raw meat in plastic wrap before returning it to the fridge. With a chuckle, he put his arms around his daughter in a heavy embrace. He followed her to the car, smoothie in hand, and let her drive him to his new home in VerHum Labs.

Chloey Jo parked in the private lot around the back of the building and met Sebastian and Wesley at the gate. Without words, they blindfolded Jared and carefully walked him through the secret entrance to the Death Lab.

Chloey Jo resented everyone for calling it that. Even most of the HPA called it the Death Lab now. No one had died in it, damn it! They were saving lives, but no one wanted to report on that. Well, she would prove them wrong. All of them. They would never call it the Death Lab again when she cured her father of his wretched disease.

After going around to the front of the hospital and walking through security, Chloey Jo took the elevator down into the basement of the building. She walked briskly to her office, passing by Peyton and Kordelia arguing in the conference room. Yeah, what else was new?

Rolling her eyes, Chloey Jo tucked her purse away and put on her white lab coat. She did not have Time for the Jericho family dramatics. A lot of experiments had been put on her plate and she had to manage her Time better. Today was the first of her round the clock four-day shift at the Lab. It was the only way Chloey Jo could see to get things done. She would extend that to five days if she had to. Anything to see her father cured.

Swiping her badge to get into the diagnostic lab, Chloey Jo sighed when Kordelia came rushing in behind her. Could she not have just five minutes without a damn Jericho ruining her good mood?

"CJ, come with me," Kordelia commanded in a breathless voice. "We need you *now*."

Chloey Jo barely had Time to climb into her chair before Kordelia dragged her into the hallway by the wrist. They jogged down the slick-floored hall to the invisible door that lead to the Death Lab.

"Dr. Danes, what is going on?" Chloey Jo said, out of breath with worry.

Rounding the corner to the first pod hall on the left, Chloey Jo saw exactly what was going on. In the pod that used to be for Subject Alpha, was Harper Corbin writhing in pain. Seeing one of Harper's hands turning into some kind of beast made Chloey Jo stop cold in front of the impenetrable glass.

James was inside the pod with Sebastian at his side. No one would let James get closer than a few feet. As much as he wanted to hold Harper's hand and stroke her hair, he was not allowed. She could attack at any minute and no one wanted to put James in jeopardy like that.

"Dr. Johnson, come in here!" Kordelia yelled from inside the pod.

Blinking at last to snap herself out of her fear, Chloey Jo ran into the pod to Kordelia's aid. Immediately, the director started barking orders about the dialysis machine. Chloey Jo grabbed the tubes and cords and began hooking everything up as she was told.

Kaylee entered the pod shortly after Chloey Jo to turn on the medication pump. They did not yet have a viable cure for Creatures, but they hoped one of these previously tested medicines would help since Harper was Human.

As the two scientists worked in tandem, Kordelia stepped out of the way to comfort James. "We will get this under control. Hopefully, we caught it early enough that it shouldn't be a problem."

As Chloey Jo worked to set up the dialysis machine, she heard the ripping and tearing sound of Harper's flesh as the infection moved its way up her body. The sound like shredding paper, made her shiver and grimace. Chloey Jo always hated that sound. Looking at Harper's left arm, she could see the slow peel of the skin pulling away as muscles stretched apart to reveal the bone beneath.

Nothing about that was natural, which was why it had to be stopped.

"Aren't we going to put her under?" Chloey Jo wondered.

"No!" James insisted. "No, don't do that, please. What if she never wakes up? Delia, this could kill her!"

"Mayor James," Kordelia said as patiently as she could manage. "I know you're concerned, but you have to let us do our job."

"Kordelia, it's okay," Kaylee chimed in. "I think she's passed out from the pain. We don't need to put her under."

Kordelia nodded and Kaylee and Chloey Jo continued working. Kaylee set up the vaccine pump and held out the singular needle for insertion. While

Kaylee could do it, she preferred not to get her hands dirty with the work of the lab staff. Instead, she waited patiently for Chloey Jo to put the dialysis machine in its spot.

Chloey Jo turned and stared at Kaylee, brows narrowed, head shaking slightly back and forth. No. No way did Chloey Jo want to stick that needle in Harper's arm. The arm they needed was the one that was changing and Chloey Jo was not okay with touching it. All the exposed muscle and tissue...It was shiny and throbbing as Harper's body tried to adjust to the disease.

Kaylee persisted, however, and cleared her throat, nodding her head toward Harper, as she held the needle out firmly for Chloey Jo to take. Closing her eyes to steady her stomach, Chloey Jo reluctantly took the needle. Her upper lip curled in a very Human snarl when she looked at Kaylee. What if Harper woke up? She wasn't on any medication to keep her asleep so they could do this. There were five people in the room who were in danger of being infected.

Still, Chloey Jo did her job. She reached her gloved hands out and touched the meat that was exposed. The last Time she saw veins out in the open this way, she was dissecting a cat in anatomy class. That was ten years ago! She hated it then and she hated it now, but she did her job, nonetheless.

Gently holding one of the veins steady, Chloey Jo held her breath and slowly pushed the needle in.

Blood seeped out of the entry wound in a thin line, but that was normal. When she finally moved her hands away, Chloey Jo exhaled, smiling at a job well done.

Kaylee turned toward the machine to start the drip and Chloey Jo took the opportunity to examine Harper since the hard part was over. She listened to Harper's labored breathing and lifted her lips to see if any dental changes were evident yet. As she lowered Harper's upper lip and clicked her pen light off, she glanced upward to Harper's eyes. They were moving frantically back and forth inside her eyelids. Curious, Chloey Jo clicked her pen light back on and leaned back in for further inspection.

Suddenly, Harper's lids shot open before Chloey Jo could touch her. Amber flakes floated in front of the blue of her eyes like snow falling on Christmas. Chloey Jo screamed and jumped back, dropping her pen light as she tripped over the cord to the dialysis machine.

Falling to the ground and scrambling for safety, Chloey Jo yanked the plug out of the wall, pulling the entire outlet with it. She skidded across the floor until she hit the glass with her shoulders and the back of her head.

Equally startled, Kaylee tripped in the other direction when Harper's beast hand moved and swiped at the medication. The entire pump came crashing to the ground, electronic components shattering everywhere, yanking the needle forcibly out of Harper's arm.

"Get out of the pod!" Sebastian called, ushering everyone out. "Get out now!"

In the hallway of the pod, Kordelia pressed the red button to slam the glass door closed. It sealed tightly with a loud click. They all stood outside and watched as Harper sat up in bed, examining herself.

Harper stared at her beast arm and screamed in agony as a bone broke in an audible crack as if a thick branch had just been torn from a tree. The bone repositioned itself and forced her left arm to expand in length as more marrow filled in the gap. Scared for her own safety, Harper jumped out of bed and ran to the glass. She threw herself against it in front of James, sobbing his name.

"James, please!" Harper cried. "Please help me. Oh, God, please don't let me die."

James put his hand against the glass over hers and leaned his head on it, unabashedly crying. "We'll fix this, honey. I promise. Just stay strong, okay?"

Dramatically, Harper slid down the glass onto the floor and continued to cry. The pain she felt was genuine and truly agonizing because it had been hundreds of years since she even thought of freeing the beast. At least the process was slow enough that she could draw it out for as long as she needed. It would be hellaciously painful, but that would lend itself better to her story.

Then Wesley rounded the corner with a pair of large metal cuffs in his hand. Harper's eyes widened with worry. If her brother got the opportunity to call her bluff, Harper was certain he would take it. He hated who they were. Why not use this as an opportunity to force her to his side?

Harper backed away from the glass and bumped into her bed. The corners of Wesley's mouth tilted upward in the slightest grin. He definitely had something up his sleeve and Harper was starting to rethink her entire deal with Lilith. It wasn't worth the risk to go against her brother. If they were both still the same Creature, perhaps she would be less afraid. Since Wesley was a living feral now, Harper had no doubt he could rip her apart if he really wanted to.

"Mayor James," Wesley said with a professional and clean smile. "I was hoping we could take this opportunity to put the cuffs to the test."

James eyed the large metal objects in Wesley's hand, suspiciously. This was Harper he was talking about. This wasn't some random Creature off the street. This was his Harper. He loved her.

"I'm not sure about that, Wesley," James said with great hesitation. "Let's let Delia and CJ do their job."

"They work," Kaylee said, stepping forward. "We've tested them. They work."

James stared from Kaylee to Wesley and then to Kordelia. "Delia, what do you think?"

Kordelia shrugged and took the cuffs from Wesley to examine them. She had read the report Kaylee wrote. The side effects; the potential for them not to work on a Creature who was already too far gone. It was all sound mechanical science. It was no cure, but it was something to keep Harper from getting worse. Time. That was what they needed. Wesley was giving the gift of Time.

"I think it's worth a shot," Kordelia said at last, looking directly into James' sad eyes. "Anything to slow the feral process down is worth trying, Mayor."

James sighed and relented. He trusted Kordelia with his Life. If she agreed it would be beneficial to Harper, then he would believe her. Besides, he knew Wesley Todd was a good man. He was a junior pastor at the church. No Godly man like that would think of hurting someone so special.

"Alright, son," James agreed. "As long as you can guarantee they won't hurt her, let's do this. We need something to keep her from getting worse."

Wesley nodded with a smile and waited for Kordelia to enter the code that would allow the pod to open. They closed it behind him as a precaution since they still considered Harper feral and dangerous. They all stood outside to watch Wesley work, hoping Harper did not tear him to shreds. No one wanted to have that conversation with Peyton, but it was a risk they were collectively willing to take.

Inside the pod, Wesley's smile expanded across his face. It did not suit him. The evil that lurked behind his eyes was unsettling and Harper wished she could make a motion to get him out of there. She was afraid now. She had no idea what was said in the hall, but she suspected she was on the losing end.

"Go away, Wesley," Harper said, climbing onto her bed. "I'm fine. I don't need your help."

Wesley shook his head. "I know you think that, but I'm not here to hurt you. I really do want to help you and whatever it is you're doing."

"Yeah, right," Harper scoffed. She allowed more of the Creature to take hold of her body, skin peeling away from her neck and down her chest as she grimaced in pain. It was all for the benefit of those watching. If she was to believed to be feral, she had to make it spread fast.

"Harper, what are you doing here?" Wesley said, studying the rips and tears as she changed piece by piece.

This was excruciating for her. Every Lycan knew how painful the change was, but Wesley and Harper faced more distress than others. They did not change as often; they were not drawn to the full moon because they were born out of the curse. As a result, their beasts were unruly and had no idea how to move quick enough that their Human did not feel the change.

"I'm feral, didn't they tell you?" Harper asked through gritted teeth. Blood trickled down her chest and shoulder as her body adjusted itself to fit the fur and lengthened muscle in her neck.

Wesley laughed, but tried not to be animated about it. "We both know you're not. Why are you really doing this? You can't keep torturing yourself. You'll end up hurt. Or worse."

"Don't pretend to care now. You won't help me, so I've gone to someone who can."

"And now you have to pretend to be feral to—what? Help James win?" Wesley shook his head and put the cuffs on the bed next to her. "God, I wish you'd let him go."

"You first," Harper spat, referring to his unhealthy relationship with Peyton. Without giving him the opportunity to respond, she looked down and eyed the cuffs, fear gripping her heart. Or, maybe, that was the pain. "So what are these?"

Wesley watched her for a moment with his arms folded over his chest. "Those are for your protection. We designed them to test our cures and keep the Creature inside from emerging. They're complete with an electric shock and everything."

"Well, that was definitely your idea," Harper laughed. "So, what? You cuff me and tell the world what I really am? That won't go well for you either, you know."

"Don't be stupid." Wesley shook his head and took one of the cuffs in his hand to show her the inside. "I've removed all the mechanisms that make these actually work. I wouldn't willingly hurt you, Harper.

I'm not a complete monster. Now hold out your hands."

Harper smiled and held her wrists out for him to cuff her. The left arm proved a little difficult, so she toned back her beast just enough that it would fit. It was tight, but it worked. And she knew she could maintain this level of change for as long as she needed. The pain of the cuff digging into her exposed muscle was enough to keep the beast at bay.

"Why are you doing this?" Harper asked at last. "I thought you wanted nothing to do with my side of things."

"Well, I figured if you're crazy enough to get yourself locked in here, then I better be crazy enough to keep you safe for as long as I can."

Harper's smile faded. "Wait. What does that mean?"

Wesley laughed and took a step back from her. "You don't think the Conquisitors are going to just let you sit here, do you? They're going to poke and prod you until they find a cure that works. At least, this way, I can say I did my part to hold them off for as long as I could."

Harper was left speechless as Wesley turned away from her and waved for the pod door to open again. He stepped out without another glance her way. It was only then that Harper realized the mess she had gotten herself into, and she wondered if she could trust anyone in this Death Lab to help her out of it.

CHAPTER 29

FAILURE

Elias' once bright green eyes were shrouded with the night. Heavy with the burden of fear. Dark half-moons took up residence beneath his lower lids. His shoulder-length hair was disheveled and tied back in a messy knot of a bun at the base of his hairline. He still wore the same clothes from the night before, and he reeked of that good old Kentucky bourbon.

When the sun rose and attempted to shine a beacon of hope on his house, Elias had lost track of Time. All night, he sat at his great oak desk with a large book open in front of him. The pages were blank. He could have willed the words as they happened, but he could not bear to witness it. Trembling hands clenched the glass of endless Woodford Reserve. A third, skeletal hand grasped his heart and squeezed without remorse.

No, he could not will the words to the page. He wasn't ready. Then again, when would he be ready?

Running shaking fingers through his long hair, which loosened the knot, Elias sighed and stroked his closely-shaved beard to give his hands something to do. Something besides reach for another drink. Something besides wring themselves with worry—and fear. Shaking his head with a sigh, Elias could not live like this. Long years of experience taught him there was so much power in knowing the truth.

The question remained: How much power did he stand to gain from this particular truth?

Blinking calmly, willing his emotions to remain in check, Elias started gradually. No need to rush into things. What happened was done and there was nothing he could do to change it. Well, even that wasn't exactly true, but Elias knew better than to mess with Time. The last opportunity he had to alter Time, he ended up alone and heartbroken. If he did not consider the situation rationally, Elias might cause a worse chain of events that would take his entire Life from him. There was nothing on Earth worth that risk.

So he started slowly, blinking purposefully, breathing deeply, as words etched their way onto the blank pages. To sit here and worry was a non-option. It did neither of them any good. Learning what happened was paramount. There was still Time to repair whatever damage Aezra might have caused. No matter what happened in the past, Elias could always correct the future.

Emerald green eyes moved, subtly, back and forth as Elias read the description of his meeting with Skyelar the night before. Reliving the moment they were in *Focus* together over and over. Regret formed in the pit of his stomach like a weight.

He had her. She was literally in his arms, and he let her slip away. Again. The fact that she was the one to turn away from him spoke louder than he wanted to hear. Something was happening with Aezra. Something she wanted to keep from him. Something that kept Elias up all night staring at the blank pages.

Yet, seeing her again, feeling the connection that only he shared with her, made Elias acutely aware of the depth of his feelings. Locked away for centuries beyond any Mortal measure, Elias' heart knocked on the door of solitary confinement. It wanted out, claiming it had so much to give, but Elias only gave it a window. Freedom came at too great a price.

Breath stifled at the image of Skyelar in his mind, Elias was treading water in a pool so deep he nearly forgot how to swim. In fact, Elias found himself more focused on how to swim lately rather than just letting the tide take him away. A normal person would just float and go where the tide willed them. Not Elias. He couldn't afford to lose control over this wave.

Reliving the moment Skyelar turned to face Aezra last night, Elias' heart slammed against its prison door, and he frowned at himself. Emotions would serve no good purpose here. This was merely an informational session. He had to know what happened to fix the problem. If there was even a problem at all.

Who was he kidding? Of course there was a problem. A big problem. Elias could perceive Skyelar at that very moment in Murlance; he hated that she was so close, but not with him. A small part of his conscience didn't want to think about it. Begged him to look away now. Put that shield back up around him so he could not hurt again.

Perhaps it would be better if he didn't know what happened. Reconciling between his head and his heart, Elias figured he could close the book right now and walk away. Go about his day and make the effort to see her later that afternoon as if nothing happened.

Inhaling deep, Elias held his breath. No. That was not who he was. He couldn't walk away from this. Charades were for his sister—and Aezra. If it was anyone else, he would close the book and let Fate do as it would. But this was about Skyelar. No matter how many mistakes she made, Elias knew in his heart that he would never walk away from her again. He could never hold it against her.

How could he? His own lengthy history was filled with more horror and bloodshed than any history book could tell in a thousand volumes. There was simply nothing Skyelar could do that would hurt him so badly to make him walk away from her.

Here goes nothing, Elias thought. He took another deep breath to try to still his thudding heart. It was Time to reveal the words. All the words. If he knew what happened, he could analyze it. Combat it. He was more helpless if he didn't know, wasn't he?

Deliberately, he willed the remaining words to appear in the book. The part of her story that he didn't witness firsthand. The memory that he hoped she did not want to keep. The words on the page sprung in to existence and shaped images in his head of the night before in Aezra's condo. Clenching his fists, Elias was angry at the physical nature of their fight. Aezra had no right to be so savage with her.

Relaxing imperceptibly when he saw Skyelar launch Aezra onto the coffee table, Elias nodded in approval. If only one of those sharp pieces of wood had pierced the Sanguis' heart. Then, Elias would have nothing to worry about today. Shaking his head, Elias read on. He could hear their voices echoing in his ears as if he were a fly on the wall.

He felt her. Every scream and yell; every violent use of her power; every stabbing pain that caused her heart to freeze over like the rivers of Hell. Elias absorbed it all into his own being. Even the torture she wished upon him as punishment for his own absent behavior. Whether she meant for it to actually impact him or not, Elias could confidently say that it was. If she aimed for him to be hurt and punished for letting her go yet again, then her mission was a great success.

Son of a bitch! He should have taken the shot when he had it. He should have held her tighter in the bar, and sent Aezra packing. He should have reveled in her touch less, and her taste more. Then his insides wouldn't be as knotted as his hair.

At least she still wore the necklace he gave her. That was something. Elias smiled.

That smile quickly faded, however, when he read about the ultimate opportunist taking the chance that was given to him. A quick brush of fangs. The wild look in Skyelar's eye that acknowledged she was too slow to stop this. Then, the worst betrayal since their falling out over his sister: fangs punctured Skyelar's wrist. Blood poured forth like a fountain. What Aezra did to Elias' sister paled in comparison with this moment. This classless attempt to throw his weight around.

Elias' face turned bright red, and his hands shook for a different reason now, as he slowly rose over the book in disbelief. Finished reading, his entire body broke into a violent palpitation. How could she let Aezra do that? One bite was impossible enough to envision and read, but Aezra feasted on her all night while taking what he wanted sexually. Shadows of a dark flame burst to Life in Elias' eyes.

Seeing nothing but blood red fire, Elias lifted the book and ripped the pages out with a loud, vibrating yell. The paper fluttered to the ground around him in a dissatisfying display. So calm as it came back to Earth, only serving to frustrate Elias more. He was a meteor set on fire as it hurtled through the atmosphere.

Glancing back at the book, he pressed his hands against the pages to stop the words from reappearing. That was the problem with these damn books of his: no matter how many pages were ripped from the binding, the story continued in perfect sequence, never missing a beat. As the words reappeared on another page, Elias shredded those as well, sending them floating in the air like the first set.

Hands still shaking, Elias watched in horror as the maddening scene between Skyelar and Aezra was written over and over again. Each Time the words reappeared, Elias fiercely tugged the pages from their binding and let them fly around the room. After four attempts to banish the event from existence, Elias snatched the freshly inked pages and set them ablaze in his hands. Balls of paper fire were launched across the room so they hit the wall in front of him, setting other books aflame.

The rancid smell of burning paper filled his nose and smoke filled his lungs, but he didn't care. Elias repeated the vicious cycle. Skyelar continued to be bitten by Aezra, and Elias continued to shred the pages apart with fire and fury. He cursed, yelled, and called out in agony so overwhelming that he could no longer control his emotions. Emotions that he had, for so long, sought to suppress and ignore. Emotions that never failed to cost him.

Elias never thought he was rich enough to pay that price.

The words reappeared in the book for the ninth Time and Elias unleashed a cry as tears stained his tired cheeks. He swiped his hand over his desk. Trinkets, the desk light, and other paperwork and accessories went flying across the room to his left and hit the wall with a clamor. The lightbulb in the desk lamp shattered, sending small shards of glass everywhere on the hardwood floor.

Yet, the book remained. Through sheer force of the most ancient magic, the words appeared, and the book remained on the desk when all else was discarded.

Lifting his hands in the air, Elias let the pain filling his heart consume him. He reached toward the fireplace on the right side of his office, and snapped so the logs were consumed in a roaring yellow flame. Turning his palm to face the fire, Elias closed his eyes and all he saw was her. Skyelar's image flooded the blackness smoldering his dark green eyes. Her smile, the flow of her hair, the thick curves of her body. It was all there as if she stood in front of him in that very room.

A shadow formed in the blackness around her. A shadow meant to harm her, meant to take her from everyone else who cared for her. The closer the shadow came, the stronger Elias' hatred and fear. His open palm pulled the yellow-orange flame from the fireplace toward him like a magnet to metal. Elias absorbed the heat into his body, fueled by these powerful emotions he worked so hard to suppress.

A river of flame floated in the air between his hand and the fireplace as Elias felt the presence of the shadow close in on his perfect image of Skyelar. At last, the shadow formed a silhouette and clutched Skyelar by the neck. Elias' eyelids shot open and he instantaneously lifted the book from his desk with his left hand. Simultaneously, the flame from the fireplace was absorbed into his right hand. When the book hovered in front of him, Elias tossed the fire back out of his fingertips like a flame thrower.

The heat beat against the book in the very middle of the open pages and cascaded off of it like water on a freshly waxed car. Scorching flames roared and burned in all directions. An exploding star, burning the velvet couch and tall backed velvet chair in front of the fireplace. When the furniture was fully engulfed in flame, Elias flipped them over so they hit the nearby bookshelves. Books tumbled off the shelves in a clatter of angry thunder.

And the book he held in the air finally fell to the ground with a crashing thud, open to the same page he desperately sought to destroy.

Dragging his feet, Elias slid across the hardwood and dropped to his knees in front of the, now, tame fireplace. He clutched the hot book in his hands, pressing it against his chest, singeing the red shirt he wore. Hints of his tattooed chest were revealed underneath the cloth. Elias rocked back and forth for a moment with his eyes closed, trying not to set the book on fire again. It wouldn't do anything if he did, anyway. Frustration scratching at his skin all over again. Feeling the flames from the couch kiss his arm, Elias released the book so he could wave his hands to extinguish the flame.

Then, he sat. On his knees in front of the fireplace, the office around him was in complete shambles. He put his head in his hands and inhaled a stuttering breath. Elias had never been so helpless in his Life. Skyelar may have always had the upper hand, but he could guide her. He could help her remain safe and alive.

In that moment, with the fading image of her smile threatening bring color to his dark world, Elias was unsure if he could keep her safe anymore. Where could he guide her from here? He failed. His mission—the only Purpose he had in this miserable Life—was an absolute failure. Now, Skyelar was stuck with Aezra until he freed her.

Or until Elias could figure out how to fix this. Yes. That was it. Even amid the despair threatening to send his heart from solitary to Death Row, a whisper in his conscience told him this was repairable. She was not lost forever. But he had to move quickly before Aezra got what he wanted and killed Skyelar.

CHAPTER 30

THE MYSTERIOUS PROTECTOR

Son of a bitch!" Bane cursed as he stood and let his fire fade back to ash atop the glass coals. Part of the damn Guardian bond was broken, but Hope managed to repair the stupid mental tether. He should be glad that he prevented her from securing the body tether, but it did nothing to calm his anger.

Watching the Sanguis feast on the Mortal was intriguing. At first, Bane thought he should do something to stop it, but he was distracted by a different force that surrounded her. It hadn't been Hope. No, she arrived later. After the first bite.

This force surround the Mortal in question was something else. Someone else. Did the Pied Piper know about this? Surely, he didn't. Otherwise, he would have asked for someone stronger than Bane. It would certainly take someone of Higher Power to sever two Angelic bonds on the same Mortal.

Yet, history reminded Bane that such a thing was implausible. There was no recorded instance of two Angels attempting the Divine Trifecta with the same Mortal. It simply did not happen. Implausible, as Fate told it throughout history.

But not improbable...

Hope was weak; Bane could certainly attest to that. Severing her bond once and for all with Skyelar would be easy enough, now that he knew what he was up against. But what of the other force?

He had to admit Skyelar was powerful in her own rite. The fight in her was stronger than whatever was there. Still, no other force could live within her without her permission. Not necessarily an expressly granted kind of permission. Rather, Angelic bonds typically derived from an unconscious desire to be loved and protected from the evil forces in the Earth Realm.

Given her surprising magical strength, Bane was positive this other force was not there by accident.

Returning to his fire to light it again, Bane studied Skyelar as she slept in Aezra's bed. Thank goodness for whatever was protecting her because Aezra wanted her power. If anyone on Earth doubted his motives, then they did not know the real Aezra.

Oh, yes, Bane knew Aezra well, but not this way. Not in this Mortal way, but the way he was before. Long ago. Before *The Fall*. They may not have spoken in ages, but Bane would never forget the destruction Aezra caused to the Realms. He was desperate back then for more than what he had. In those days, however, Aezra had power. These days, Bane supposed "weak" was a term to add to Aezra's long list of vile personality traits.

That little feast last night was a prime example of desperation caused by weakness.

Bane remembered the curse placed upon Aezra, and he was afraid of what would happen if the Sanguis broke it. Free to return to the Life he owned before. Somehow, Bane thought this version of Aezra was far more wicked than the one of old.

But Aezra was not his priority right now. A cautionary tale to keep in his periphery, but nothing more. Right now, Bane desired to inspect Skyelar without the threat of Hope trying to piece together her pathetic little bond. Something about Skyelar caught his eye, knocked on the door to vague memories that he could barely visualize. Who was this Mortal, exactly?

The tattoos scattered across Skyelar's body told an interesting story. Pieces of an incomplete puzzle. They were scattered here and there around her legs, arms, and chest. Plenty of the tattoos were related to animals or nature. Wolves, panthers, roses, dandelions. She was a tapestry, unfinished, and Bane was surprisingly anxious to help stitch in the remaining threads.

Glancing at her wrists, Bane noted the bites were already healing without scars. That was good. She didn't need another grim reminder of this night. This mistake.

Bane empathized with her pain when she was bitten. The sharp sting surged through his own wrists, and he did not care for that at all. It nearly faltered his concentration. If it hadn't been for whatever that other force was, Bane worried Hope would have succeeded in her mission of bonding with Skyelar's body.

So, that was the real mystery. This Mortal was important to Fate, but why? And who else was protecting her?

It was too tempting to enter her mind and try to read her memories to see if he could have some sort of hint. His master would remind him that the more he knew of his adversary, the better prepared Bane would be. But who was really his adversary here? Remembering her reaction when he watched her in her lab yesterday, Bane decided not to do anything. He could not risk waking her and having her discover him. He would just have to regroup and approach this from a different angle.

The green emerald around her neck caught the light peeking through the bedroom window, glinting into Bane's eyes. He stopped and stared. A chill darted down his spine. He had seen a lot of gems in his long Life. Most of them, worthless. A few of them critical to Angelic survival. But this emerald? Well, Bane hoped his gut warning was wrong.

Should this emerald be what Bane worried it was, fear of a different kind would take him over, paralyzing him. The entire deal with the Pied Piper would be broken. And there would be nothing anyone could do about it.

No, Bane thought, a poor attempt at arrogance. Paranoia. That's all this was. When battling an enemy Angel, it was easy to allow doubt to creep in and create the most unlikely scenarios. Besides, Samuel would not have given him this mission if there was any risk that Bane could suffer for it in the end. Right? Right.

"Okay, Skyelar. Who are you, really?" Bane wondered out loud, trying to regain his concentration. "And who else is protecting you?"

The way Bane saw it, Hope did not work very hard to bond with Skyelar in the first place. He was willing to bet she waited for the perfect opportunity when Skyelar was at her weakest before she pounced.

How very un-Angelic of the would-be Wielder of Fate. And how very familiar. Bane had seen this movie before with Aezra. Only, this Time, Bane could control the ending.

Clearly, something was keeping Hope from bonding with *The Hand*. Why else would she need a Mortal as strong as Skyelar? He had a feeling Hope planned to absorb Skyelar's power so she could force *The Hand* into a bond with her. How predictably cliché! Why did so many Heavenly Angels seem to lack forethought?

Bane knew how this worked. He was a Guardian in another Time. Witnessing *The Fall* and the introduction of Death to the Realms, he knew how dark minds thought. That was why he was now a proud Dark Angel in Hell.

Sitting up straighter, Bane decided this was going to be a little tougher than he originally expected. He didn't know who Skyelar was, or who else was trying to bond with her. All he knew was he did not want to be on the other end of that power when it found out what was happening in the background.

So, Bane would lay low and stalk Hope's every move. He would be the thorn in her side, thwarting her every plan to bond with Skyelar, until he got the answers he wanted. Then, he could break Hope completely. There was no way he was going to lose everything he earned to some half-wit Guardian.

CHAPTER 31

THE FAMILY CANCER

Nole enjoyed being alone, at last, in his house. No more science degrees or lab coats to remind him of the cold heart that used to be his wife. The tough rigamarole of emotions that plagued him the day before finally relented today. Bringing home a signed separation agreement was overwhelming, to say the least. Regret hit him first and hit him hard. This was the woman he loved. Could he really give up on their Life together that easily?

As it turned out, he could. Sadness and fear of the future came to him next, but Nole managed those better than the regret. Now that he was rid of anger and frustration as well, Nole could breathe. He inhaled the oxygen of his home like it was his first Time breathing free air at all.

Nole was unabashedly thrilled when Kordelia was shocked to the point of denial. It was Time for her to wake up. They were broken. No glue was strong enough to adhere them back together. The sooner she accepted that fact, the sooner she could move on. Hell, even their own children knew it long before either of them did.

That was not to say Nole did not love Kordelia anymore. He did. Very much, in fact. Nole would likely never stop loving her. But he couldn't be married to her anymore. Not if she was determined to murder their children. Nole could not tolerate the eye-for-an-eye motif. Losing one innocent Life in *The Incident* was enough to last him for two lifetimes.

That day, all Nole wanted was to enjoy a leisurely late morning breakfast as a free man. Dressed in his casual jeans and a white polo with the Church of Life logo on it, Nole sat at the dining room table, drinking his coffee while scrolling through the news on his phone. He would make eggs and bacon, momentarily; first he wanted to enjoy being a little lazy for once. It wasn't every day he got to be on his own schedule.

Startled from his private Time, Nole jumped when a crazed pounding sounded on his front door. His first thoughts went to Skyelar, and Nole rushed to his feet to answer the door, fearing the worst. He stopped and narrowed his brows in question when Lola was on the other side of the door. She was a complete mess with her hair pulled back in a messy ponytail and her makeup smudged from evident crying.

Nole stepped aside so she could come in. She was visibly shaking; eyes vacant but frantic, searching for he knew not what. Lola was never this unkempt, let alone nervous. She toyed with the edge of her oversized blue tee shirt and wiped her sweaty hands on her dark jeans.

"Lola, what's wrong?" Nole asked, leading her to the dining room to sit down. He went into the kitchen to get her a glass of water.

"I didn't know where else to go," Lola whimpered. "I'm sorry. I don't know who else to turn to."

Kneeling in front of her, Nole took her hands in his. "That's just fine, Lola. Tell me what's wrong."

Just when she thought she was unable to cry anymore, a monsoon of tears flooded her eyes, washing her face and dampening her clothes. Fighting back her hiccuping breath, Lola tried to stay strong. She had to stay strong for those she loved.

"Reygal's missing," Lola sobbed. "He didn't come home last night, and his nurse said he never made it to his last surgery. He won't answer his phone. Nole, I can't find my husband."

"It's going to be okay," Nole said. "We'll find him. Can you think of anywhere he might have gone?"

"Nole, come on!" Lola sniffled, frustrated. "We both know what happened to him. That's why I came to you."

Nole shook his head. He knew his father had plans for Reygal, but he did not think it would involve something as drastic as abduction. This was taking it too far. For years, Nole tried to remain neutral in his family's feud for the sake of being a role model to those who needed one. Well, not any longer. He finally had to choose a side. His congregation could scold him all they wanted, but it was more important to help those around him than stand by and let others cause harm. Especially when they were all in his family.

"Did the nurse or security see anything?" Nole wondered, grasping at straws for a lead.

Lola frowned deeply. "Security at the hospital work for James and Sebastian. They aren't going to talk to me."

Nole was disgusted. He rose to his feet and paced, taking another sip of his coffee. Just when he thought he got rid of the cancer in his Life, his father had to remind him that they were all a shared disease hellbent on attacking each other until the host they called Earth died.

"Okay, what about Ava?" Nole asked, hopeful. "Maybe she's heard something."

Lola let out another sob and put her head in her hands. "I haven't been able to get in touch with her either. Nole, if they took either of them..."

"We're not going to think like that right now," Nole insisted. He had to keep her thinking positive and affirmative thoughts. Even if Reygal and Ava were at the Death Lab, the Conquisitors wouldn't kill them instantly. Not without running some experiments first. So there was hope. Albeit a sliver, but it was something.

Nole grabbed his cell phone and pounded on his little sister's name in his phone book. If he could get answers from anyone, it would be her.

"Hello?" Kaylee answered, her voice barely a whisper.

"Kaylee, are you there?" Nole asked, pressing the phone hard to his ear. "I can barely hear you."

"What do you want?" Kaylee asked, daring to speak a little louder. "I'm in the middle of something."

"That's why I'm calling," Nole said. "Did the Conquisitors take Reygal into custody?"

There was silence on the phone, but Nole knew Kaylee hadn't hung up. She was likely at the Death Lab that very moment. She knew every answer to every question he had. If Nole asked those questions in the correct way, he hoped she would answer them.

"I don't have Time to talk about this," Kaylee said finally. "Subject Beta was brought in last night and we've had an emergency come up with Harper. Everyone's here."

"Just answer me 'yes' or 'no', Kaylee," Nole insisted, failing to understand her code.

"No, you don't get it," Kaylee insisted in a measured tone. "*Subject Beta* is here and I have to get to work. I don't have long to do my job before CJ gets to do hers."

"Wait. What's CJ's job, Kaylee? What are you guys doing to him?"

"I have to go."

Just like that, the line went dead.

"Oh, God, he's there, isn't he?" Lola cried.

"I think that's what Kaylee was trying to tell me, yes," Nole replied, sadly. "And it sounds like Dad wants them to move pretty fast on whatever they're doing, so we don't have much Time."

"Then we have to go down there," Lola insisted, demanding her tears remain behind her eyes. She took Nole's hand without telling him where they were going, but stopped before she reached the front door.

"Lola, we can't just go marching in there," Nole said, somberly. "That will only make things worse for him."

"What about Ava?" Lola yelled. "They might have her, too. They can't keep my family from me like this, Nole!"

Exhausted with crying, Lola collapsed to her knees, dragging Nole down with her. In one long exhale, she released a gut-wrenching sob. Her heart shattered to pieces on the floor in front of her. Nole held her for a few seconds, getting his polo soaked in her tears.

"I can't let them hurt my family," Lola choked. "Please. We can't let them do this."

"Don't you worry, Lola," Nole said, confidently. "We'll find a way in there. You'll get your family back."

CHAPTER 32

DEFICIENCY

It was well after noon by the Time Skyelar woke. That was so much later than she expected. Feeling Aezra dead-to-the-world and snoring next to her, Skyelar groaned softly. Oh, God, what had she done? Well, she crossed a line she swore was hard and fast.

As it turned out, the only thing hard and fast was last night's sex.

Risking another low grumble, Skyelar carefully rolled out of bed. Bite marks scarred her wrists and arms lightly as they healed. Interesting that no tattoo was forming. Hopefully, that meant the scars would fade. Skyelar did not need a reminder of this mistake.

Walking down the hall to the guest shower, Skyelar turned on the water before she even got there so she could stumble into the tub. The water poured over her in therapeutic pulses as it cleansed her of the night before, washing red down the drain. Skyelar leaned her arms against the wall and sighed. She was exhausted. How much blood did the Sanguis steal?

She hoped it was enough to last him a very long Time because there was no way this could happen again.

After cleaning up, Skyelar made her way to the living room to quietly collect her clothes as she dressed. Aezra still snored loudly in his bed. Good. She was in no mood for a confrontation. Shuffling her feet with what little energy she had, Skyelar took the elevator down to the lobby and left the condo building. The summer sun was warm on her skin, returning some of the Vitamin D she was certain she lost to the monster on the top floor.

Looking around the parking lot, Skyelar shielded her eyes from the bright light of the sun. Well, this was just great, she thought. How the Hell was she supposed to get home? Maybe she could call Peyton. No, Skyelar remembered Peyton had to work today. Well, that was fine, she supposed. She would just call her dad. Maybe he wouldn't judge her so harshly. Maybe.

Lifting her phone to press Nole's name, Skyelar's hands jittered. The phone nearly slipped from her hands as she was too weak to grasp it. Her magic still flowed through her just as strong as ever, but she was so physically weak. Her body desperately needed replenished of what it lost.

Skyelar looked around and saw a patch of dandelions behind her on the edge of the park. She stumbled over to the grassy area between the residential building and Freedom Park to pluck a large handful of the weeds. Blowing away the seeds, she nibbled on the stems. It wasn't much, but it was iron. Much needed iron.

Turning back around, flower stems in hand, a blue Nissan truck slowed to a stop in front of her. She frowned and squinted her eyes to try to see the driver in the bright sunlight.

"Skyelar?" Derek asked, cautiously, as he rolled the passenger window down. She looked like the woman he saw in pictures. A bit disheveled, but he presumed this was her. "Skyelar, is that you?"

Skyelar stared at him as she swallowed another stem. "Well, look who it is! Derek Noble, in the flesh. I was starting to think Peyton had a fever dream about you."

Derek chuckled. "I was just coming to see you. What are you doing?"

"You mind your own business, Noble," Skyelar joked with a grin. "Can't a girl go flower picking anymore?"

"And eat them?" Derek wondered, eyebrows raised in confusion.

"It's just the stems," Skyelar laughed, taking a nibble of another one. "I'm not an animal."

Derek was unsure if she was trying to insult him or not, but he decided he didn't care. He could smell her illness, and when he saw one of her knees buckle and give out, he jumped out of the truck and ran to catch her. She almost hit the ground, but he was just in Time. Skyelar didn't even fight him; she was aware how weak she was. Having Derek arrive in the knick of Time made the entire situation much easier. Whatever she did to earn this blessing, Skyelar was certain to give extra thanks.

Derek put her in the cab of the truck and jumped back into the other side to start driving. He did not even have to ask for Skyelar to give him directions to her own car. The Mountain Highway that led out of Murlance was a straight and narrow road. Simple enough to navigate. Derek seemed to remember it, but not this Devil's Fountain bar she described.

They sat in silence most of the way into Falshooke Mountain. Derek enjoyed looking around at the familiar scenery while Skyelar was still too exhausted to engage much. Given the stench radiating off of her, Derek was unsure if he should ask.

Everyone presumed he remembered Skyelar clear as day. As if she'd always been there. Derek may have forgotten a lot of things since his break up with Peyton, but there was no way he would forget someone like Skyelar. Even in her, apparently, exhausted state, this woman claiming to be Peyton's sister was beautiful. She was no Lycanthrope, but she was something powerful. He could smell it all over her. Feel it oozing out of her to tickle his skin.

Asking if she was well would open a door to a room Derek was unsure he wanted to enter. The question was not simply if she was healthy or how she had been during the last four years. The question also indicated who she was and why the Hell Derek couldn't remember more than what Dr. Danes and Harper had told him.

It was like some sort of spell had been cast on the Jericho family while he was gone. To him, Skyelar was a new person infiltrating their lives. To the rest of the family, she was a Jericho, through-and-through. A dangerous and ostracized Jericho, but part of the family nonetheless. A mass collection of memory could not be wrong, could it? Hell, in this world they lived in, Derek wouldn't be surprised by much anymore.

"Skyelar, are you okay?" He finally asked, deciding it was better if he knew.

He was her HPA now. That entitled him to privileged information about her. Habits, personality traits, interests, dislikes. He had to know it all to properly protect her. Perhaps his personal line of questioning to get to know her wouldn't be so unusual after all.

Rolling her head to face him, Skyelar sighed. "I fucked up, royally, last night, Derek. It's a shame you didn't come see me this Time, yesterday."

"I'm sorry," Derek said. "I was going to, but I had to finish another job last night."

"It's fine," Skyelar said, waving him off and rolling her head back to face the road. "I'll fix this."

Entering Falshooke Mountain, the truck bumped on the uneven pavement. Just a few miles in on the left,

Skyelar directed him to turn into the parking lot of The Devil's Fountain.

"Are you sure you should drive right now?" Derek wondered. "I can always bring you back up here after you've gotten some rest."

Ignoring Derek's concerns—sweet as they were—Skyelar waved him off. She had every intention of getting out of the truck and leading him to her house, but something in his wolf eyes caused her alarm. He spoke to her as if he knew her well, but he stared at her as if he was trying to learn who she was.

"Why are you looking at me like that?" She asked suddenly. If this was some sort of trap set by her mother, she would be damned if she fell for it.

Derek stared at her, blankly. "I don't know what you're talking about."

"That weird look in your eyes. We've known each other for years, Derek. I was there four years ago when—" Skyelar cut herself off.

Four years ago, Skyelar had just been brought into the family. Although she had memories of Derek, those were implanted. She knew that now. Her father confirmed it.

For the first Time since her mysterious and unmemorable arrival to Murlance, Skyelar was sitting face-to-face with someone who had no clue who she was. In fact, Derek would have all the memories of Life before Skyelar. That might put things into perspective for her. If he even had information he could provide. That was doubtful, but worth exploring.

"What?" Derek asked, probing her to finish. "'Four years ago when', what?"

Skyelar's lips curled ever so slightly and her eyes softened into a smile. "You don't really know who I am, do you?"

"I'm sorry, Skyelar, but I don't." Derek exhaled as if he'd held that breath all morning. "I don't know why, either. Everyone's updated me about you like I've known you for ten years, but…Maybe it has to do with what the Conquisitors tried to do…"

"It's not your fault," Skyelar said, shaking her head. "I got here after you left, so it seems you remain largely unaffected."

"By what? What the Hell is going on?"

Skyelar laughed and closed her eyes. She didn't have the energy for this right now, but if Derek was going to be her Human Protection Agent, she had to trust him. She had to let him in. Not all the way; that could be dangerous. She could to let him into her Life just enough that he could trust her in turn.

Who knows? Having him around might keep her from getting into so much trouble. Like the trouble she stumbled into last night.

"Okay, if I tell you the bare bones of what you need to know, will you save the probing questions for another Time? I just need to get more energy before we get into this, you know?"

"Uh, sure," Derek agreed, unsure what choice he had. He was stuck with her, so he might as well agree to things that would keep her happy.

"You don't remember me because, apparently, I'm not really a Jericho." When Derek narrowed his brows and opened his mouth, Skyelar held up a hand. "Hold your questions, please. I don't have all the answers. I just know some Mythic in town has altered the memories of the entire Jericho family to make them all think I've been part of this fucking family all along."

"But you haven't."

Skyelar shook her head.

"But you have the same memories as the rest of them."

Skyelar pressed her lips together and nodded.

"So how far back does your memory go?"

Sighing, Skyelar shrugged and shook her head. "All the way back. I remember growing up with Peyton and getting into all kinds of fights. Protecting her when she was bullied in school. Uh, when you and her got together…I remember how much she loved you…And I definitely remember how badly she was hurt when you ditched her."

Derek frowned. He didn't know Skyelar very well, but he could tell in this moment that he would like her just fine. Her no bullshit approach to Life earned his respect. If he had found out his entire memory and the Life he knew was a lie, Derek would probably lose it and go on a killing spree. Skyelar, on the other hand, seemed to be introspective about it. As if she was sorting everything into neat little boxes to rationalize later.

He was surprised to find respect for her coming so easily. Since she felt she knew him, she didn't hesitate to call him out on his wrong-doing. The rest of the family still danced around it. Perhaps they were fearful of angering him. But this woman? She had guts, and Derek appreciated that. At least someone was being honest with him. Even if her words cut deeper than he cared to admit, he respected that she brought it up.

"I know I hurt Peyton," Derek confessed, choosing that weight to bear. "But I had no choice."

"Well, that's bullshit, and you know it," Skyelar huffed. "There's always a choice. You just made a shitty one."

"I wish that was true for me. Looks like we both fucked up royally, huh?"

Pursing her lips, glancing at him from the side of her eyes, Skyelar sensed his truth. If she really wanted to know, she could read his thoughts and he couldn't stop her. But she felt bad for him. Something about his utter sadness and vulnerability was all the truth she needed.

He was genuinely apologetic. How he would make it up to Peyton would remain to be seen. For now, though, he was alright in Skyelar's book. This whole HPA thing might work out.

"Have you talked to Peyton alone?" Skyelar wondered.

"I can't," Derek shrugged. "Wesley's being pretty possessive."

"Yeah, I'm not surprised. He's an asshole. You do remember that, right?"

Derek laughed and nodded, but a frown quickly followed. He had one question that he wanted to ask Peyton, but it was clear he wasn't going to get the opportunity. Not yet, anyway. Since Skyelar seemed to know so much about Peyton, he figured it was worth a shot. At least Skyelar would actually be honest with him.

"Is she happy with him?" Derek wondered, gulping down his fear.

Skyelar just shrugged. "She says she is, but we all know better. You just—You hurt her so much, you know? My heart still breaks when I look at her. So she leaned pretty hard into the shit-hole that is her relationship with Wesley."

Derek glanced at Skyelar with his wide and sparkling sad wolf eyes. They were a soft hue of amber and they tugged at Skyelar's heart.

"Are you kidding? You just meet me and you're already asking me for a favor?" Skyelar laughed. She had to look away before those puppy eyes made her cave. "Boy, you are a gutsy little wolf."

"Nothing little about me," Derek said without thinking. He stared straight ahead, waiting to see if she would be upset with his remark. Meanwhile, he cursed himself for letting his guard down. If that didn't say something about how she made him feel...

Skyelar suddenly broke into a chuckle with a big grin on her face. "Since you're, clearly, still the Derek I remember, even if you don't remember me, I will see what I can do to get the two of you alone."

"Thank you, Skyelar."

"It's 'Skye'," she corrected. "With you, it's always been 'Skye.' Don't make my fake memory weird by changing things now."

Derek laughed, but stopped when he saw her shiver. In the ninety degree June heat, she should not have been cold. He reached over and took her hands, feeling that her fingertips were ice. Turning to face her in his driver's seat, Derek put both his hands around hers and rubbed them to warm her. He didn't know what kind of trouble she was in, but it was his job to make sure she was alive and well. If she needed to be warmed in the middle of summer, then he supposed that was in his job description.

"Listen, Skye, if you need help with your issue—"

"Let's get reacquainted first, okay?" Skyelar laughed, taking her hands back, and getting out of his truck. "Once you see what my world is like, you might be tempted to run the other way. And I won't hold it against you like my sister does."

As Skyelar jumped out of Derek's big Nissan, she turned toward the road and saw a familiar car abandoned at the edge of the dirt path leading to Alchemic Falls. For a moment, she just stared, trying to figure out if she was hallucinating.

"Skye?" Derek asked, leaning into the passenger side. "You okay?"

"Do you remember my cousin Ava?" Skyelar asked, walking away from the truck.

Derek jumped out and jogged around the side to stand by her. "Yeah, I remember Ava. Why? What's wrong?"

"I think that's her car," Skyelar said, pointing to the car left abandoned on the side of the road. Shadows lurked around it like agents of Death seeking their next soul. "Something doesn't feel right."

"Come on," Derek said, taking her hand. "We'll go check it out together."

CHAPTER 33

THE PROPOSAL

Sitting in the velvet chair, Elias stared into the ignited fireplace. He had cleaned off that chair alone so that its destruction was never evident in the first place. Otherwise, his office was still a mess and he wanted it left that way. He needed to live in the emotional distress a while longer. Let it sink into his skin, driving his next move.

The book was in his lap now, but he kept it closed. The words would remain no matter how many pages he ripped out. And he ripped out most of the book. So many of those pages became kindling for the fire. Now that he'd calmed, Elias had to formulate a plan.

Interrupting his thought process, Lilith entered the office with a soft knock, pushing the door open without waiting to be beckoned. Her heels clicked against the floor and her short little summer dress, with chunky red horizontal stripes, hugged her body tight. She tried to smile at him at first, but when she saw the destruction in his office coupled with his shirtless physique, her brown eyes widened with worry.

"Shit, Elias, what happened?" she asked, stepping into the room, over fallen books and piles of ash.

Casually, Elias opened the book, revealing only the words he wanted her to see. "Have a seat."

With a wave of his hand, he flipped the velvet couch upright so she could sit on it near him. As it landed on its legs, the ash and burn marks dissolved, leaving it brand-new, as if it had never seen a fire at all. Concern fluttering her heart, Lilith did as she was told and sat, taking the book that he handed her.

Heartache resonated from his hands to hers when her fingertips grazed his by accident. This was going to be bad, she just knew it. Glancing down at the book when Elias nodded, Lilith read the words on the pages. The concern in her heart faded to mutual affliction, and she had to work hard to maintain an unmoved composure.

Her fingers tightened around the edges of the book until her knuckles were sore from the tension. Lilith was not naïve. She knew this day would come. In fact, she fully anticipated it happening last night. Aezra promised. He would get what he needed and be done with Skyelar. He promised her.

Lilith knew very well what had to happen to keep her lover alive. She was just hoping to avoid all the filthy details. All the things that would stab at her pride and make her question their relationship yet again.

Elias grinned as he analyzed her thoughts. The woe; the concern; the heartbreak. Most of all, the uncertainty. Sure, the job was done, but would Aezra remain faithful?

Good. His misery did not typically love company, but he would make an exception for this. Elias wanted her to feel everything. Needed her to sit with all those things just like he did. Aezra was her lover, and she deserved to hurt just as badly as Elias was over last night's events.

Whereas Elias knew Skyelar would put her foot down, he could not say the same thing about Aezra. The Sanguis had a track record of never being faithful to anyone except himself. Elias cared about Lilith. Genuinely. This desire to find joint bitterness stemmed from his anger; that was a given. More importantly, Elias wanted Lilith to open her eyes to what Aezra was and always would be. He cared about her too much to see her continue to suffer more than she had already endured.

The ancient couple had been apart for so long that Elias doubted if Lilith altogether understood what Aezra needed to be the man she remembered. Ironically, it was not anything she could provide. That hurt. But had it sank in yet? Had she allowed herself a moment to consider the consequences of the previous night's scandal?

Normally, he would pity her for it, but today, he laughed at her for it. He taught her better than this.

Foresight was critical when agreeing to ultimatums. Had Lilith thought with a clearer mind instead of the shades of jealousy that she wore lately, they might not be in this mess.

"It would appear, Lilith, that you're the other woman yet again," Elias commented dryly.

"I am not," Lilith insisted as she snapped the book closed. "This is just for Aezra's health. A one-Time thing."

"So you say." Elias shook his head, retrieving the book back from her with only a magical finger wave. "Just what do you think Aezra needs? Where do you go from here?"

"He's already gotten what he needs," she said, sharply. "This is it for him. He promised."

Elias shook his head sadly. "Oh, *Lily*, you're so blind sometimes. It distracts you from your Purpose."

"Me?" Lilith wondered, her pitch rising. "What about you? What about your Purpose? Clearly, you threw a tantrum over this last night."

Elias smiled and nodded. "Yes, much like the one you're throwing now. Don't try to guess what my real Purpose is, Lilith."

"Why? Because it'll prove you're a hypocrite?"

"No, because it'll prove how wrong you are about yours."

Gulping to swallow her dread, Lilith refused to bicker with him about this. She knew what Aezra needed. Everyone knew what a Sanguis needed, especially the Original Sin Sanguis. But that didn't mean she had to acknowledge it. That didn't mean she couldn't still be his lover. Besides, now that he got what he needed, he could be done with Skyelar. He promised her as much.

Startling her, Elias rose from his place on the chair, setting the book down in the seat. He stood in front of her and leaned over her, holding her chin in his hand to keep her in place. Rage and contempt radiated from his pores, dripping onto her skin, warming her to the point of sweat.

"If *anything* happens to Skyelar," he warned with bite. "I will ensure the rest of your existence is nothing but torment."

Lilith's breath hitched and her eyes magnified with alarm. Then, at the worst possible moment, the doorbell rang. Her palms instantly dampened with sweat and her stomach rolled, paling her.

That was surely Aezra, coming to tell her the good news. Just as he promised. Damn it all! For once in his miserable existence, Aezra kept a promise to her and it put him in danger. Shit! Lilith had never considered the consequences if the two men encountered each other after Aezra encroach Elias' turf. Then again, Lilith stupidly thought they could keep this a secret from Elias. At least until this whole Skyelar-thing died.

With all the nervous energy in her body, Lilith lifted out of her seat, surprised Elias moved out of her way so easily. Eyeing him as she ran to the office door and left, Lilith was grateful. He was giving her Time. She had to correct this before Elias came in and unleashed his anger.

Throwing the front door open, there was Aezra just as he promised: wide grin on his beautiful face. As much as Lilith wanted to bask the moment, she had to get Aezra out of here.

"Aezra, leave," she insisted. "You have to go *now*!"

Ignoring her, Aezra lifted his hand to her face to reveal the massive diamond in his palm. It hovered there and spun, glittering in the mid-afternoon light. Lilith couldn't help but gasp as tears flooded her eyes with excitement. This was it: Aezra was fulfilling his promise to her.

CHAPTER 34

FIRST BLOOD

Unable to restrain herself, Lilith squealed with glee at the diamond floating in Aezra's hand. This was what she always wanted: commitment. For the first Time in their long relationship, Lilith won. She was *the* woman, and she couldn't wait to wear the ring to prove it.

Until she heard Elias' heavy, determined footsteps approaching from behind. She turned before she could take the precious gem from Aezra's hand, and was shoved out of the way by Elias' magic. Evidently, Time was up.

Throughout the ages, Lilith idly wondered how Elias would behave when he was scorned beyond repair. She had seen him angry numerous times. Today, though, she was about to see his true colors. If honesty prevailed, Lilith was not ready for the scorned and fiery Elias Luck experience.

Trying to fight back, Lilith attempted to stop him from whatever he was about to do to her precious Aezra. But Elias—in his infinite wisdom—had her confined with his magic. She was trapped in the far corner of the room where he knew she would be safe from the impending danger. It was her own invisible prison cell, and all she could do was helplessly watch, banging against the air like a mime.

Aezra remained just outside the door since he had not yet been invited inside. Studying Elias' dark green eyes, Aezra held his hands up in an effort to make peace between them. Unfortunately, Elias was in no mood to hear it.

Using all the anger still boiling in his veins, Elias threw his right arm and punched Aezra square in the jaw, cracking it in two upon impact. Aezra's right fang flew out of his mouth, plinking onto the ground. Elias stomped on it to crush it against the hardwood of his living room floor. The light summer breeze carried the tooth dust outside.

The diamond flew from Aezra's hand, as his body rotated, and floundered onto the hardwood next to Elias. Blood sprayed from Aezra's mouth as he fell backward toward the porch, but he never landed. Elias reached out and grabbed his stained white shirt to pull him inside.

Using brute strength alone, Elias turned with Aezra stumbling against him and tossed him into the nearby coffee table. The table shattered upon impact and Aezra groaned loudly as some of the wooden pieces splintered into his back.

Bleeding, but determined, Aezra tried to get back up. Slivers of wood embedded themselves into his hands and arms as he applied pressure on them in an effort to stand. Blood trickled out of his body, but he managed to get his shoulders off the ground before Aezra realized Elias had other plans.

Waving his arm wide, Elias used his magic to bring a tall shelf across the room. It scraped the wooden floor, and he threw it on top of Aezra's body. Pressing his hands downward in the air, Elias crushed the seventy-five pound oak shelf into Aezra's bones just below his heart. The Sanguis was pinned; only his head was able to move as his chest heaved for breath.

Elias walked over, grinning devilishly, and stood on top of the shelf, certain to press it down harder with the combination of his body weight and magic. The sound of bones crushing beneath him was like music to Elias' ears. He had wanted to do this for so long.

"So I guess this means you know about last night," Aezra slurred with a choked chuckled. His cracked jaw hung awkwardly toward the left side of his face and bobbled as he coughed up a bubble of dark blood.

"Oh, I know," Elias said. "And I'm going to kill you for it."

He knelt down and slammed his fist into Aezra's face again, sure to hit on the other side of his jaw this Time. Lilith's screams were muffled in Elias' ears as he viciously pounded on the Sanguis, making more blood spout out of his mouth. The blood fountain splashed back onto Aezra's face in a puddle, threatening to drown him. Some of the splatter landed on Elias' face and bare chest, but he didn't care. He meant what he said. He was going to kill this asshole once and for all.

Grabbing an edge of the shelf, Elias dug his fingers in and ripped a piece of wood off to use as a stake. Fueled by jealous rage, Elias did not hesitate. He held the stake above his head and drove it, forcefully and purposefully, into Aezra's heart.

Calling out in unbearable pain, Aezra gushed enough blood to fill a mug. He clutched the stake just below Elias' hands to prevent it from driving deeper. Blood pooled around him and seeped into the wood of coffee table in a deep maroon lake, adding a grotesque shimmer to Elias' dark hardwood floor.

"Didn't I promise I wouldn't miss again?" Elias taunted.

Aezra gurgled, gasping for breath, as he chuckled. "I never doubted it, but don't forget the head."

Stretching out his left arm while his right kept the stake in place, Elias summoned a large kitchen knife. "Trust me, I won't."

"Elias, no!" Lilith screamed, finally capturing Elias' attention and halting him in his tracks. "Please, Elias, don't kill him."

She screamed out a sob when Aezra coughed and blood ejected from his mouth at the same Time as it spouted out of his chest wound around the stake like a volcano erupting.

Elias remained bent over Aezra contemplating. As much as he wanted to do it, the red began to fade from his eyes so he could see clearly. Somewhere in his intellectual processes, he knew it would only make things worse. Killing Aezra would cost him what he really wanted: Skyelar. And he could not risk hurting Skyelar like that. Hell, if he was honest, he couldn't hurt Lilith like that. She was among his closest and dearest friends.

Damn these women. He didn't used to have such a soft heart.

Jumping off the shelf and onto the floor, Elias tossed the knife aside. With a wave of his hand, he lifted the shelf off Aezra's body along with the stake in his heart. Gasping in a deep, wheezing breath, Aezra's body instantly started to repair itself, but the blood loss was great. For the first Time in his Life, Aezra was uncertain he would live.

Pushing against the force field that was meant to protect her, Lilith nearly fell onto her face, tripping over her high heels, when the invisible prison was abruptly removed with a wave of Elias' hand. Kicking off her shoes, she did not hesitate to run over to her lover so she could try to lift him onto the couch.

"Now, *that's* the Elias I remember," Aezra joked, still bleeding, but not as profusely as before.

"Shut up, Aezra," Lilith demanded in a harsh whisper. "You've stirred up enough trouble."

Holding out her hand in the same fashion as Elias, Lilith summoned several kitchen towels to her side so she could clean up Aezra's broken and bruised body.

Using the same kitchen knife that was meant to sever his head, Lilith slit her wrist and let Aezra feed to replenish his loss. Hopefully, he could keep it down now that he had his fill of the Life-Blood.

Elias casually walked over to the large diamond that still sparkled on the hardwood floor by the open entrance. He picked it up and toyed with it in his hand for a minute before reminding Aezra of its existence.

"Lilith, I know Aezra is your Purpose, your Life," Elias began. "He always has been, even at everyone else's expense—including my own sister."

"That was a long Time ago," Lilith mumbled without looking at him. She continued to clean Aezra's wounds to prevent an argument.

Elias walked over to the side of the couch so he was in Lilith's periphery. "Regardless, it's clear to me that you will never be Aezra's Purpose. You forget that Aezra will always need his Life-Blood...until he kills her. And if he thinks his Life-Blood is Skyelar, well, I will not allow that to happen. Thus, is the cruelty of Fate."

Lilith turned to stare at Elias now, her brown eyes sad and resentful. "He promised me he was done. That diamond proves it."

"What, this old thing?" Elias laughed, tossing it into the air and holding it there with his magic. "I could destroy this right now, and it wouldn't make a bit of difference."

"No!" Aezra coughed so more blood splattered out of his mouth. His words were still slurred and twisted as his jaw took its Time healing. "You can't. You don't know what will happen."

"Oh, I think we all know exactly what will happen," Elias grinned. "Don't we, *Lily*?"

Lilith remained silent. Contemplative, even. Elias was right. They all knew what it meant to destroy a precious gem. Among other things, the destruction of a precious gem would separate the soul it protected from its true home. What Lilith had to determine was if that would work out in her favor. Damn, Elias, for always being so clever!

"Please, Elias," Aezra coughed and choked again. "I can't lose my last link back home."

"Sure you can," Elias laughed. "Earth is your home now, and I think you deserve to be just like everyone else on Earth. What do you think, Lilith?"

She watched the diamond spin in the air between them. With a flicker of fear and jealousy, Lilith was tempted to agree. She could have Elias destroy it and Aezra would be weak. Losing most of the magic he possessed that was not natural to the Sanguis species. But at least his dependency on Skyelar would be cured.

Elias smiled wide when he heard Lilith's thoughts as she contemplated what to do. "Now, Lilith, it is my obligation as your dearest friend to remind you of that pesky little thing known as the Mortality Rule. If you break it, you will face dire consequences."

Damn, Lilith cursed quietly. Elias was right. Again. Her face twisted as her confidence wavered. This was a bigger conundrum than she had ever been in before. She knew the potential for those consequences, and no one in her position would want to face them head on like this.

"I won't destroy it right now," Lilith said at last, turning her gaze onto her bloody lover. "But, Aezra, you have to promise me you're done with Skyelar."

Aezra nodded his head, weakly. He just wanted to close his eyes and heal. He would have agreed to massacre all the children in the world if she'd asked him in that moment. As long as he could just lay there and heal first.

"Listen to me," she said, slapping Aezra's cheek to get his attention. "If you break this promise, I will not hesitate to break this diamond. Bit by bit you will learn that I will not be betrayed again."

Elias winked at Lilith when she turned back to him with a nod. Proud of her decision, Elias floated the gem to her and she wore it as a ring on her left hand. Of course, she did not have the courage to break the diamond right now, but she would. Elias did not trust Aezra to remain faithful, but he did trust Lilith. That woman had centuries of pent-up rage just waiting to boil over the surface. When that finally happened, Aezra would be truly remorseful.

Walking over to Aezra, Elias slapped him on the chest, causing him to cough up one more spout of blood. "Didn't I tell you to be careful who you give that gem to? You have an awful habit of not listening to me. I'd take on a different habit, if I were you."

Elias smirked with glee. Although he wanted nothing more than to end the Creature, having Lilith torture him in her own special way was somehow far more satisfying. Aezra was naïve enough to think that Lilith would never hurt him, but Elias knew otherwise. Elias was the one who had to deal with Lilith while Aezra was absent; he knew exactly how much resentment she had against her lover.

Yes, this would justify having Lilith around, after all.

CHAPTER 35

PARALYZED

Following the path from the main highway in Falshooke Mountain to Alchemic Falls, Skyelar's hands were clammy. Her fingers kept slipping out of the tight hold Derek had on her. It wasn't unusual for cars to park on the side of the road by the Falls. It wasn't even unusual for Ava's car to park by the side of the road that way. There was only a walking path leading up to Alchemic Falls, so it made sense.

What was unusual were the shadows that lurked around Ava's car. The cold aura encapsulating it. Skyelar did not have a habit of seeing shadows when they were not attached to a person. Either she had some kind of untapped magic that was suddenly surfacing or she was losing her mind. Coupled with an unnerving twinge in her heart, and Skyelar was unsure which would be worse.

Grazing the car with her fingertips as Derek led her down the path only confirmed her fears. Ava was in distress; something bad was waiting for them at the Falls.

Readjusting so she could better link her hand with his, Skyelar squeezed Derek's fingers until his knuckles were white. They heard the waterfall crashing into the pool at its base long before they saw it. This was always such a beautiful place. So many fond memories that Skyelar wanted to hold on to. One in particular with Elias that she wished she could relive right now. She prayed she did not come upon something that would sour the beauty of it for her.

Feeling Derek reciprocate the pressure of her grip for the first Time, Skyelar could never prepare herself enough for what she saw when they cleared the trees and came upon the rock ledge.

There, floating in the pool of Alchemic Falls with three of the Mer-folk tending to her, was Ava's body. Her short black bob barely floated around her to give her face any definition. Bloated from the swelling, Ava's sharp features were blurred like an eraser to a drawing. Her once brown and amber eyes were forced to close and her complexion was inordinately pale. The reflection of the blue-green water washed all the color out of Ava's body.

Skyelar's chest tightened when she gasped as if a boa was constricting around her body, crushing the wind right out of her. She dropped Derek's hand and could not control her legs. With barely any breath to aid her, Skyelar took off running to the rock ledge around the pool.

"Ava!" she screamed. As she slid to a stop, she fell onto her knees, hitting them on the rocks to leave small gashes and a smear of blood. "Oh, my God, Ava!"

"Is this your Creature?" one of the Mermaids asked. She had long blonde hair flowing down by her waist. Her face was soft and those blue eyes were curiously inspecting Ava's body. In the blink of an eye, she could transform to her true form, but she was not threatened by Skyelar's presence.

"Yes," Skyelar said, quickly, through a fog of tears. "Yes, that's my cousin. Please, bring her to me. I can help her."

The trio of Mer-folk did as they were asked, although they doubted Skyelar could do anything. Ava's body was stiff and heavy in its prostrate form as if she was made of lead. If they let her go while she was in the water, she would sink to the depths where they could feast on her flesh. That had been their plan until Skyelar and Derek showed up to claim her.

"I'm afraid she's already gone," the Mermaid said in a lyrical voice.

Skyelar refused to believe that. She motioned Derek to her so they could remove Ava's body from the water. Taking Ava in her arms, Skyelar was woefully unprepared for the weight of the dead, and dropped Ava's head and shoulders onto the jagged ground before she could catch her. The Mer-folk winced at the damage they worried would be done.

Residual blood began to ooze out of the wound on Ava's neck and shoulder, but not in the steady stream of a fresh wound. Just old, dark blood that had coagulated hours before. Seeing the wound, Skyelar knew that was likely the reason for Ava's current disposition. If she could just heal the nasty gash...Maybe she could pull the infection out like she had with Peyton.

In spite of Ava's frigid body turning blue from the cold of Alchemic Falls, Skyelar tried. She tried to save her cousin. She had no choice. If she could heal wounds, she could save lives. That was how it worked, wasn't it?

Holding her hands over the destruction in Ava's neck and shoulder, Skyelar attempted to feel something, anything. Some sort of warmth that let her know a pulse was still there, regardless of how faint. When she felt nothing, Skyelar closed her eyes and tried to encourage the infection to come out. If she could just remove the sickness, she might be able to bring Ava back.

"Skye," Derek said, softly.

Skyelar refused to hear him. She was busy. Never mind the jagged flesh around the edges of the wound. The tissue turned black as it died with the rest of Ava's body. That was no big deal to Skyelar. She could repair that. If she could just get Ava awake, she would be good as new. A violet-colored light flowed from

Skyelar's hands and was absorbed into Ava's decaying body. This should be working. Why wasn't it working?

Derek took a few steps closer to Skyelar to get her attention. He put a hand on her arm gently, trying not to startle her. "Skye..."

Ignoring him, Skyelar kept one hand over the gaping wound, and moved her other hand to Ava's chest cavity. C.P.R. That was what she needed. Pushing all of her concentration into this, Skyelar used her magic to force Ava's lungs to inflate with air. Nothing. She encouraged the heart to fill with blood to kick-start it again. Still nothing.

Much to her dismay, her magic was halted before it could even begin. Something dense and heavy inside Ava prevented Skyelar from being able to help her.

No. That wasn't possible. Skyelar could help her. Skyelar could always help people. She helped Peyton all the Time. Healing. That was her thing. Nature and healing. At the thought of nature, Skyelar looked around for any flora she might be able to use to aid her desperate endeavor.

"Skye, stop," Derek pleaded, somberly. When she refused to acknowledge him in her frantic search for healing flowers, Derek raised his voice. "Skyelar!"

Her head jerked around to stare at him, grey eyes glossy and cloudy with sadness. He expected her to be afraid, but he couldn't read that on her face. Instead, he only saw the sadness. The failure.

Derek may not have known her very well, but he got the feeling this was about so much more than saving her cousin. They both knew Ava was dead, but Skyelar's instinct was to try. She had to try to save her. It was her job to save people. Yet, why try so hard when it was evident there was no bringing her back? Skyelar's frantic behavior, in that moment, was definitely about much more than Ava.

"I can't do it, Derek," Skyelar said at last. She choked on a cry that she didn't realize she longed to release. "I can't save her. I want to save her. I want to make things right. I don't know how. I don't know if I can do this."

Derek nodded his head and took her hands as they hovered over Ava. He held them tight so she would stop trembling. He didn't know what she had going on in that pretty head of hers, but he smelled her fear like it was a new brand of perfume she was sampling. He had to get her away from this before she had a breakdown.

Holding her hands to keep her focused on him, Derek forced her stand so he could move her out of the way. She tried to help; now, it was his turn to take control of the situation. He couldn't let her contaminate the body any further before the rest of the HPA arrived. Sitting Skyelar on one of the flatter rocks on the ledge away from the body, Derek removed his phone from his pant's pocket.

"I'm going to call Sebastian, okay? Don't move. I'll handle this."

Skyelar nodded, obediently, and wiped her left eye as a small tear escaped. Her mind was racing with suspicions of what gave her cousin that awful wound. Whatever it was, it had killed her. Between the sizable gash and the location of her body, Skyelar wondered if Ava had been on her way to see her for help.

If Skyelar had been home...If she hadn't gone to that fucking Sanguis' condo last night...If she had just stayed at the bar with Elias instead...God, if she would have just stayed in that protective little bubble with Elias, she wouldn't be in this predicament right now! Skyelar wouldn't be faced with the consequences of the worst mistake she'd ever made. One of which was seeing her cousin as a lifeless corpse. Such a stark contrast to who Ava really was.

"I'm sorry your cousin is dead," the Mermaid said, swimming over to rest her arms on the rock near Skyelar.

Skyelar jumped and put her hand to her heart. She did not realize the Mer-folk were still there. Actually, she hoped they swam away into the deep so she wasn't bothered. Since they were there, however, Skyelar figured she might as well take advantage of what they might know. Mer-folk saw a lot more than they were given credit for.

"Do you know what happened?" Skyelar asked, turning to face the Mermaid.

Her blonde hair stuck to her shoulders and she had to swipe it away from her rib cage so it did not hinder her breathing through her gils. She was nude from the waist up. A long, elaborate fish-like tail from the waist down. As she leaned against the rocks, her breasts were covered from view.

"We found her about fifty feet below the surface," the Mermaid said. Her lyrical voice bounced off the rocks like a song.

Confident she could not scare this interesting Creature away, the Mermaid lowered her magical guard to reveal her ghastly face. Sharpened teeth extended well-beyond the boundary of her lips, which recessed into her face. Her cheeks sank into her jaw and her eyes bulged so they appeared as opaque crystals in her skull. Blue veins decorated the thin flesh of her face like paint poured over her.

Skyelar tilted her head in wonder, having never seen a Mermaid in her true form before. Horrifying as they were, Skyelar managed to find a sense of peace in the Mermaid's appearance. Odd, she thought. But, then, Skyelar was more emotional than usual. Watching a Creature shift into its natural form was something normal. And alive.

"Do you know how she got into the water?" Skyelar asked at last, when the Mermaid ceased her shifting.

"No one saw. But she was falling fast. Much heavier than any other body we've caught. When I found her, she was already dead."

"Why was she so heavy?" Skyelar wondered aloud, not expecting the Mermaid to know.

The Mermaid shrugged and her tail gently cracked the surface of the water, making a small splash as she dipped it back in.

"Sebastian's sending a team out to come get her," Derek said, returning to Skyelar. "Why don't you go on home? I can wait here with Ava. I'll make sure she's take care of."

Skyelar hesitated. She wanted to be there to make sure Ava was treated fairly by the Human Protection Agency, but she knew it wouldn't matter. Once Ava was taken to the Death Lab, none of it mattered. It was unfortunate, but Skyelar couldn't deny that an ending as shocking as this was not expected for her cousin. Ava's party lifestyle was bound to get her in trouble, eventually; it was just a damn shame Skyelar couldn't be there to help her.

"Thank you, Derek," Skyelar said, softly. "I'll light the path for you to find my house. The door will be open. Just...make yourself at home in the lab."

"I appreciate it," Derek said with a smile. He took her hands and squeezed one more Time. "And I appreciate your trust in me. I'm guessing that probably doesn't come easy."

She managed a laugh as she shook her head. "No, it doesn't. So don't screw up."

Skyelar walked back to her car alone. Another tear snuck to the edge of her eyelid and dove down her cheek. Thankfully, her house was just across the street. She could go inside and soak in the tub for a while until she felt like being around people again. Until she felt like she was worthy of the sunlight again. Maybe she would go see her father later; that would cheer her up.

Driving down the long path to her house, Skyelar shook her head at the other tears that threatened to bombarde her face. Just a few more minutes, she thought. Just get inside the house and she could curl up in her bed and cry, if that's what she needed.

As soon as she parked, Skyelar fled from her car and waved her arm wide to open the lab door ahead of her. She heard the car door slam at the same Time as the main entrance to her home, and she tossed her keys on the work bench to her right. At a jogging pace, Skyelar rushed through the second open door to the rest of her house, and slammed it shut behind her.

Through the kitchen and living room, she took a sharp right to run up the stairs. At the end of the short hallway was Skyelar's bedroom. The plush, gold cotton sheets beneath a navy blue comforter beckoned to her and she gladly fell onto them. Sinking into the abyss of the bed, its warmth swallowed her whole.

For a few minutes, Skyelar simply sobbed into one of her pillows, allowing the bed to open up and cocoon her in its safety. No one could hurt her here. Least of all, herself and her own reckless decisions. Her chest heaved with each sob, and her breathing hitched. The burden, the shame of the last twelve hours weighed on her. She worried she would succumb to her sorrow and sink to the depths of her own emotion with no hope of escape.

Maybe she would be better off that way. No Death; no one to drain the Life from her; no one to reject her. Just the comfort of her own heartache caressing her pain away. Once she bled enough of it out, she would be numb. That was easier than facing the truth. Easier than confessing what she had done. Easier than facing the disapproving eyes of Elias. And ten times easier than confronting the shame-filled liar she would see in the mirror.

Abruptly sitting up in her disheveled pile of blankets and pillows, Skyelar pulled out her phone and pressed Elias' name at the top of her "favorites" list without a second thought. As much as she liked Derek, he would not be able to help her when he came back. She could barely help herself in the moment. And, if she didn't call Elias while her heart forced her into it, she would surely drown just like her cousin.

Staring at the fading scars of bites marks on her left arm, a small chunk of her heart cracked and fell to the pit of her stomach. First, she let herself become

Sanguis food and now her cousin was mysteriously dead. Her Life was starting to spin out of control. She needed someone to help her piece it back together. Here's hoping Elias was still willing to share his glue after he learned how badly she screwed up.

"Skye?" Elias asked, breathlessly, on the other end of the line. "Is everything okay?"

Before she could speak, Skyelar choked on another sob. She quickly covered her mouth and considered hanging up, but stopped herself. That would only make him worry more.

"Ava's dead," Skyelar hiccuped through her tears. "And I did something…awful…I'm sorry. Eli, I'm so sorry! I never meant—"

"Where are you?" Elias asked, trying to maintain his composure for her sake. He would hear what she had to say in person. It would be better for them to go through their mutual suffering together. "Are you home? Are you safe?"

"I'm in my room," she said. "Please come over. I don't want to be alone anymore."

"I'm on my way," Elias said without hesitation.

Even after he hung up, Skyelar kept the phone pressed against her face, drenching it in her tears. She fell back into the mound of comfort that was her bed. Someone needed to be there with her; someone who understood her. Someone who was worth more than the blood pumping through her veins.

CHAPTER 36

LAST CHANCE

Peyton white-knuckled the railing as she walked down the steep, spiral stone staircase on her way to The Devil's Playground. She thought the hard part would be opening the door, but she was wrong. The hard part was moving through the candlelight in the pitch black dark as the bright daylight was closed off behind her. The hard part was trying to sneak into Elias Luck's basement undetected.

It wasn't that Peyton didn't want anyone else in the club to know she was there. Lycans could hear and smell things long before they saw them, so other Creatures would know she arrived. On the contrary, Peyton hoped she lost whatever was tracking her outside. Rumor had it the entrance to The Devil's Playground was only for those who drank from *The Fountain*. She hoped they were right.

While she hunted last night, Peyton smelled foulness all around her. She was being watched. Was this what her prey felt like? It was unsettling, if so. Peyton was not used to being on a lower rung of the food chain. Something was out there, stalking her, waiting for her to lower her guard so it could pounce. Or whatever it was this abhorrent Creature did.

It had to be the same Creature that scratched her the day before. The same foul stench of Death lingered in the woods around her. Whatever this thing was, it had died a long Time ago. Now, its sights were set on Peyton for some sick reason.

Feral beasts could live for many long years if they managed to maintain a fresh food supply, although it was not common. But this one had been alive for too long. As if some sheer force of will prevented it from just giving up and dying. Most feral beasts did not outlast their first year because they either got killed when they were discovered or they ran out of food. That was what they were told in the history books, anyway. Today, Peyton was willing to question the history books.

Going to The Devil's Playground was not her first choice of ways to handle this deadly stalker. She hoped it would just leave her alone. Hadn't it been after the panther in the woods, anyway? Peyton should be in the clear. Yet, here it was, back to finish her off. That worried her and she had no where else to go right now. No one she trusted to hunt with her. To keep her safe.

If only Derek wasn't Skyelar's Human Protection Agent. They had a long and steamy history of hunting together in Liberty Forest that Peyton wouldn't mind repeating.

Pushing through the multitude of heavy black curtains, Peyton ignored the sex and feasting around. She followed the scent of stale iron until she came upon a door in the common area of the club. Knocking on it, Peyton was positive Aezra was inside. Judging by the staleness of the blood, Peyton figured he finished eating a few hours ago. She knew from experience that he liked to sleep it off for hours afterward.

When the door slowly opened and Lilith answered, Peyton took a startled step back. Was it possible she had the wrong room? Peeking around the tall redhead, Peyton saw Aezra's body lying across the bed. His chest heaved hard with each wheezing breath. Blood stained the room. It looked more like a massacre than a feeding.

"I'm sorry," Peyton flushed. "I didn't mean to interrupt. I just…Is Aezra okay?"

Lilith stepped out of the room, closing the door behind her. She put her delicate, but dangerous hands on her hips where her shirt brushed against her jeans.

"Who are you?" Lilith asked.

"Um, I'm Peyton," she said slowly, not sure why it mattered.

A light came over Lilith's brown eyes. Had Peyton not been used to catching shadows and changing colors in Creature eyes, she might have missed it. Since she saw it, Peyton swore that flash turned Lilith's eyes from brown to red.

"Oh, you must be Skyelar's sister," Lilith said with disdain. "What do you want?"

"No, not before you tell me who you are and what the Hell is wrong with Aezra."

Lilith rolled her eyes and relaxed her arms, leaning against the door. "You know, I can't get over how little it seems Aezra has talked about me while I was gone."

"So are you, like, an ex-girlfriend?" Peyton guessed, waving her hand in an attempt to extract more information.

"I suppose you could say that." Lilith pursed her lips in a smile. "Aezra and I go way back. All the way back to the beginning, actually. I'm Lilith, his lover."

Peyton jumped backward a few inches when Lilith stuck her right hand out for Peyton to shake. She had no doubt Lilith was Aezra's lover. The woman carried herself in the same manner: cocky with an heir that she always knew something no one else did. Peyton used to like that about him, but the more she saw him away from Skyelar, the more she realized he was just an ass. Simple as that.

Still, he was an ass that was good at hunting and good at getting into her mind. She could use a little of both right now, if she was honest. And she would overlook his attitude for the sake of it.

"Great," Peyton said, shaking Lilith's hand with a secure grip. She thought she felt something tapping her on the shoulder, forcing her to let go and turn around. Paranoia. That's all it was. There was no way that thing could get in the club; the doors were sealed to trespassers.

"Everything okay, Peyton?" Lilith asked with smiling eyes.

"Huh?" Peyton asked, turning back to Lilith to remember why she was there. "Oh. Yeah. I just—I really need to see Aezra."

Lilith nodded, but made no motion to move out of Peyton's way. "I'm sorry to be so protective. It's just that Aezra was in another fight with Elias—over your sister, actually. I wasn't sure if you came here to finish the job."

Peyton laughed. "Elias doesn't trust me like that. And they're always fighting over Skye."

"Not anymore," Lilith said, suddenly very serious with a darkness seeming to creep in around her. "Aezra belongs to me now."

Holding up her left hand, Lilith proudly flashed the large diamond ring as confirmation of her words. Peyton's bottom jaw lowered and she hoped her mouth was not hanging open. That was the same ring he had given to Skyelar just last year. Damn, this man was eager to tie someone down!

Quietly, Peyton wondered what lies he fed to Lilith to convince her to marry him. Then again, she seemed crazy enough that she didn't need much of a lie to get her to agree to do whatever that gross blood drinking thing was. It gave Peyton a chill just thinking about it.

"Congrats, I guess," Peyton said, finally. "But I was hoping to talk to Aezra about this beast that's stalking me. I know he can help me find it—"

Lilith shook her head and stood straight again, taking a step toward Peyton. "Aezra won't be in the condition to hunt for several days, maybe longer. He needs to heal. Elias nearly killed him."

Shrugging, Peyton spoke before she could stop herself. "Well, he deserved it after the way he hurt Skye."

That flash reddened Lilith's eyes again and Peyton took a step back, kicking herself for even saying anything. Sure, she knew Aezra deserved to be punished, but she also knew better than to confess something like that to his lover. Fiancée? Whatever the Hell Lilith was.

As Peyton continued to back up, Lilith stepped forward to close the gap, the red filling her eyes. Oh, shit, this was going to be bad. Peyton took one more step back and stiffened her body to prepare for the change. When she felt someone else's body brush up behind her, however, Peyton jumped toward Lilith, and turned on her toes, nearly falling over into Lilith's angry clutches.

Elias caught her before she could fall and pulled her into him. For the first Time, Peyton felt the strength of his muscles as he steadied her. The comfort in his power washed over her, soothing her anxiety. He pushed her to the side to stop Lilith in her tracks. Was that what Skyelar felt when she was around him? Now, Peyton began to understand the attachment. She was still uneasy about it, but she could understand it better.

"Peyton, you shouldn't be here," Elias said, sternly. "You're going to be needed at the Death Lab."

"What?" Peyton laughed. "I paid for my right to be here."

"Skye just called me," he confessed. "She found Ava's body in Alchemic Falls."

A soft gasp escaped Peyton's mouth before she jumped yet again at her phone buzzing in her pocket. Damn it all! She hated being so on edge like this. Removing her phone from her pocket, a text message from her mother explained Ava's delivery to the Death Lab. Before she could say anything else, Peyton fled out of the club to her cousin's aid, forgetting about her stalker waiting just outside. She would run there as the wolf. Give both of them some exercise.

"Lilith," Elias began after Peyton left. "You wouldn't happen to know anything about this tragedy, would you?"

"Elias, come on," Lilith said, nervously. Now, it was she who backed up and cornered herself against the door to Aezra's room. "I loved Ava. I would never hurt her. You definitely made it clear I couldn't."

Elias smiled and nodded his head as if he believed her. In reality, he knew better. He knew better than anyone that Lilith had everything to do with this. He hoped she would be honest with him, especially after the morning they had. Nearly killing her lover should have reminded her that Elias never forgot a bargain. Since Lilith had clearly forgotten the deal she made, it was Time for him to remind her—for the second Time that day—how deadly the consequences could be.

Lifting his hand in the air, the door behind Lilith flew open and he shoved her inside. Slamming the door behind him, Elias marched over to his cowering friend and grabbed her by her bright red curls. With his other hand, Elias summoned serpents to slither up through invisible cracks in the stone floor. The obedient reptiles tangled themselves around Lilith's legs and hands tightly, pinning her to the cold of the stone in submission.

"Elias, please!" Lilith cried as she was forced onto her hands and knees.

Elias ignored her pleas and knelt down in front of her. On her right wrist, Lilith wore a beautiful white gold bracelet with a shining red ruby in the middle. Smiling, he reached between the tangled serpents on her arms and plucked the stone from its nest on her wrist.

"You might be inclined to spare Aezra the pain of shattering his gem, but I don't necessarily feel the same for you right now." Elias threatened it, holding the bright red gem tightly between his fingers to apply pressure.

"No!" Lilith screamed. "Please, Elias, have mercy! There was nothing I could do. She was feral. I just eased her suffering."

"Didn't I tell you not to harm her? Not to harm Skyelar as a result?" Elias asked, using his free hand to tilt her chin up so she was forced to look at him. As he did, the deadly serpents snapped their sharp fangs. "What's the matter, Lily? I thought you enjoyed having fangs in your face."

Lilith let out a choked sob and dropped her head as tears splashed onto the stone below her. "Please, Elias, please. Don't damn me to this Life. I'll do anything. Anything you want."

"You will confess what you've done," Elias said, stoically. "You'll go to Skyelar and tell her what you did. Tell her everything. And you will gladly accept whatever punishment Skyelar decides suits you. And you'll do it all without a fight."

Defeated, afraid of losing everything, Lilith nodded her head as she continued to cry. Lucky for her, Elias did not require verbal acceptance of the terms of her punishment. Fear and regret spoke volumes on her behalf.

He rose to stand over her, still holding the precious ruby, and waved the serpents away. They hissed and slithered back into the stone floor from whence they came. Pocketing the ruby, Elias turned to leave without another consideration for the Creatures in this room. He had to get to Skyelar. The sound of her sobbing echoed in the chambers of his heart and he had to go comfort her.

"Elias, wait," Lilith said, finally standing on unsteady legs. "My gem…"

"No, I'll be holding on to that," Elias rebutted with a grin. "When you confess your sins to Skyelar, you can have it back."

"You can't do that!" she complained without thinking. The moment the words came out, Lilith regretted them and covered her mouth with her hands.

Elias turned back to his confidant and friend, quickly closing the distance between them. "Never forget that you could face so much worse for what you've done. Be grateful I have the ability to show a little mercy while I still have some in stock."

Lilith quickly lowered her head and closed her eyes in obedience. She might have been frustrated with him for doing this to her, but she had to concede he was right. He had always shown her more mercy than most. She owed him her allegiance for that. Still, it didn't mean she had to like it.

"Oh, and Lilith?" Elias said, walking away again. "This is your last chance. If you pull another stunt like this, I'll gladly feed you to the wolves."

CHAPTER 37

BLESSED IMPLOSION

Patrise was in the Garden on that pleasant afternoon. The light of the sun shone on her face, warming her heart. Gently, she unfolded her wings and stretched them out wide. As the sun's rays collided with her strong, soft white feathers, Patrise's soul found inner peace.

With so much disarray all morning in the Earth Realm, a little sunlight was good. It reminded her that the light would always conquer the dark. She knew this path was for Fate. Everything she did was for Fate. Yet, she couldn't help question the pain and suffering that had to go along with it.

The Earth Realm was sick. Even if she wanted to, Patrise could not save it. Not on her own. The Angels of Wisdom could only help the Mortals with Divine Intervention. That was something Ginysis would not willingly provide. Not unless the Earth was on the very brink of complete destruction. So the Mortals were left to sort it out on their own.

If they had a proper Wielder of Fate, things would be drastically different. Patrise would not have to get involved this way. As it was, Fate required assistance from a trusted source. Who was more trustworthy than Death?

Waiting by her Tree of Death, Patrise smiled at the small green apples flourishing nicely. It mattered not that Carmen thought so ill of her. Life and Death were symbiotic. They could not thrive without each other. Carmen was just afraid. Her fear was a reflection of most Mortals who begged for Life at the end when Death would ease their suffering.

After the Earth was healed, Patrise hoped to understand such Mortal choices better. Until then, however, she remained the outcast of the Angels of Wisdom. Fine. She could enjoy this moment alone before the next soul arrived to the Garden.

Carmen and Theo finally stepped out of the castle. They should have been out there before now, but Patrise was not going to criticize. Their recent debate about Hope's suitability as the Wielder of Fate only worked to drive them further apart. It was exhausting.

The most important thing to Patrise, now, was this Earthly Guardian that she only recently learned about. No one would tell her who the Guardian was; only that this Angel was on Earth completing a Divine mission. Naturally, the nature of the mission was also a mystery. Evidently, the Guardian in question would be called back to the Kingdom soon and they could make everything right again based on what the Guardian learned.

Carmen was starting to believe this missing Guardian was the reason Hope was unable to bond with *The Hand*. Patrise did not think so at all, but she would not argue anymore. She would stay the course that Fate had laid before her feet and see where it led her.

Finally, the newest soul to enter the Kingdom of Heaven appeared in the Garden of Eden. Patrise tucked her wings away and turned to face the soul along with her brother and sister in wisdom.

"Welcome, Ava Jericho, to the Kingdom of Heaven," Carmen said with a soft smile.

Ava's soul stood before the Angels of Wisdom as she was on Earth. Her black bob framed her round face and she stood tall and strong. Confident as she ever was on Earth. Best of all, the bite on her neck was gone. Ava was healed, but also sick. Empty. Alone. She looked around at all the flowers and golden castles in front of her and her heart was so overwhelmed that she started to cry.

"Do not be afraid of this Life," Carmen continued, "for it is yours to choose. You have led a good Earthly existence and, now, have a choice of Time before you. I am Carmen, and I am the keeper of Knowledge. Should you choose to follow me, I will grant you Angelic wings and you can watch over those you loved on Earth."

Ava stood, staring and silent, even as tears flowed down her cheek. She wrapped her arms around her stomach, clinging to her Human flesh, knowing it was all she had left.

"And I am Theo," he said, taking his turn. A small cough ruffled his throat before he spoke, but he maintained his composure. "I am the keeper of Life. Should you choose to follow me, I will help you become reborn, and you can live again on Earth in a new Mortal skin."

"And I am Patrise," she said, stepping between Theo and Carmen. "I am the keeper of Death. Should you choose to follow me, I can help you rest. Your deeds are done, and you do not have to carry the burden of Life any longer."

Ava looked at all three of them, sadness and pain in her eyes. She knew she was dead the minute she got out of the car at Alchemic Falls. The harsh whisper within killed her faster than anything Lilith could have done. Reflecting on her demise, Ava was convinced Lilith did what was necessary to ensure the feral beast did not harm anyone else.

Still, Ava was dead. She always thought she would be ready for it. Living Life to the fullest and all that. Yet, when she was faced with it—when she was given the choice to continue forward or even live all over again as someone else—she was afraid.

She lost her beast. Somewhere between her last memory on Earth and waking up in front of the Pearl Gates, Ava's panther abandoned her. She could feel the vast emptiness inside her, as if someone ripped out half of her organs to leave her Human shell only half filled.

Ava continued to cry, wishing for the comfort of the Life she knew. In that moment, Ava realized that it wasn't her family or friends she feared leaving behind. Now that she was given the choice to start again, she feared losing herself. If she could not carry her beast, then she was no longer whole.

"I don't want to keep living, if I can't be who I was," Ava said at last. "I can't carry this emptiness forever."

"Then come with me, Ava," Patrise said, holding out her hand, for the choice was clear. "I will let you taste the sweetest fruit, and you will finally be at peace."

Ava nodded her head and the gate to the Garden of Eden swung open on its hinges. Taking Patrise's hand, she walked to the tall Tree of Death with the Angel of Wisdom. The sparkling green apples shimmered in the sunlight. Ava smiled.

"You may pluck the fruit from my Tree and feast," Patrise said. "Then, you shall rest and find peace within yourself for eternity."

Without hesitation, Ava reached up and plucked the largest apple she could find, although they were all rather small. Biting into it, Ava closed her eyes as the sweet taste of the fruit moistened her tongue and filled her body with warmth. Before she could take the second bite, the light in her soul began to fade as she was removed from the Garden and sent to the Eternal Pool where she could find her peace in eternity.

Sighing, Patrise watched as another apple grew in place of the missing one. She always felt a sense of relief when a tired soul chose her Tree. Sometimes, rest was all they needed to help the Earth heal.

"Why would she choose your Tree?" Carmen asked, folding her arms in a pout. "I don't understand how souls keep choosing you."

"We are all chosen at random, sister," Patrise said, trying not to pick a fight. "You have had many souls choose you, and I do not lie down with jealousy."

Carmen huffed, unable to believe how Patrise was willing to speak out to her lately. "Come, Theo, let's retire to the dining hall. Alone!"

As Carmen swept passed her brother in Wisdom, she thought he followed, but she was alone in her march. Turning, wondering why he would also choose Patrise over her, Carmen screamed in horror as Theo's body grew weak and he fell to the ground before her.

Patrise ran to Theo's aid before Carmen could get there. They were both pushed away by his Defender quickly flying in to lift him and carry him to his chambers in the Castle of Wisdom. Carmen did not hesitate to follow, but something caught Patrise's eye and made her linger in the Garden for just a moment longer.

As she turned toward Theo's tree, the Tree of Life, she witnessed the fig fruit showing signs of age. Some of them were even starting to rot. What kind of dark magic was this? The fruit on their trees was meant to last well beyond Time itself. Glancing over her shoulder, Patrise could see Carmen's pomegranates still shining and healthy.

Her heart skipped a few beats, and, as she turned to further investigate the Tree of Life, she caught a minuscule movement out of the corner of her eye. There, in the distance, the Balance of Power tipped as the hand that clutched the apple fell an inch closer to the serpent. This could only mean one thing: the Kingdom of Heaven was danger.

READ ON FOR AN EXCERPT FROM

BLESSED IMPLOSION

BY STEVIE JO

Fifth in the Angel of Death series.

Coming Summer 2023!

With the Fourth of July picnic just fifteen hours away, the Death Lab was akin to a shopping mall the last weekend before Christmas. Scientists ran everywhere, pushing carts, carrying syringes of mysterious elixirs, and barking out orders. The Creatures being kept in the Death Lab were howling and crying in pain as they suffered every little experimental drug the Conquisitors could create.

Fifteen hours remaining until showtime and they were still no closer to a cure than when they started this stupid competition a month ago. Ten days ago, Kordelia Danes might have believed they could do something. She might have been inclined to have a little faith that her Conquisitors would pull through and cure one of those obnoxious Creatures.

Then, nine days ago, Harper came into the Lab with a furry arm. She had been attacked by a Creature and was turning feral. Nine days ago, Kordelia knew they would never find a cure because her entire focus had to shift to saving a Human.

While there was a possibility that whatever they found to heal Harper of this slow-moving poison would work on the other Creatures in the Lab, Kordelia seriously doubted it. Treating a feral was not the same as curing a Creature of its illness.

Kordelia still managed to keep some of her Conquisitors on other projects, but she assigned the task of saving Harper's Life to Peyton and Chloey Jo. The way Kordelia saw it, if she had to suffer James' wrath, then so did they. Especially Peyton.

As much as she loved her daughter, Kordelia was quite worried about Peyton's loyalties. The girl would come in to the Lab to work for a shift, then leave and take a day off in between. She kept all of her notes with her and was often seen taking things in and out of the Lab. If it was any other Conquisitor, Kordelia would fire them for stealing her property. Yet, she couldn't do that to Peyton.

Her biggest fear was that Skyelar was getting to Peyton, converting her to their side. In that respect, Kordelia supposed it was a good thing they did not yet have a cure. She did not need Skyelar screwing things up for her yet again. Kordelia was still recovering from the last Time Skyelar destroyed the cure for Creatures.

Still, Kordelia tried to remain positive. Perhaps she was just taking things home to work on it there. Or, perhaps, Peyton had convinced Skyelar to help them. Wouldn't that be something? Well, if anyone could do it, Kordelia had her money on Peyton.

She was not oblivious to the lengths Skyelar would go to for her sister. As often as they fought and hurt each other, Kordelia knew that Skyelar would always be the one to make the sacrifice in the end if it meant Peyton could be happy. Everyone thought Kordelia was blissfully unaware of that dynamic, but she was not.

That was why she continued to allow Peyton to take things home and take days off. It bothered her endlessly, but if it brought them a cure, she would allow it. Then, she just might have to go easy on Skyelar for once. Maybe.

Kordelia always thought it was a shame she and Skyelar did not get along better. Her personality was perfect for taking over VerHum Labs. Watching Peyton straddle both sides of the fence worried Kordelia that she might never have someone she could trust to take over when she was ready to retire. And, at the rate they were going with this cure, Kordelia was ready to retire tomorrow.

When she thought about Peyton's persistent absence and blatant disregard for their goal, Kordelia was infuriated. Chloey Jo was overworked as it was. The case load was massive and they were running out of Time. Thank goodness Chloey Jo had been at the Lab every day and night for the last nine days. She barely slept, barely ate. Kordelia noticed because she was in the same routine.

Little did Kordelia know, Chloey Jo was not working on anything to cure Harper. Since checking her father in to his own pod last week, Chloey Jo worked tirelessly to find a cure for him. She had to. She couldn't just bring him here and then watch him die. The problem was, every Time she thought she took a step in the right direction, she was pushed two steps back. Jared just was not taking to anything like she thought he would.

Damn Aezra. If only she had some of his blood to try. She was sure it would be different coming from the pure source rather than recycled through her own body and mixed with something else.

They were running out of Time. Fifteen hours, she knew. Kordelia had an announcement over the loud speakers that announced as each hour ticked away. But Chloey Jo was not worried about James' campaign. She couldn't care less who won or who lost. What she cared about was healing her father first, then herself.

Chloey Jo was starting to really feel the effects of being infected by a Sanguis. Her hunger was off the charts, but regular food did nothing. So, she had to resort to sneaking sips of the blood they kept on hand in the Lab. It was despicable, but it sustained her for a few hours here and there.

She hated to admit Aezra was right. She was becoming the very thing she hated.

On the other hand, at least she wasn't Harper. The poor thing was slowly changing into a wild feral beast. Thank goodness all Chloey Jo had was a little Sanguis inside her. That should be easy enough to eliminate once she figured out how to cure the Zombie killing her father.

Walking by Harper's pod on her way to Subject Zeta, Chloey Jo glanced over her shoulder to monitor her progress. Harper's entire left arm was some sort of deformed Creature. It had spread to her neck and chest by the Time Wesley and Kaylee came forward with their little invention.

Docility Cuffs. That was what they called them. Clicking them around Harper's wrists, they kept her from changing any more, but they did nothing to reverse the change she had already begun. Although James considered that a failure, Chloey Jo saw it as a success. It did exactly what Wesley advertised it to do: keep the Creature inside the Human docile.

The fact that those cuffs worked on a feral beast was a bigger deal than James could realize. If all else failed, maybe Chloey Jo could have some made for Jared. It would likely keep him from changing and killing anyone, but it wouldn't cure him. That was why it was a last resort.

Stopping to see James inside the pod with Harper, loving on her as he was wont to do, Chloey Jo realized docility could be all they could ask for sometimes. If she could hug her father that way without worrying if he had eaten or not, Chloey Jo would consider her Life returned to normal.

"Dr. Johnson," James said, catching Chloey Jo's eye from inside the pod. He waved for her to come over to him.

Damn. She lingered too long. She really did hate the Jericho family, most of all the mayor, but he was the lesser of two evils right now. Obediently, Chloey Jo walked over to the pod and smiled at the mayor and Harper.

"Dr. Johnson, do you have anything you might be able to try on Harper to cure her?" James asked. "I assure you she's strong enough."

"Oh, I'm sorry, Mayor," Chloey Jo said sincerely. "I, uh, I have something in the works for Harper, but it's not ready yet."

"Well, what have you got there?" James wondered, pointing to the syringe in her hand. "We've got to try something."

Chloey Jo shook her head and took a step back. "No, Mayor, she can't have this. Since Harper is primarily Human, this would likely kill her."

"We're losing Time," James grumbled, frustrated by the lack of progress.

"Mayor James," Kordelia said coming around the corner for her hourly check on Harper. "You can't keep harassing my staff for a cure. They're working on it. I promise."

Seeing her opportunity to slink away, Chloey Jo did just that. The mayor and Kordelia could argue all they wanted, but Chloey Jo had things to do. In the last pod on the right of the hall was Ava's body. Kaylee had modified the pod so that it served as a cryogenic chamber. The goal was to preserve her body for study in hopes that they would find a cure faster. The problem was Ava's body had been poisoned so not all of it was salvageable.

Lucky for Chloey Jo, some of her organs were still safe. For the last nine days, she had come in the pod to cut out little pieces of Ava's liver to feed to Jared. It wasn't much, but it was something. He was still starting to deteriorate, but it wasn't at the rapid rate that he would if he had not been fed.

Across the hall was Subject Zeta, Jared Johnson. There was a note signed by Kordelia plastered on his pod that denied him food. Chloey Jo hated it. Had she known Kordelia would be so cruel, she never would have agreed to bring her father in there. Although Kordelia claimed it was for Chloey Jo's benefit, the young scientist failed to see how.

By all appearances, Jared was not the father Chloey Jo grew up loving. His body was on the path to deterioration and would soon turn completely feral if he did not keep eating what little Chloey Jo could sneak to him.

Jared's muscles were exposed in places where the skin fell right off his body into a wet heap on the floor. As Jared walked around the pod, he stepped on the skin pieces and they squished to the concrete. Where he still had some skin on his body, it was swelled up in puss-filled boils. Soon, he would start rotting from the inside out as the muscles gave way and the organs fell out of him one by one.

Pushing the piece of liver through the small feeding port in the thick glass of the pod, Chloey Jo tried not to cry. Watching him swallow the organ without even chewing, Chloey Jo mustered her courage and beckoned him to stick his arm near the feeding port. Carefully, she inserted the needle into Jared's arm and injected him with what she hoped would cure him.

Then again, she had already tried at least a dozen of these things and none of them seemed to work. She feared she was actually accelerating the process. She would never be able to live with herself if she was the cause of her own father's demise.

"Dr. Johnson!" Kordelia exclaimed when she saw Chloey Jo at Subject Zeta's pod. "Just what do you think you're doing?"

Chloey Jo straightened and look at Kordelia with eyes that she hoped weren't too glossy. "I'm just checking in on him, Dr. Danes."

"Have you been injecting him with something?" Kordelia asked, closing the gap between them. "Because I believe I specifically asked you not to give him anything if you brought him in here."

"Yes, ma'am, but he's so sick," Chloey Jo said, trying to find a little empathy in her boss. "I can't just watch him die when I might have the cure right here."

"We all have to make sacrifices, CJ," Kordelia said. "It's not your place to decide which subjects deserve a cure more than others."

"Kordelia, please," Chloey Jo begged. "He's my father. How would you feel if Nole was in here? Or even Peyton?"

Kordelia did not even hesitate to respond. She couldn't. Too much was at stake to play favorites right now.

"If they were in the pod, they would be treated like the rest of the subjects. They will get their own cure in their own Time."

"So you expect me to work on someone I don't even care about and watch my father die?"

Kordelia stepped so close to Chloey Jo that her exotic perfume wrapped around the young Conquisitor and nearly choked her.

"I expect you to do your job," Kordelia insisted. "We have fifteen hours left. Subject Zeta's disposition is deadly and historically irreversible. If you fail in your assignment, I will make sure Subject Zeta is unable to infect anyone else. Do you understand?"

Chloey Jo nodded, but maintained the bitterness in her eyes. As she walked around Kordelia, she swore she was going to give Kordelia a taste of her own medicine. She may not be able to cure her father, but she could certainly cure the city of the likes of Kordelia Danes and James Jericho.

ABOUT THE AUTHOR

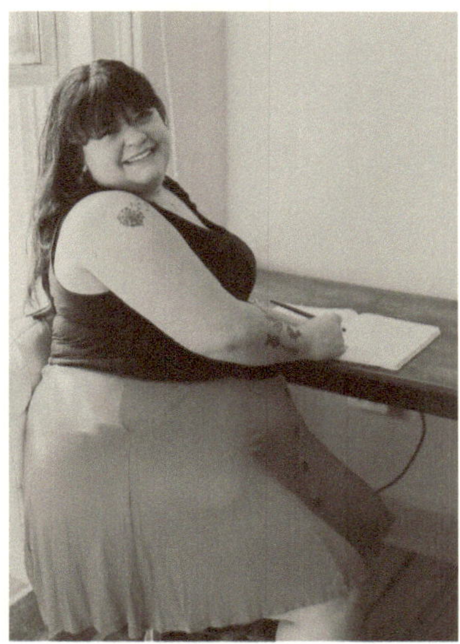

Stevie Jo has always been passionate about writing fiction. Throughout the years, she has honed her skills so that she enjoys most forms of writing. Her series, *Angel of Death,* continues to thrill readers by blurring the boundaries between imagination and reality. Although not a Mythic, she believes in the magic of love, family, and experience to elevate us where we need to be.

Currently, Stevie Jo lives out her own fun and wild romance in Lexington, Kentucky, where she is busy trying to keep plans running smoothly for Murlance's annual Independence Day Festival. You can find her on the social platforms below; she would love to hear from you.

www.steviejoauthor.com
Fb, Ig, TT: @StevieJoAuthor
www.YouTube.com/@StevieJoAuthor

Author photo by Jesy Bowling.
Cover illustration by Keith McCafferty.